The Children of Allura

Green Valleys Series: Book 1

Elaine Santos

Book Cover by Betty Martinez

ISBN 978-1-7390208-0-4 (pbk)

ISBN 978-1-7390208-1-1 (ebook)

1st edition 2023

Contents

Preface

Dear Reader,

I am delighted to guide you through the lands of Green Valleys. This is not only an enjoyable read, but it also offers a profound message of connection, healing, and self-discovery. The book takes you on a journey of self-reflection, where you will learn the importance of connecting with nature and how it can have a healing effect on us.

You will meet a wide range of characters—you will root for some, and wish for punishment for others—but I am sure you will find a special connection with them. This book offers more than just an escape to a world of action and adventure. It delivers a powerful message that there is still love, kindness, and selflessness in the world.

I hope this book will bring more beauty to your life. May the stories of the people from Green Valleys bring out the same emotions in you as they did in me when I wrote them. Close your eyes, take a deep breath, and step into this marvelous world!

With love,
Elaine

P.S: If you would like to add music to your reading experience, I invite you to listen to the songs that inspired me to write this book. Please scan the QR code below.

To the Good Friends, always!

Prologue

I heard the bells. The Temple's bells. It reminded me of just how much I hated going to the Temple. Once a week, the Society citizens had the duty to go to the Temple. The preacher transmitted the Holy Teachings. Teachings you would be damned if you refused to follow.

Women must care for their husbands, children, and their houses.

Children and women must show obedience to the men in the house.

Men are the heads of their families.

Everyone must work for the good of the Society.

The guttural preacher's voice echoed in my head. "I, a humble man, remind the residents of Green Valleys of their responsibilities to the Society." His opulent solid gold necklace covered his chest like a sort of golden armor. The silver belt buckle in a shape of a thick open book showed otherwise. The Temple's emblem. The book was merely symbolic, since there was no such thing as an actual book. There were only the same statements to be followed by the loyal citizens of our Society.

Going to the Temple was torture for me. I had to sit still for two hours and hear the preacher talking about things that seemed alien, almost an unfamiliar language. Or maybe it *was* an unfamiliar language after all.

All those holy words and teachings on how to live our lives, how to behave. Laws we had to obey and men we had to obey. Everything was ready for us. There was no need to think for ourselves, no need to come to our own conclusions, let alone question these teachings. All we had to do was say yes and be good citizens, which often meant keeping our heads down, doing as we were told, never asking questions, staying out

of trouble, working for the well-being of our Society, obeying the men in power, and knowing our place in our circle. That was how we learned, and no one dared to disobey the Law or they would face the consequences. These were the holy teachings. But were they indeed holy? Does holy mean punishment to those who disagree with these teachings?

Well, it is irrelevant right now. I am not going to the Temple today. I am lying on the ground. My face is against the dirt. I can taste the earth and...BLOOD? Why blood? Am I hurt? I cannot feel my body! I feel warm and cold. I feel exposed and covered. I feel empty. My eyes are closed. Should I open them? I would rather not! I am scared! I am scared to learn what happened to me. Why am I here? What happened to me? Can anybody see me? Hear me? I am...invisible! **I thought.**

"Enough! Open your eyes!" the man said.

I opened my eyes and saw him standing next to my bed. Although it was just a shadow, I could feel his eyes on me. He was watching over me, and that was enough to slow my racing heart. At least a bit. I knew he was there to protect me. He had stopped the dream to save me, as he had done before.

His shadow vanished within a few seconds, and Aura was lying in her bed, in the dark.

"It was just a dream. Nobody can hurt you. There is no blood. You are not invisible. You are fine! Life is good!" Aura told herself, repeating the words her parents used to tell her when she was a child.

"Dreams cannot hurt you," she took another deep breath and looked around. The bedroom was dark, but she could see the moonlight through the curtains. Aura got up, reached for a glass of water, and took two small sips while she looked at the stars.

"It is a full moon. It looks so big and bright. What a beautiful sky! So many stars!" she whispered. "Please, no more dreams."

Aura went back to bed, closed her eyes, took another deep breath, and tried to sweep the floor of her mind and clean up her messy thoughts. After sweeping, she clapped her hands in the empty room of her mind, nodded, and smiled. Finally, it was dark and quiet.

Chapter One

Life Is Good

Aura lay in bed with her eyes closed. Sunrays invaded her bedroom like dancing fairies. She smiled as she imagined some colorful little fairies with tiny bright wings flying around her bedroom, bringing so much life into her big white room. She saw them landing on her white dresser and spreading magical dust on her oval mirror, then flying to her little white chair and spreading some more magical dust on it. Next, they were flying in a circle around her tall wooden bed. Finally, the fairies flew around Aura's head like a wreath. Suddenly, they stopped in a straight row, pointed their magical wands at her forehead, and with a smile, they released a rainbow over Aura's head. It was beautiful, shiny, and magical. The multihued rainbow bathed Aura's forehead, cheeks, mouth, neck, chest, arms, legs, and feet. Soon, the light involved her entire being. She kept her eyes closed. The peaceful feeling running through her body was almost palpable. It was quiet and safe inside her head — a rare feeling.

"I wish fairies were real." Aura sighed, but she laughed right away. "I am too old to believe in fairies. I am almost a woman now."

Aura's thoughts were abruptly interrupted by a familiar woman's voice.

"We are the obedient children. 'A delight to the eyes,' like our fathers say. The perfect daughters, little birds in cages, because that is what we are supposed to be. We are there to be seen, never to be heard, never to ask questions, never to disagree, and never to cause problems. Just out of everybody's way. We are nameless, darling. We are invisible to man's world. But soon they will all be invisible, as we are, for it is coming, my darling. It is coming for our kin."

Aura turned and tossed in her bed with her eyes closed. It was that relentless voice in her head again, talking about things she did not want to hear. She took a deep breath.

"It is just in my head. There is nobody here." Aura reluctantly opened her eyes.

Then I saw her looking at me. Tears inundated her face. There was sorrow in her eyes, pain in her voice. I trembled because I could see her face. I had heard her voice so many times inside my head, sometimes whispering in my ears, but her face was new to me. Until then.

"Listen to me, please!" the woman said.

My body froze. I felt like a heavy burden was pressing my chest against the bed. I could not breathe. My head hurt. I felt cold. So cold! I attempted to move, but I couldn't. I tried to close my eyes, but they stayed wide open. I tried to open my mouth to scream, but the sound did not leave my throat. I tried to think, but thoughts did not come to my head. I was no longer the mistress of myself.

"You must listen, Aura! We are running out of time. It is coming! Can you feel it?" Her voice trembled as tears rolled down her cheeks.

Yes! I could feel it. I could feel my skin grow cold. The pressure against my chest. My throat closed. A hole in my stomach. Yes! I could feel panic, fear, and pain. I felt, I felt...invisible!

The sad lady's eyes shone like bright stars. She knew I could feel it. I saw a glimpse of something on her face. What was it?

"Hope, my darling," the lady said, almost as if she could read my mind. "Feel, see, listen, and be brave when the time comes, Aura."

Aura blinked a few times. Her white bedroom looked dimmer than before. She noticed how cloudy it was outside. She was still trying to process what had just happened when the door opened.

"Good morning, baby!" Aura's mother kissed her as she engulfed her daughter in a tender hug. Aura smiled and wrapped her arms around her mother.

The best hugs in the entire world! Aura thought as she tried to get back to reality.

There was something magical about her mother. She always made things better, and that was why Aura admired her. Everything always fell into the right place when she was around.

"Good morning, Mother," Aura replied. "I am sorry I am still in bed. I will get up and help you with breakfast."

"There is no rush, baby. I already kneaded the dough for the bread." Her mother smiled.

"My apologies! I will finish preparing the breakfast." Aura's cheeks flushed. She had strict chores, which were her responsibility. And helping her mother with breakfast was one of them.

Her mother took Aura's face in her tiny white hands. There was something wrong with her daughter. Aura did not have to tell her; she was her mother. She could see it in her eyes.

"Did you have another nightmare, baby?" her mother asked, noticing her daughter's paleness.

"Yes, Mother." Aura lowered her eyes. She was almost a grown woman. It embarrassed her that nightmares were still a source of unease for her.

Although it wasn't a nightmare. It was much more than that! she thought, trying to paste a smile on her face.

Aura's mother hesitated for a second, biting her lower lip. "Did you see the man standing next to your bed?" Her eyes showed she didn't want to hear the answer.

It was much more than that! There was the woman's voice...then her face...her face! I know that face! How is it possible? Aura thought as she inspected every inch of her mother's face. *No! It was my mother! The woman was my mother! Younger, but still my mother!*

Aura's mother could see the terror on her daughter's face. She tried to keep her voice low and calm, but it was hard to see her daughter so distressed.

"Are you feeling unwell, my baby?" She tried to look composed.

"I am fine, Mother. I will be downstairs in a moment." Aura took another deep breath.

"They are just dreams. They are not real. Try to forget about them."

Aura nodded but didn't reply.

"And remember to keep it between us," her mother said, trying to smile.

She knew something was wrong with Aura, but her husband had strictly advised against talking about the girl's dreams, and it was her duty as a wife to respect her husband's demand, even if it meant burying all her worries about her daughter away from everyone.

"Let's not worry your father and brother about these dreams, Aura." Her mother forced another smile to cover up her pain at the sight of her girl's disturbed eyes.

Aura's cheeks flushed again, this time even deeper than before. It was not common for her mother to call her by her name. It was not common for a woman to be called by her name at all.

"Yes, Mother," Aura whispered.

"I will leave you to get ready. We still have an hour before your father and brother get up. You know how hungry they are in the morning." Her mother flashed a smile one last time before she closed the door behind her.

Aura sat on her bed for a moment, trying to digest all the events of that morning. The pain in the woman's voice was engraved in her mind. And her face! She looked exactly like Aura's mother but seemed much younger. She had the same kind eyes, but they were filled with pain and sorrow.

And what she said: 'it is coming.' What is coming? Who is coming? What does it have to do with me? I am just a woman, Aura thought.

"Women are meant to be at home taking care of men in the house and doing chores. Women are not meant to do those silly things," she told herself, repeating her father's words.

Aura tried to forget the mysterious vision. She kept herself busy preparing breakfast. After all, she had much to do with her mother before the men in the house woke up.

By the time the two women were done setting the table, they heard footsteps.

"Good morning, baby girl. Good morning, wife." Her father was standing in front of them, smiling.

Aura rushed to kiss his hand. He kissed her forehead and gave Aura one of his secret smiles. As a man of Law, he was not exactly famous for smiling. He was stern and focused. A serious man. At home, however, he was a different person. Themis occupied a prominent position in their circle: he was the Magistrate. The Law itself was above everyone and everything, even above the Leaders. People sought Themis for advice because they considered him a just man.

"Good morning, Themis." Aura's mother smiled.

"This smell woke me up! There is nothing better in life than fresh bread! Good morning, my beautiful flowers!" There was Aura's brother, a big and handsome man with a bright grin and brighter eyes.

"Good morning, Anandy," their mother said as she kissed him.

Anandy was everything a man was supposed to be in Green Valleys: strong, brave, handsome, and intelligent. According to his professors, he had a bright future ahead of him, and he enjoyed an excellent position in Green Valleys as the most valuable warrior in the city.

It was time for breakfast. The men had a ferocious appetite, as usual. The women were never hungry. They had a slice of bread, some butter, and a glass of milk. The men had two sausages each, two fried eggs, some freshly baked bread, a glass of milk, and strong coffee.

"You look a bit tired, sister. Did you sleep well last night?" Anandy asked.

"It was just a nightmare." Aura cut a small piece of bread.

"Was the weird big guy looking at you again? Oh, I guess it is time for you to get married, my beautiful flower. Then you will have a weird big guy staring at you every night." Anandy chortled.

Aura blushed and tried to smile. She knew Anandy's playful nature, and his joke was only meant in jest.

Themis did not laugh this time. He was gazing at his daughter. She was pale and looked uneasy and scared.

"Did you say your prayers last night?" the Magistrate asked.

"Yes, Father." Aura's voice was faint.

Themis's eyes were still fixed on her. Aura could see the worry in them. "Daughter, perhaps you should finish your breakfast and fulfill your duties at home today. Let your mother run the errands for the day."

Aura nodded and smiled. Her parents tried their best to teach her how to please everyone, and so she did her best to please her father. But she knew very well why he had made this request. He did not want others to see his daughter looking pale or sick. After all, it was all about appearance.

It is all about what others think about us. This thought used to keep her up at night.

Do we really have to live our lives out of fear of displeasing others? Why do others' opinions dictate our actions? Isn't it our life? Shouldn't we live as we please? But it doesn't matter! Life is good! We have everything we need. We have a magnificent house and an excellent position in the Society. The future is bright; we have everything, Aura thought as she smiled weakly at her family.

Chapter Two

The Council

Themis glanced once again at the heavy black book in front of him, hoping the numbers would miraculously change. All eyes were on him. He could feel the tension and impatience growing in the big Council Room.

How did it even happen? he thought as he avoided the other leaders' gaze. *How could I be so blind that I did not see it coming?*

A harsh voice abruptly interrupted his thoughts. *Dansa!* the Magistrate thought as his eyes met the Leader's scornful eyes.

"What do you suggest, Themis?" Dansa asked impatiently.

The Magistrate did not reply. He glued his eyes to the book in front of him as if he was trying to make those numbers change. Themis couldn't believe what he was seeing. It made little sense to him how everything could possibly go downhill after an exceptional year of profit and abundance.

"Farming and fishing are Green Valleys' major activities." Dansa clenched his fists, raising his voice. However, he remained comfortably on his high-back cushioned silver chair.

Just like a throne, Anandy thought, examining the great oval room. Each leader was sitting on a silver chair resembling the throne from one of his sister's fairy-tale books. The clan leaders and the Magistrate were the only ones granted a seat in the Council. The heavy, dark wooden table was a symbol of equality and unity. *All Council members hold the same power*. Anandy chuckled at this thought. *Everyone must bend to the Law, and Father is the Law!*

Anandy was standing behind his father. As a warrior, and as the son of the Magistrate, Anandy could join the council as a witness. He was there to learn because he would get a seat one day. *A seat to blah blah blah the whole day away with a bunch of old folks who have nothing left in their petty lives but to talk. I would rather be training, getting stronger, and being out there solving the problem!*

The Magistrate's son studied the room, as he did in every council. Such events were not very common in Green Valleys. Actually, there were only two annual Councils, one at the beginning of spring, which had the purpose of planning for the abundant months of fishing and farming, and the second and last Council of the year at the end of fall with the purpose of analyzing the numbers of the year and creating a contingency plan for the winter months, when fishing and farming would be scarcer. This Council, however, was atypical. It was the first one in Anandy's memory when the Magistrate and the clan leaders had faced such a problem.

It is concerning, he thought, lowering his eyes and glancing at his father.

Themis was staring at the black book. Anandy felt an unexpected unease. He turned his attention to the Council Room. The big oval room was not richly furnished. Besides the heavy wooden table, the Magistrate's and the leaders' silver chairs, there was no other furniture, which was intentional, since it was expected each leader would be accompanied by their own committee of warriors, advisors, and a few vendors, bringing the clan's goods to sell in the city. Anandy still refused to look at the leaders or even at his father. He knew what he was going to see on their faces.

When will this be over? He resisted the urge to rest his back on the thick white column behind him. *How many columns are there in this room?* he thought as if it was his first time in the Council Room. *Whatever!* He silently counted the columns holding up the domed roof. *Ten.*

Anandy was still distractedly running his eyes throughout the Council Room when he placed his gaze on Dansa. He was still vigorous, but age was catching up.

I wonder how much longer he will be around. Who will succeed him? He has only two daughters. Huh! The poor fellow didn't get any men in his family. Well, I could be his successor, but those girls are not even beautiful! Argh! The mere thought of him marrying one of Dansa's girls gave him shivers. *Whatever! To be important, I don't need to marry an ugly girl. I am the Magistrate's son and the fiercest warrior of Green Valleys. I will be the most powerful man in our Society, like Father is.* This thought brought a proud smile to his lips.

"Dansa, sir," Conrad called, "the crops are dying, and the Great River is not giving us enough fish to export." His tone was respectful but confident.

"Talk only when you are asked a question, kid," spat Ansel, the Leader of the West.

"The name is Conrad, Ansel. I am not a kid. I am a man and Leader of the North," he replied calmly. "I will talk as I please."

Conrad's father had passed away three months earlier. After leaving for a hunting trip with Cato, his main advisor, and Erhart, the High Captain of the North, he never returned. Anandy remembered the previous Leader of the North from previous councils. His calm eyes and the wisdom of his words were respected by other council members. Everyone highly valued and appreciated his opinion.

It was Conrad's first council as a clan leader. Being from the farthest point of Green Valleys, close to the Mighty Mountains, the Northerners were very reserved and rarely visited the City. People knew little about this young man other than he was a man of letters, an academic, not a warrior. He was confident and eloquent, like his late father.

Ha! The new kid is sharp-tongued. This council is getting interesting! Anandy thought as he covered his mouth, coughing to hide his laughter.

Ansel's face turned red. Being the leader of the smallest clan didn't match his exalted view of himself. Ansel was famous for considering himself far more important than he really was.

Proud Ansel smashed by a thin kid. Ha! What a day to be alive! Anandy struggled to keep a straight face.

Ansel abruptly got up, but before he could say a word, Themis spoke in his deep and slow tone. "Leader Conrad is right, Leader Dansa. The reports are not favorable to us. The truth is plain. We barely have enough food to sustain our families."

Anandy felt his left hand slightly tremble as he heard a murmur of discontent from the council's members and witnesses. The young warrior quickly folded his muscular arms, covering his enormous chest. He tried to lower his shoulders and roll them back to ease sudden neck pain.

"Then let me ask you once again." Dansa grinned sarcastically. "What do you suggest, Magistrate Themis, the Just, the Wise?" As the leader of the financial center of Green Valleys, the clan to which Themis's family belonged, Dansa somehow believed he was above Themis.

Fool! Who are you to challenge the Magistrate? I should give you a taste of my iron, old man! Anandy thought. He clenched his fists, feeling a sharp pain running through his left shoulder to his neck, followed by pressure on his forehead. As he slowly opened his hands, he took a step back. His father had clearly instructed him not to interfere in the council's affairs. He was there to listen and learn.

Don't be reckless, Anandy. Learn, and someday you will be the Magistrate. It is your birthright to lead. You were born to it. He remembered Themis's words before every single council. It was the Magistrate's attempt to restrain his son, controlling his behavior with an iron hand.

Anandy had been trying not to speak, trying to control his actions wisely. Pleasing Themis and adjusting his behavior to make his father proud was a constant in his mind.

You're too loud! Serious men never laugh! You have too much fun! Speak lower and deeper. True leaders are well mannered, Anandy. Learn today and lead tomorrow. These were Themis's daily criticisms.

Wait, Anandy! Control your tongue. Remember who you are. He exhaled heavily, rolling down his tensed shoulders once again. *You are the Magistrate's son.*

"Should we perhaps...hunt?" There was a nasty smile on Dansa's face. "We don't hunt, Themis. We leave hunting to animals in the woods."

"No living soul would go deep in Sankul Woods. It is not a place to go." Ansel was eager to make himself sound important.

"We should not trust those inhospitable places. We stay together with our kin. My people stay together, and that's what makes us strong," Old Gilbride, the Leader of the East Lands, solemnly declared.

Of course not, Old Gilbride. You folks are farmers. For thousands of years, you have been living on the land. You are not strong or even large. Most of your lands are fields, Anandy thought, biting his lower lip to hide a scornful smile.

"The Great River of crystal waters. Green fields that extend beyond the human eye," Faron said, standing up.

The handsome Faron, Leader of the South, the second largest clan among them all. The military heart of Green Valleys.

"The largest and strongest horses in the world come from the North." He raised his glass to Conrad, who smiled politely, returning the gesture.

"We train our men in the art of war since an early age at the army camp in the South. Green Valleys' warriors are fearless, strong, and merciless. The best iron from the mines of the Iron Mountains and the most skilled blacksmiths and sword makers are also found in the South. Our Society thrived among all the others because of our fertile lands and great people! No other society dares to challenge us. They fear us! Nothing and nobody can defeat us!" Faron's voice was deep and passionate.

The large, oval room exploded into a thunderous roar. All warriors in the room howled in approval. The Leader of the South was a legend among warriors. Anandy kept his composure. He didn't like this sudden turn of events.

Faron looked around, showing his pearly whites. His turquoise eyes shone.

A man of legendary beauty. A celebrated warrior. The man is a god himself! Anandy thought, wanting to spit on the floor. *He thinks his words covered in honey and sugar will hide the truth. What a bunch of idiots!*

Anandy was reckless and quick to act, but he was no fool. He could understand the gravity of the situation. He knew sweet words wouldn't put food on their tables. As he looked around at all leaders, Conrad's face caught his eye. Although there was a pleasant smile on the young leader's face, there was something else in his eyes. Anandy couldn't tell for sure what it was, but he could read deception in those light blue eyes.

Suddenly, the roaring stopped. His father had stood up.

That's a man whose simple demeanor inspires respect. A true leader! Anandy thought, grinning proudly.

Themis looked around, examining each face. Listening to each voice. Watching each move.

"Eagle's eyes. Tiger's moves," Anandy whispered inaudibly, remembering how the other kids used to describe his father when he was a little boy. *The great Magistrate! The most powerful man in Green Valleys!*

"My friends," Themis's voice was calm but firm, "as Leader Faron reminded us, we are a great Society! Our green fields, the mines from the Iron Mountains, the Mighty Mountains, and the Great River are our blessings. They have been sustaining this community for thousands of years. We made a living out of exporting our goods to the Oisan Clans down the river. We are powerful because we are united. Five clans are under the same sun. Being as one is our greatest strength." Themis paused, glancing at each man's face in the oval room. "Friends, let's not divide ourselves in this hour of need. The annual reports collected by the military are clear. There is not enough food, as Leader Conrad clearly pointed out. I called upon you to discuss our options."

Dead silence filled the room. Each member of the council had their eyes fixed on Themis.

Father will solve this problem. The wisest man in Green Valleys. Anandy nervously rubbed his hands. He gazed at his father. Sitting behind Themis, all Anandy could see was the back of his father's head and the right side of his face. It was enough for the young warrior to read tension. Anandy's left hand trembled once again.

"Answering your question, Leader Dansa, I suggest we ration our food. You are right. We are not hunters or barbarians. We will use our intellect. Let's be reasonable and save our portions until the land and the river give our blessings back to us. Rationing our provisions will help us get through the winter months," Themis announced.

Rationing? Using our intellect? What the hell is Father talking about? Anandy felt as if the thick white columns crushed him.

"Agreed." Dansa nodded impassively.

"Agreed." Faron, Ansel, and Gilbride nodded too.

"Leader Conrad?" Themis turned to Conrad.

"Magistrate Themis, if I may," Conrad said, standing up slowly, "I disagree."

Things just got interesting. This lad really amuses me! Anandy thought, biting his lower lip again to prevent a smile.

"I beg your pardon, Leader Conrad?" Themis's eyes looked even darker.

"I said I disagree, Magistrate Themis," Conrad repeated, louder and slower. "Rationing our food doesn't seem to be a rational solution in my not-so-humble opinion, sir. Perhaps it would be a good start, but it is not a solution. I believe we must sort out this problem. As you said, sir, the river and the fields were our blessings for thousands of years. So, why are the reserves becoming scarce?"

I admire this kid's courage to go against the council members and the Magistrate. Clever young Conrad, indeed. Anandy fought the urge to speak or laugh. Those were the words he had been expecting his father to utter.

"The lad is speaking nonsense. You have four votes, Themis. It is settled." Dansa avoided Conrad's penetrating eyes.

"It is settled!" all the other leaders echoed.

"Let's see how long the rationing plan is going to last." Conrad ignored the interruption, gazing at Themis. "I hope I am wrong, but I know I am not. We don't need a quick fix, Magistrate. How long are we supposed to ration our provisions? How sure are you it won't last months or even years? How sure are you that our reserves are ending?"

The Magistrate avoided the young leader's gaze. As the Magistrate, he did not have the right to vote. He was a mere mediator in these councils. He had the right to comment or even suggest a solution, but the leaders were the ones in charge of voting and having the last word.

Anandy caught himself staring at Conrad and smiling. He was pleased to see someone challenging the Council. He was pleased to see someone challenging his father. But those feelings only lasted for a moment.

That's not right! Focus, Anandy. Control your emotions. Don't be reckless. He lowered his eyes, feeling shame invading his heart.

"That's enough, lad. You are too young to worry this much! All this worrying will give you wrinkles. Soon you will look older than I am," Faron joked, grinning. Although Faron was older than Conrad, he wasn't by much. The Leader of the South was young, handsome, and adored by everyone.

Laughter filled the room, and an air of joy and celebration replaced the curtain of tension.

"Bring beer! Let's celebrate having all the leaders together! Let's celebrate Leader Conrad's first council!" Faron gestured to his advisors, who promptly left in search of beer.

Conrad sat down. Although he felt his face burning and his hands sweaty, he allowed Ansel to fill his glass. He drank to his first council. To the prosperity of Green Valleys. To their good people and brave warriors. He drank with a smile on his face and pleasant words coming from his lips, as his father had taught him. There was the moment to speak and the moment to remain silent. And this was the moment to retreat and join the majority with a smile on his lips, beer in his belly, and pleasantries on his tongue.

Chapter Three

Empty Words

Dansa took a small sip from the wooden cup placed in front of him. The dark beer was a delicacy from the east. Its delicate bitterness and full-bodied characteristics made it a staple in Green Valleys, also appreciated by the Oisin clans. The Leader took another sip, scrutinizing the Council Room. The deafening sound of dozens of men laughing and celebrating almost made him puke.

The calm before the storm, he thought. *Folks do what they do best: they drink!*

Sitting across from him was Themis. The well-known burning feeling growing from his stomach to his chest was there again, which only aggravated his nausea. Dansa placed his cup on the wooden table and fixed his eyes on the silent figure of the Magistrate sipping his beer.

Themis, the fool, Dansa thought, amusing himself with the thought of "rationing food."

You always opt for the fastest and easiest route, old man. You will never change, he thought, examining the lines on the Magistrate's face. *He knows he's a fool.* Dansa wrapped his fingers around his cup and took it halfway to his mouth. His fingers pressed tightly on it. *The question is when the other fools will see the truth.*

Sitting next to him was Faron. *The handsome warrior. Deadly with a sword. Suave in his words and ways. His beauty and sweet words hide his lethal true nature*, thought the Leader of the Central Lands.

"Enjoying your beer, my good friend?" Faron placed his turquoise eyes on Dansa, grinning.

Dansa got caught up in the intensity of his eyes. *There is no other man with such beauty in all clans*, he thought, analyzing the perfect symmetry of the warrior's face. Faron ran his fingers through his wavy brown hair while sipping his beer. His red lips gently touched the cup. His muscular arm was bent while he drank, revealing his sculpted biceps and shoulder muscles.

"Yes, my dear friend." Dansa blinked twice, taking another sip of the dark beer. "The East has the best wheat in Green Valleys!" he added, speaking loud enough for Gilbride to hear.

"Kind words, my esteemed friend," Old Gilbride replied faintly across the table.

That's what we do best in our Councils. We exchange empty words and give orders to lower men, Dansa thought. These empty little compliments deeply amused him.

"My friends, honorable Magistrate, and fellow leaders, I must bid my farewell. The North awaits me. My journey is long, and I shall depart now." Conrad raised his glass, bowing slightly out of respect.

The lad is no fool. He is already playing the game. Sharp tongue and sharper mind, Dansa thought. *But a weak body. Weaker than a girl! Just like his old man.*

"Leader Conrad, thank you for joining our council today. I send my regards to your family and to the good people from the North." Faron rose from his chair with his characteristic charming smile.

Conrad returned the smile and nodded politely.

The fools are playing gentlemen's games now. Well, I had better join them, Dansa thought as he was about to stand up.

But Old Gilbride was quicker. "Young Conrad, may good fortune be with you on your journey." His shaky, faint voice matched his tired eyes as he struggled to raise his glass. His High Captain, Evander, helped him to stand, but he was already done speaking. Gilbride murmured a few inaudible words while the warrior gently helped him sit down.

That old crow should have died long ago! Dansa thought, glancing disgustedly at the old man. *He must be close to a hundred years by now. His son is older than I am! The poor fellow will never be a leader!*

"Safe trip, young man!" Ansel cheerfully placed his hand on Conrad's shoulder, gulping beer from his cup.

Typical Ansel. Quick to jump into quarrels and quicker to forget them.

Dansa stood up. *Learn how it is done, fools!*

"Leader Conrad," he called in a thunderous voice. The room was instantly silent.

Conrad turned his head from Ansel to Dansa.

"Good! Look at me, little men!" he whispered. It gave him instant pleasure to feel all eyes on him and the expectation of his next words.

This is power, Dansa thought.

"Leader Conrad, I welcome you to our circle of leaders. Your brightness makes up for your young age. I am positive you will bring reason and clarity to our Councils! May your return be safe!" Dansa raised his glass, pasting his best smile on his face.

Conrad's eyes shone for a second. There was a spark in them. Dansa did not see it because he was still staring at Themis in vain. The Magistrate seemed to be absorbed in his own thoughts. Anandy, however, noticed the strange shine in the northerner's eyes.

Loathing, he thought. *The lad hates Dansa!*

Makes up for my young age? Being young is not a flaw, sir! Conrad thought.

But he was well-trained. He knew how to play these little games. "*It is all games! Just play your part, Conrad. Pick your battles wisely.*" He could hear his father's voice in his head.

The Leader of the North bowed his head submissively. He lowered his eyes. "Your kindness, good leaders, fills my heart with gratitude. May your clans be prosperous and peaceful," he replied, leaving, followed by his main advisor and high captain.

Interesting! Themis did not bid farewell to Conrad, Dansa thought. *He is in his own head again!*

He was not the only one who had noticed that. Anandy took a deep breath, rubbed his hands, and approached his father.

"Father, forgive me." Anandy hesitated. "But you haven't bidden farewell to Leader Conrad." He rubbed the sweat from his hands as he felt his heart racing in his chest. Pointing out his father's mistakes wasn't something he was comfortable doing. However, it was his duty to highlight such a lack of etiquette.

Themis did not reply. The Magistrate had his gaze placed on an empty cup in front of him.

"Father," Anandy called once again, staring at Themis's face. "Are you unwell?"

"I heard you the first time, boy. I chose not to acknowledge your impertinent comment," Themis replied. He was still staring at the empty cup in front of him.

Anandy clenched his fists, feeling uncontrollable heat growing inside him, the same burning fire that had put him in so many fights in the past. "You could have prevented my impertinent comment if you had fulfilled your duties as the Magistrate. It was your responsibility to welcome Leader Conrad to his first Council and to conduct the farewell wishes, sir." Anandy spoke bluntly, turning his back to his father and leaving the Council Room.

"That insolent brat will pay for his recklessness!" Themis spat. He clenched his jaw. Then, calming himself down, he whispered. "Let it be! We never chase our little ducks, for they always come back home. And this little duck will get his punishment tonight." Themis repeated these words with shivers going down his spine. The same words his late father used to say before every beating.

"*You will be a man. So I will beat you like a man. Don't be a girl! Stop crying! I am teaching you to be a man.*" He could still hear his father hissing in his ears.

Themis had to put his cup on the table and hid his hands in his lap. He was shaking. It was as if his guts were being pulled down. A line of cold sweat ran down his spine.

"Be a man!" His father's voice rang again in his ears.

The Magistrate looked at his hands, reminding himself of how his late father's beatings had helped him to mature and how beating his son would teach him the same.

But Anandy is already a man, Themis thought, staring at his trembling hands placed on his lap. He rubbed his sweaty palms on his cotton pants.

There will be no beating tonight, and even if there was, it wouldn't improve his flaws. The boy is reckless, insolent, and fearless. He fears nobody, not even his own father. Themis rubbed his palms on his pants once again. *We are so different. The boy is too impulsive. He knows no fear. Anandy is so different from Aura, my obedient little girl.* Themis's face softened as he thought of his daughter. He could almost see her face.

"Magistrate Themis, I came here to pay my respects and bid my farewells." It was Dansa, standing in front of him, showing his fangs.

The viper is here to spit its venom, Themis thought.

"Thank you, Leader Dansa." The Magistrate glanced at Dansa, returning his gaze to the cup in front of him.

"I noticed you missed your chance to bid farewell to Leader Conrad. That was a fault, indeed. So I welcomed him to our council myself, as you failed to do." His eyes were shining with pleasure. "No need to thank me, Themis. That's what friends are for." Dansa smiled, revealing his yellow teeth.

Come on, Themis. Play our little game with me, he thought, feeling that burning feeling growing in his chest.

Dansa the Viper is trying to bite, the Magistrate thought. But he did not reply.

Well, then. Next move, Dansa thought, disappointed at his opponent's unresponsiveness. "Before I leave," he added, "I think it would be prudent to set a meeting to discuss what the next steps of the rationing will be, *Magistrate*."

"I beg your pardon? What is there to discuss?" Themis raised an eyebrow.

"You know. The rationing will not be for everyone. It is a symbolic term and solution. We will exempt the leaders' families, and yours, from such a vicissitude. After all, we are above these decrees, or laws, or whatever you call them."

Themis clenched his right fist but quickly covered it. *Restraint*, he reminded himself. The Magistrate nodded politely. "Indeed, Leader Dansa. I will send a message to you for a meeting. Thank you for coming. I bid you my sincere farewell."

Dansa smiled, pleased, and left. Themis placed his troubled gaze on the Council Room. The clans' representatives had left.

"Sir," called Mattas, his advisor, "I took the liberty of bidding farewell to the leaders and their committees." His voice was low and respectful. "I understand you must be tired. Should I close the Council Room now?"

"The Magistrate must be the first to arrive and the last to leave, Themis." There was his father's voice echoing in his ears.

Themis ignored his father's words. "Thank you, my friend!" He ran his eyes over the room, expecting to see his father's ghost standing next to him. There were only him and Mattas in the room. "You might go now. I will close the Council Room myself."

Mattas nodded and left.

Themis watched the old man leave. A sudden sadness invaded his heart. *Father's ghost must still be here, watching every word I say. Every move I make. The old bastard is laughing at me now!* Themis clenched his jaw uncomfortably, but he quickly pushed those childish thoughts away.

"No," he whispered. "The old bastard must be playing his little political games with the Devil in Hell."

CHAPTER FOUR

I AM THE ONE WHO HIDES

Anandy shivered when a chilly wind blew into that gloomy fall afternoon. He rubbed his gloved hands, tucking in his chin. The young warrior felt as if the dark, heavy sky was getting lower with every step he took.

"It's always cloudy in this hole of a city," Anandy murmured as he wandered the streets.

The Central Lands was the capital and financial heart of Green Valleys. Being home to all the trading houses, stores, and export firms made the City the busiest of all five clans. The houses were large and comfortable. The streets were peaceful to navigate. Busy, but still pleasant.

The clans were under a system of codependency. Each clan had their staple products, which were sent to its local Central Building for division within the clan. Then they would send the surplus to the City, which would sort them out for distribution to other clans and for export to foreigners. They divided the profit between the City and the clan that produced the product. The Oisin Clans down the Great River were Green Valleys' biggest importers.

The North had the best and strongest horses in the world. Their strength resided in raising cattle and exporting meat, wool, and dairy. The East was home to vast fields. One could find the best yeast in their crops. Given the temperate weather there, the easterners grew a wide range of fruit and vegetables. Blessed by the Great River, the West offered a variety of fish such as salmon and trout. The high-quality iron from the Iron Mountains in the South was world-famous. These lands were home to the most talented blacksmiths and crafters. Due to the warmer climate, the South Lands' wine was a delicacy appreciated even by foreigners.

Anandy, however, didn't care about the hustle and bustle of the Central Lands, or even about Green Valleys' import and export system. His head was exploding, his hands were sweating, and his heart was pounding.

I have to punch something, or someone, he thought. *There is something wrong with Father. I can feel it!* He tucked his chin in even more to avoid the chilly wind and the overcast sky, which almost seemed to touch his head.

Anandy kept walking. Nasty thoughts filled his head. Anger populated his heart. He walked until his legs felt heavy. Each extra step felt like a struggle. *I feel like I am dragging a horse attached to my legs*, he thought. His legs refused to take another step. Anandy looked around, and to his surprise he found himself in the middle of the road.

"Why the hell have my feet brought me here?" He gave his legs a little shake to ease that heavy sensation. "It's time to go back home. The sun is setting. I must have walked for hours. Bloody hell!" he said, trying to understand how he hadn't noticed the hours passing by. *How deeply lost in anger and self-pity was I?* he thought, noticing frustration growing inside him.

As he stopped to turn back on his heels to the City Center, he heard a long whistle. The slight tremor returned to Anandy's hands. He rubbed them once again.

"Well, well, well, look what we have here," said a man's voice.

Anandy quickly turned and saw a group of five men standing in front of him. *Vagabonds! I could punch them and let off some steam*. The idea was tempting but reckless. As the Magistrate's son, he shouldn't be involved in street fights. *"It is all about appearances. What will the others think of us?"* He remembered his father's words.

"I don't have time for this right now!" he heard himself saying instead and kept walking.

"Not so quick, handsome," an older man said, showing his brown teeth. "Your clothes are nice. You must be a wealthy young man, and as such, you wouldn't mind showing generosity to some poor souls." He was still smiling.

That smile intensified Anandy's trembling. *You are just tired and hungry. They are harmless vagabonds in search of a coin*, he thought, trying to convince himself.

Anandy nodded impatiently, reaching for the little coin bag on his belt, but it wasn't on his waist.

I must have forgotten it at home this morning, he thought.

Carrying money was not a custom among the wealthy families in Green Valleys. As Themis's son and the best warrior in the Central Lands, nobody expected Anandy to pay for anything. It was not uncommon for powerful families to get gifts as a way of saying thank-you for their hard work to keep the Society working smoothly.

Although the men had noticed Anandy didn't have his coin bag, they didn't seem to care.

"I have nothing to offer you. Farewell now." Anandy resumed his journey back home. That strange feeling was there inside him. Something did not add up.

Steps! They are following me! He reached for his small golden pocketknife. *"Small, but deadly if handled properly."* Themis had uttered these words to Anandy on the day he left the Army Camp.

It was a graduation gift for successfully enduring ten years of grueling training to be a warrior in the South, or, as the young cadets used to say, "The Hellish Lands," where the minority of the kids sent to the Camp at the age of six finish their training. The others would fail and carry this shame to their families and find employment in their own clans as lower men. Anandy, however, was a king in the Camp. He succeeded in every single task, almost to the point of perfection. He was one of the best cadets the Hellish Lands ever had.

These vagabonds are making a serious mistake. I cannot be defeated! He remembered how the other cadets used to refer to him as "The Undefeatable Anandy."

"As a matter of fact, good sir, you can still give us something valuable." A bearded man came from the back of the group.

A foreigner! Men in our clans shave the hair on their faces. Anandy's heart was beating faster. *They are all foreigners!* He examined each man standing in front of him. *Their accent and clothing are different. They are carrying weapons.* His heart raced. *Healthy men! Not vagabonds.* He finally understood. *They are mercenaries!*

The young warrior looked at the five men and finally *saw* them. They were five well-built, vigorous men. Their worn-out cloaks hid shoulder armor and weapons.

Anandy remembered his training in the Hellish Lands. "*Always see your opponent. Each detail counts!*" His old master's voice echoed in his mind. Anandy tried to control his breathing and took in his opponents. *There is an old man*, he thought. *The bearded man is not young, though. He must be as old as Father. The other three are still kids... I can see knives, swords, light body protection, daggers... Bloody hell! These bastards are ready for action!*

Anandy held his knife tight as he analyzed his chances. *I can take them down. I have done it before in the South. There is nobody more powerful than me.* Fighting multiple opponents was part of the warrior training in the South. Although it wasn't training or a silly fight with some other young warriors, Anandy was still confident in his skills.

"Go home if you don't want to bleed."

The young warrior placed his hand on the pocketknife. The golden handle felt cold against his gloved hands. Anandy's right hand trembled once again. He squeezed the golden handle.

"It isn't me who will bleed today, Anandy, son of Themis," the bearded man replied.

What? How does he know who I am? Anandy couldn't believe his ears. He knew his name!

"How do you...?" Anandy could not finish his sentence. There was a soft whistle coming from behind.

My chest burns! Anandy hurriedly placed his hands on his chest. *No! Blood? Why am I bleeding? Oh, God! The arrow came from behind and...and...oh God! It went through my chest!*

He was still processing what had happened when the second arrow hit his right thigh. Falling to his right knee, Anandy tried to lift himself up, but his body was not responding to his commands. His chest and right thigh were burning. The warm feeling of blood running down his torso and leg felt as if he was dreaming. Small drops of blood touched the ground.

There are more of them! Cowards are attacking me from behind! Come and fight me like men! Get up and kill them, Anandy! his brain told his body, but the latter was unresponsive. The world around Anandy was spinning. It was getting dark. *I can't die here! I am a warrior! I will fight until my death!*

Anandy was still trying to take control of his body and pull himself up when he heard steps.

Someone is coming, he thought. *Get up! Fight! Kill them all!*

With difficulty, he looked up and saw the old man and the bearded man walking toward him, side by side. The bearded man held a black dagger. Anandy could feel a third man stopping behind him. He couldn't turn his face to see him, but he could sense the mercenary's presence.

"I will give you a quick death, boy." The bearded man grinned.

With a sudden adrenaline rush, Anandy squeezed his knife's handle. Pressing his toes against the ground, he pushed himself up into a jump and with a precise move cut the bearded man's throat. Blood squirted in all directions. The bearded man dropped his dagger and instinctively grabbed at his throat. Anandy took advantage of the old man's confusion and stuck his knife in the man's chest. The old man collapsed to the ground. His lifeless eyes stared at the cloudy sky.

"Here's to your quick death, old devils," the young warrior grunted.

For a moment, the pain had left his body. He was numb. Every muscle was numb. He felt his soul numb too as both men's blood covered the ground in front of him, forming two small, dark red puddles.

There was a moment of silence. Surprise had rendered the mercenaries speechless. They hadn't expected this half-dead boy to kill their leaders. Anandy didn't hesitate and stabbed a third, younger man, three times, in his chest, throat, and left cheek. The man didn't have the chance to defend himself. He fell next to the dead body of the other two men.

Anandy was still numb. There was no reasoning or emotion. Only survival. He had to kill in order to live.

"Three down!" he whispered. *But I don't know how many they are or where they hide*. His legs failed him. He fell to his knees.

Three men came for him. Two were holding his arms, and one was standing in front of him.

"You just killed my father, and now I will kill you," a young man said. His black eyes shone with despair. "Let's end it here and go back to claim our payment, men!"

Anandy spat in the young man's face, releasing himself from the grip of the other two men. The young warrior elbowed the mercenary to his left in the nose, punching the one on his right straight in his left eye. Both men fell to the ground. Anandy punched the young man's face twice. Blood covered his face. The warrior had broken the mercenary's nose. The man took his hands to his face and groaned in pain, taking five steps back.

The other men quickly got up and pushed Anandy face down to the ground. *Dirt and blood!*

Far South, he heard the bells. *The Temple's bells! How is it possible? I am on the borders of the Central and the South! How did I walk so many kilometers?* He could taste a mix of dirt and blood.

Anandy was no longer numb. There was pain. He was cold and warm. He felt exposed and covered at the same time. He felt empty, like there was nothing inside of him, only a black hole. His eyes were closed. He dared not open them. The warrior felt scared for the first time since childhood, when he used to hide from strangers behind his mother's skirt. There was fear in his heart. Fear was the enemy. They did not allow fear in the military. Fear was for the weak, but fear was what the great warrior felt. Anandy felt weak and *invisible.* He felt unseen, unworthy. He no longer existed. He was forgotten. Simply invisible to the world.

So, that's how it ends? he thought, still fighting to release himself from the heavy foot on his back, forcing his body against the ground. *I, the great warrior Anandy, will die at the hands of filthy mercenaries.* A tear rolled from the corner of his eye.

There was something growing inside him. It differed from everything he had ever felt before. It was a new feeling. He did not even know he could have feelings other than anger and scorn.

I was proud and reckless my entire life. I thought myself untouchable and invincible, but I am not, he thought. Anandy opened his eyes and stared at the puddle of his own blood next to his mouth. *I am just a boy who hides behind titles and possessions. The one who hides behind his family's name. I am the one who hides behind his father's power. And behind his military title.*

He hesitated as light filled the dark emptiness inside him. A sudden beam of light. Weak at first, but perceptible if he kept his eyes open to it, and Anandy's eyes were quite open. The beam of light was getting stronger and stronger.

"I am not him..." Anandy whispered inaudibly. "I am Anandy, I am... I am..." It was clear now what he was feeling. He felt peace and humility. These two new feelings were bathing his being. He was not cold or warm, covered, or exposed. Anandy was no longer empty or *invisible*. He struggled to lift his head and looked at the green grass in front of him.

Anandy thought of his sweet mother, who loved him and his sister above all things. *My angel of a mother, please forgive me!* He thought of his quiet and innocent sister. *My beautiful little sister, grow up and be as good as Mother is. Please, forgive me!* He thought of his serious and strict father. *You were right, Father. I am reckless. Please forgive me.*

Someone violently turned Anandy's body. There was a blade pointed at his throat, but he did not look at it. Instead, he looked at the skies and smiled.

"At last, blue skies," he murmured, wondering when that cloudy day had turned into a glorious one. The warmth of the sun touched his face and the softness of the grass caressed his body. "I am ready. I go in peace." He closed his eyes peacefully.

There was a sharp scream of pain and the swish of a blade. People running and screaming. The well-known sound of steel echoed in Anandy's ears.

"It is a battle! Someone is fighting the mercenaries!" Anandy whispered, opening his eyes.

The blade pointed at his face was gone. Anandy tried to get up, but pain had invaded his body. He could not move. A muscular arm grabbed his arm. It was the young man. His nose was still bleeding. Fear clouded his eyes. "I said you die today." There was determination in his voice.

Anandy tried to reach for his knife but it was gone. "My pocketknife," he murmured.

The young man smiled. "Looking for this?" He was holding Anandy's golden pocketknife. His expression turned into a scream of agony. He let go of Anandy, falling dead to the ground.

He has the same lifeless eyes as his father, Anandy thought, remembering the man he had killed. The *first* person he had ever killed in his life. Grief invaded his heart as the realization of being responsible for ending someone's life hit him.

That was when he saw a slender figure behind the young man. Anandy tried to make sense of who it was, but all he could see was a small shadow standing in front of him. Looking at him.

Who are you? Anandy wanted to ask, but words would not leave his mouth. His voice was stuck inside his burning chest. There was a shiver of terror as he noticed the shadow was staring at him. But it only lasted for a moment. The shadow did not waste time but ran to the other mercenaries.

Anandy observed in dismay as the shadow moved hastily through the grass. *He is fast! I can't see his feet moving! What kind of sorcery is it? He jumps high in the sky, as if he is flying. He's fast as the wind but small and thin like an ant.* He partly opened his lips. *He is not one of Green Valleys' warriors. We are big and strong, and that's not how we fight! It differs from everything I have ever seen! He is not dressed in light armor, like us. He was not trained in the South, for sure. Who is he? I can't see his face. All I see is a shadow. Is it black magic?* Anandy's head was spinning. It was getting dark. He understood it was time.

Anandy raised his chin to the skies, allowing the chilly wind to kiss his forehead. The young warrior smiled as he contemplated the rare vision of a blue sky.

"I am dying." He lay on the grass under the blue skies. "I die in peace, for I know who I am."

Anandy closed his eyes.

Chapter Five

Blue Skies

The dull afternoon was coming to an end. The pale shadow of the sun hidden behind gray clouds was making its way to the horizon. She observed the majestic white tree out the window. Its thin white branches moved in a fall's dance.

Aura smiled at such a poetic thought. *"The world is brighter when you see trivial events through the eyes of a poet."* She had read these words in an old, thick book that belonged to her mother when she was a child. Her mother only allowed Aura to read this book when her father and Anandy were somewhere else, busy with their duties. Aura loved the tales in it.

"The Sun and the Moon started their battle," Aura whispered. Her lips were partly opened in a dreaming state as she remembered her favorite tale from the book: the daily battle between the Sun and the Moon to be the Ruler of the Sky and their eternal raising and falling. Aura loved the illustrations in the book, especially how the author depicted the Sun as a stern old man and the Moon as a cheerful young woman.

Perhaps that's why Mother always cautions me against telling Father about this book, she thought. *Women will never rule. Not even in fairy tales.*

The girl sighed dreamily as she rubbed herbs on the last of the six fish her mother had brought from the market. "Anandy will love it! It is big and fresh. It just needs some lemon juice, salt, pepper, and paprika to be perfect." Aura smiled, imagining her big brother getting home and announcing how he could smell the fish three blocks away. "This has been our favorite dish ever since we were kids." She revisited sweet childhood memories.

Aura could picture them as little kids impatiently waiting for their mother to set up the table for dinner, their little noses sniffing all those delicious aromas while their bellies roared. Anandy would always convince their mother to give them a small piece of bread with butter and a chunk of cheese while they waited what felt like hours for the fish to be baked.

Silly us! she thought, reaching for the lemons. Aura suddenly stopped and looked at her hands. They were shaking. *What's happening?* She was panting, sweating, and cold.

Then all she felt was pain. Falling on her knees with a sharp scream, Aura tried to reach for the counter to give her some support to get up, and that was when she saw it.

***Blood inundates blood! Pain! So much pain! God help me!* I thought, crying desperately.**

Horses? A breeze! I moved my neck up and gazed at the sky. "Blue skies?" I whispered, wondering what had happened to that gloomy afternoon. "Am I dreaming?" I looked around, trying to understand where I was.

I was on a road. I could hear bells ringing. It was just like in my dream. The world was spinning and getting darker, despite those blue skies.

Fear was consuming every part of my body. I could taste blood in my mouth. I couldn't move!

Someone or something threw me to the ground. Another wave of pain hit my body. I fell face down on the dirt. My torso was pressed against the ground. I closed my eyes, choking on the unpleasant taste of blood mixed with dirt. Should I dare to open them? Better not!

"It is just a dream! I am dreaming!" I murmured. But that wasn't true. "I was in the kitchen cooking dinner, and now I am here in pain and hurt."

Strong arms pulled me up from the ground. "I must see and understand what is happening!" I murmured, gathering all the courage left in my

being and forcing myself to open my eyes. What I saw made my blood run cold.

There was a battlefield. I saw violence, death, fear, pain, and evil. Men were fighting, killing, and dying. I saw swords, arrows, bows, knives, daggers, and, and...a little golden pocketknife? Anandy!

Unwillingly, my eyes scanned the battlefield in search of my beloved Anandy. But he was nowhere to be seen. I didn't allow myself to feel relieved, though. I could feel evil on that battlefield.

"Oh, God! No!" I gasped at the sight in front of me. I saw a pair of dark eyes lurking in the darkness of madness. I saw a desire to kill in those evil eyes. A desire to kill me.

"You die today," those dark eyes said to me.

I looked at the blue skies and saw a light shining straight into that deathly camp of desolation. It shone behind those dark eyes. Then I saw it. A golden shadow was in front of me. I felt at peace. I felt humbled. Horror consumed me once again when I looked down at my chest.

"No! It is not me! This is not my body!" I screamed.

For a second, I saw a muscular warrior's body where my torso was supposed to be. I saw his broken shoulder armor. His strong white hands were covered in blood. Then it was my own thin hands. I was myself again.

I looked at my feet and cried bitterly, for I saw the body of my beloved Anandy, destroyed by arrows, lying on the green grass of that red day. His body was fading from in front of my eyes. Darkness took over my world.

★ ★ ★ ☾ ★ ★ ★

"The doctor is waiting for you in the living room, Themis," Mattas informed him, handing the Magistrate a cup of tea.

Themis motioned to reach for it, but he hurriedly placed his hands on his lap under the table. It didn't escape Mattas's trained eyes. He could perceive the smallest details. That was his job as Themis's senior and most trusted advisor.

His hands are shaking, Mattas thought. He smiled sympathetically, placing the cup on the Magistrate's wooden dining table.

"Thank you," Themis murmured. He gazed at Mattas, realizing how discreetly his advisor had handled this situation.

Themis held the cup with both hands, which he thought would probably ease the tremor, and sipped the tea. It was warming and soothing. *But it can't soothe all my sorrows.*

"My only son went missing, and my little girl is...she is..." Themis didn't finish the sentence. His voice was coming from a dream. He stared at the dark liquid in his cup.

"Themis?" There was kindness in Mattas's voice.

The Magistrate turned his attention to him. Mattas read confusion in Themis's dark eyes.

"The doctor is waiting to talk to you, Themis."

Themis nodded, blinking as if he was trying to wake from a nightmare. "Yes, send him in."

Mattas left the room, and a few seconds later a muscular man entered the room. It was Doctor Valens.

Valens went to the South Lands' Army Camp with me. He would have been a great warrior. Instead, he chose his father's path and became a doctor. I am glad he did. He is the best in the City, Themis thought. His eagle eyes examined the strong man standing in front of him.

Valens was dressed in fine clothing. His light blue cotton pants carefully matched his white long-sleeved shirt. The sleeves were folded to his elbows. His light blue jacket was in his left hand and a small black leather medical bag was in his right. Themis gazed at the emblem on the front pocket of Valens's jacket, the coat of arms of their clan.

The City and the Coin, the Magistrate thought. The sight made him feel uneasy.

"Greetings, Magistrate. I truly hoped my visit would be under better circumstances." Valens fixed his straight brown hair behind his ear.

Themis nodded slowly. He stood up, entwining his fingers behind his back. He felt as if his soul wasn't in his body.

"I just examined the girl." Doctor Valens paused, searching for the right words. "Well, she's delirious, sensitive to light and sound. Probably because of headaches. Her cheeks are flushed, and she has a high fever. It seems to me, Magistrate..." He paused again.

"What does it seem to be, Valens? Just say it!" Although Themis's voice was low and controlled, his hands were shaking uncontrollably behind his back.

Valens looked Themis straight in the eyes and said the fearful words. "She's in shock, Magistrate. It seems to me that it is not a physical problem. I would rather say," he paused once again, trying to choose carefully his words, "it is a state of mental shock."

Themis felt like the ground underneath his feet disappeared. He lost balance. Valens rushed to hold his arm, helping him sit down.

"No! It's impossible! My daughter is young and strong! Young and strong!" Themis said deliriously.

"Mattas, come here! Help me take the Magistrate to his bedroom." Valens grabbed Themis's left arm and pulled him up.

The advisor hesitated for a second when he saw Themis. The Magistrate was pale and weak. He looked hopeless.

"Mattas, help me take him upstairs," Valens repeated, not so calmly this time.

Mattas rushed and grabbed Themis's right arm. The men made their way upstairs, taking Themis to his bedroom, where they helped him lie down.

The doctor gave the Magistrate a small glass of liquor. "Drink it at once. It will put some life back in you."

Themis drank it and felt the liquor burning his throat and mouth. "Thank you, Valens," he murmured. Then he turned to Mattas, who was putting a pillow behind his head. "Thank you, Mattas. Thank you, my friend."

Mattas nodded. "Is the Magistrate sick?" he asked Valens.

"I am fine. The unfortunate news caught me off guard. That's all. Valens, let's talk about my daughter." Themis struggled to sit down and keep his eyes open.

Mattas motioned to leave, but Themis held his arm. "Stay. I need a friend with me now, Mattas."

The advisor nodded and smiled. There was kindness in his eyes.

Doctor Valens assented. "The girl should be fine. Her mother told me she left her daughter in good spirits cooking dinner this afternoon. Upon the mother's return from her last errands of the day, she found the girl on her knees crying and screaming her brother's name," he explained.

Themis's heart almost stopped. "Was she calling for Anandy?" His eyes were wide.

"It seems so, Magistrate," Valens replied. "Their mother has provided little information. Understandably, the whole thing has shaken her."

Mattas noticed a cloud on Themis's face. "Can we do anything to make the girl more comfortable?" he asked.

Valens nodded vigorously. "Yes! It is important to keep her covered with blankets to make her sweat as much as possible. Keep the windows closed during the night and open them during the day for fresh air. Change her bedsheets every morning. Give her warm baths, and," Valens paused and turned his attention to Themis, "*talk* to her. Try to bring her back to us."

The Magistrate nodded eagerly, but he didn't reply. He felt as if hope was returning to his heart.

"She is young. I am confident she will recover soon," Valens said, looking at Themis. "Your color is coming back, Magistrate. I shall bid my farewell and return tomorrow to check on the girl."

"Valens," Themis said, trying to get up, "please, keep things private between us. I don't want people talking about my daughter."

"I never discuss my patients' affairs, Themis. It is against the Code of Medical Honor," Valens replied as he was leaving the room and closing the door behind him.

"I will send word to my wife to come and help," Mattas said. "No need to worry. We will keep it private. My lady is very fond of the girl, and it will please her to help nurse her back to health."

"Thank you, Mattas." Themis was gazing at the closed door.

He is at a loss, Mattas thought. *I have never seen Themis so defeated in my entire life*. The advisor could feel his friend's sorrow.

"Themis," Mattas called softly, "the girl has your family's blood in her veins. She will fight her way back to us. Everything will work out just fine in the end."

The Magistrate looked at his friend. He couldn't help but notice how shiny Mattas's green eyes were. "Hopeful Mattas!" Themis whispered. "You always see positivity in dark moments. How can you truly believe everything will turn out just fine? It was you who came to my office to tell me that my son was missing. Then we got word from my wife about my daughter." Themis kept his eyes fixed on the closed door. "Both of my children are in danger! My lineage is in danger! How can you have hope in such dark moments? My poor wife is suffering in silence at our daughter's bedside! My family is ruined!" Themis seemed to be in a trance.

Mattas smiled compassionately. He took a seat next to the Magistrate's bed, his eyes shining. "Because when there is life, there is hope, Themis." He grinned. "There is always hope."

These words hit Themis deep inside. He felt like the darkness the day had brought him was dispelled.

Mattas placed a hand on Themis's shoulder. "It is not the time to despair, but to act."

Themis nodded but remained silent. He didn't know what to say.

"I believe," the advisor said, "it would be prudent to talk to your wife about what *really* happened to the girl." Mattas stood up slowly. "I will send word to my lady to come at once."

"Anandy." Themis's heart sank when he pronounced his son's name. "I must find him! I–I must find out what happened to him... I must..." The pain was unbearable. This pain was guilt, and it had been growing in his heart since Mattas brought the news of his son going missing. "I should have listened to him. He was trying to be useful. But I repelled him and called him insolent. It's all my fault." Themis buried his face in his hands.

"Themis, it is not the time for lamentations. I have a feeling that your conversation with your wife might offer a valuable lead. Meanwhile, I will send a patrol to look for Anandy in the City and within our borders. I will caution the men to keep a low profile," Mattas added. "Now, go to your wife. She needs you. I will make all the arrangements." The advisor helped Themis to stand up and guided him to Aura's room.

Taking a deep breath, Mattas left the house on that chilly evening. "I believe! I believe!" the advisor repeated to himself, trying to regain his composure. *My friend needs me to believe. These kids need all my hope and good thoughts. It is not time to let them down. But first, it is time to fulfill my real duties.* The advisor headed for the busy streets of the City Center.

Chapter Six

The Garden

The pain and terror were unbearable to my weak body. I felt like I was breaking from the inside out, trapped in a dark room. No. It was more than that. Darkness and terror wrapped their long, thin arms around me. Pain consumed my very being. I couldn't see. All around me was dark. Only one thing was clear: the torment of those souls lying on the battlefield. I could feel their pain and the evil lurking around them.

"Please, help me! I don't want to see it! Why do I have to be here?" I implored, closing my eyes.

Then I heard his voice, the well-known strong and deep voice of the man who watches over me during my nights of torment.

"Open your eyes and come to me, Aura."

"What?" I froze. "Did he just say my name? A man saying my name? I am scared!" Tears of despair inundated my face.

"Have no fear! You are not alone, Aura. Trust and follow the path to me," the man said.

I opened my eyes. I was mesmerized to see that the darkness had cleared. I was barefoot, and somehow I could see my figure standing on a staircase. It wasn't the one in my father's house, though. It was different. The steps glittered gold. The delicate light silver handrail was shaped into a beautiful circular pattern. I saw myself wearing a long white dress. My blond curls gently moved free on my shoulders and down my back. At the top of the staircase was a magnificent wooden door. Although it looked heavy, it opened easily, leading to the most beautiful garden I have ever seen.

The sky was blue, and there was a soft breeze playing with my dress and curls. I stepped into the garden, and the sunshine bathed my body. The warmth of the sun above me and the softness of the grass underneath my feet healed instantly all my aches and sorrows. I could feel a calm and joy that I had never experienced in my brief life. The world seemed to have slowed down, and everything fell into place.

I walked into that magical garden, running my hands through those magnificent flowers of various colors and shapes. Some of them were unknown to me but no less spectacular than the others. The birds were singing their joyous song above my head. I saw some beautiful little brown birds on the branches of a white tree. I smiled at the sight of them. My ears caught an insistent honking sound. I turned my gaze to the right and saw a flock of geese making their way to a distant land.

I walked over the bright green grass while my pale hands touched the robust trunks of ancient trees. My hand gave a small twitch. I could feel those majestic trees' strength and wisdom. I felt calm, at peace. I was at home.

Sitting on a big rock in front of a pond was the tall shadow of the man who had been standing next to my bed since I was a little girl, always telling me to open my eyes and come back to the waking world when things got too scary in the sleeping one.

He was there, looking at me and smiling. I approached him. I felt drawn to him. He smiled even broader. And he hugged me! No man besides Anandy and Father had ever hugged me. At first, I didn't know what to do, but his warm hug felt right. There was love in it. I wrapped my arms around him. The pain and fear were gone.

"Thank you for coming to me, Aura." His voice was firm but gentle.

I stared at him while taking a mental picture. He was tall and blond and had deep blue eyes and the most beautiful smile I had ever seen. He looked young and old at the same time. It was like it was impossible to tell how old he really was. He was dressed in a white, loose long-sleeved shirt; its cuffs were star-shaped. His pants were a light shade of blue. He was barefoot. I gazed at his outfit, realizing how foreign it was. Men in our Society didn't dress in such a manner.

"Why am I here?" I heard myself asking.

The man hugged me once again. There was something about his hugs that filled me with warmth and love.

"You came to me, Aura. You found the way to the Garden. You were and always will be welcome here." As he spoke, his form changed. He became younger and older, taller, and shorter, his hair changed colors, his eyes changed colors, and his skin changed colors. It was like he was becoming a different person with every word he said.

"You came here with a heavy heart full of questions, and I am here to answer them," he said when his face changed into the woman's face I saw in my room.

"You look like my mother, but you are not her. You look younger than her. How can you change forms? Who are you? What are you?"

She engulfed my hands in hers. "Appearances are irrelevant, Aura. It is easier for people when we take on the appearance of a loved one."

"We? Who are *we*? What are we? Are you even human? Are you a demon?" I asked, mesmerized, watching the being change into an old man.

"No, sweet child. We are no demons. We are humans' very essence. Human consciousness." The old man smiled kindly.

If it was under different circumstances, I would have been frightened, but I wasn't. This being in front of me fascinated me.

"I don't understand. What's your name?"

The old man turned into a child of no older than eight.

"We had names when we were alive. We had families, lives, titles, and possessions, but all these are earthly things. They do not belong here, Aura." The child spoke to me in his childish voice.

"Why do you keep saying my name? I am a woman. The men and women in our Society call me 'girl'," I said while gazing at his soft, delicate child's face.

"Humans have the need to put a name on what they consider important. Why did you receive a name if you cannot use it?" The child smiled wisely.

I didn't have an answer for that. I simply looked at him. My eyes and heart were wide open.

"I lived many lives, and I was called by different names. I can give you a name, if that is what you wish, but it is irrelevant because I am more than a name, and so are you, Aura." The child turned into the tall blond man who had welcomed me into the Garden.

"No. I am only a girl. I am nameless. I am the Magistrate's daughter, the famous Warrior's sister, and someday someone's wife and mother." My heart was heavy, and there was a knot in my throat.

"Do you really believe in it?"

"No," I said without hesitation. I couldn't believe I said that out loud.

"Then you must find who you really are." The man took my hands. I felt a warm, pleasant feeling radiating from them. "Close your eyes and tell me, Aura. Who are you?"

I closed my eyes. I kept my gaze down. The warmth from his hands sent a white-bluish light into my small fingers. I could see it in my mind's eye. It started as a beam of light. It was weak at first, almost faint.

"Feel the warmth, Aura," the man said. "Focus on the light."

And so I did. I turned all my attention to that faint beam of white-bluish light. Slowly, the beam became stronger. I felt as if it was dancing in front of me, just like the little fairies dancing in my bedroom every morning in my mind. I smiled as I remembered my little friends.

"Tell me who you really are," he repeated.

"Who I really am." The words echoed from my lips.

The light got stronger. It was a big white-bluish circle.

"Keep breathing," he said. "Focus on the light."

I realized I was holding my breath. I took a long, deep breath and once again turned all my attention to the light. This time, I reminded myself to keep breathing.

Light surrounded me. All I could see was that.

"Breathe into the light." His voice was inside my head.

I did it. Then I saw fire. Bright yellow-reddish fire flames replaced the light. A large red dragon flew into the sky, spitting fire. I smiled at the sight. I could feel its power. Its blaze was warm and pleasant, just like that white-bluish light. The dragon and I locked eyes. Its large yellow iris and black vertical pupil were placed on me. I could see myself in its eyes as if it was a mirror. I took a step forward, and the dragon showed me its long, pointy yellow teeth. There was a flame inside of it. And I understood. *I* was the dragon!

The dragon raised its scaly body into the air and spat fire. From the fire, the image of a great phoenix emerged screaming and putting out the fire in the skies with its wings. I gazed at it, amazed. The phoenix gave a strident scream and looked down at me. I took a step forward. I could feel the wind of its wings flapping. The fire was growing inside me. *I* was the phoenix.

Next, the dragon and the phoenix were gone. The fire was gone. The white-bluish light was gone. There was only a black circle. I was no longer the dragon or the phoenix. I focused my attention on this black circle, and I realized it was flashing in my core. It expanded slowly to my entire body. Soon, there was no Aura. There was nothing, only a black circle. That was when the truth hit me.

"This is who I really am," I whispered.

I opened my eyes. I was back in the Garden. Everything seemed peaceful. The man was standing in front of me. "Now you know." He smiled.

"Yes," I said, "but what should I do next?" I was eager to learn more.

"You will do what humans are supposed to do when faced with the truth. You will act, Aura."

I stopped for a moment. How could I act? What should I do? I wanted to ask him so many questions. I felt so overwhelmed!

"Why do I see and dream about things that come true?" I heard myself asking the question that had haunted me my entire life.

"You are not the only one, child. There are a few people who are like you. Actually, everyone is capable of hearing and seeing us; however, they choose to close their ears and eyes to us. A few, like yourself, are more sensitive than others and decided to open their hearts to us, which makes me grateful to have this conversation with you." The man looked pleased with my question, as if he had been expecting to answer it for a long time.

"There are others like me? I always thought I was an outcast. I always thought I was alone." I grinned. I felt good knowing that I was not somehow broken or Nature's mistake.

The man took my hands again and kissed them. I kissed his hands as well.

"Are you an angel?" I asked shyly, immersed in his deep blue eyes.

The man gave a good-humored laugh. "Remember, once you name something, you limit it." Then, looking into my eyes, he added, "But, since you insist, you can call us Good Friends. It is our duty to help humanity in times of need to advance through goodness, kindness, and honesty."

"The woman. I mean, you. You told me there was something coming to my kin. I could feel the emptiness inside me. I had this feeling of hopelessness. What is coming?"

"There is a shadow coming to your people, Aura. It will take many lives, and it will change the course of your history forever." There was urgency in his voice.

"What is coming?" I felt a shiver of fear on the back of my neck.

The man looked deep into my eyes, as if he could see my soul. I could feel his eyes searching. After what seemed an eternity, he finally said, "A monster. A monster is coming, Aura."

Among all things, a monster wasn't exactly what I expected to hear. For a second I thought it was a joke, but I saw a shadow covering his deep blue eyes, and a chill travelled down my spine.

"You don't mean that a...a...an actual monster is coming, do you?" I hesitated.

"It is as I said, Aura. A monster is coming to your kin. As a matter of fact, it is already among your people. This monster can take thousands of lives if it is not defeated."

His words went against everything I had ever learned. Monsters do not exist. They are old wives' tales to scare the little ones to go to bed early and to behave. How could a monster come to Green Valleys and kill thousands? However, here I was in this magical Garden, talking to a spirit, having visions of dragons and phoenixes.

"Why is this monster coming to us?"

"Because your people attracted it. Your people invited and welcomed the monster to stay, Aura." There was sadness in his eyes.

"How is it possible? Nobody would consciously welcome a monster into their homes. If there is someone hiding this monster, I must warn the warriors, and we need an army to defeat it!" The chill had spread to my entire body now.

The man looked at the pond as if he was trying to meditate or in search of words to use. "Aura," he finally said, "you came here with a heart full of questions, and I am here to answer them all, but you are not asking the right questions."

I looked at the pond, at the ducks with their ducklings and a couple of swans with their babies on their backs. Then it came to me.

"What do I have to do? What does this monster have to do with me?"

He flashed his beautiful smile again. "Now you are asking the right questions," he said. "*You* will defeat the monster, Aura."

Chapter Seven

Fear

Themis stood still with the white door in front of him. His heart was pounding. The slight tremor in his hands was there once again. He knew all he had to do was open it and talk to his wife about Aura and Anandy, but he couldn't. There was no strength left in his being.

"Fear lurks in every man's soul and waits for the right moment to bury its teeth in their minds. It makes you weak. Fear makes you less than a man. Never allow it to enter your house or it will eat you alive." His father's words echoed stubbornly in his mind.

"You are weak. You are scared." The Magistrate could hear his father spitting these words in his ears. *"You are pathetic. You ended our bloodline!"*

Themis closed his eyes for a second and took a deep breath, hoping to shut out the voice.

It's not real, he thought. *That old bastard died years ago.* A chill travelled through his entire body. *He's burning in Hell!* The mere thought of his father's suffering was enough to ease the shaking of his hand. The Magistrate opened his eyes, placed his hand on the silver doorknob, and turned it.

Aura's white room felt darker and suffocating. Themis stood by the door. Lying in bed, pale and motionless, was his sweet girl. Her lips were as white as the bedroom's walls, and her cheeks were as red as flames. A thick blanket covered her. Sitting next to her, weeping quietly, was his wife.

Themis felt the urge to leave, to run from that place. *I can't do it! I can't see them like this.*

"Husband!" His wife ran into his arms. Her small body shook as she wept for her daughter. Themis hugged her and ran his fingers through her long, straight, blond hair. The muscles in his shoulders relaxed a bit.

Her hair always smells good, he thought, closing his eyes as he inhaled the sweet aroma.

"Oh, husband!" she whispered. "Our poor little girl!"

She doesn't know about Anandy! Poor soul! What a tragedy in our family! Themis kissed her forehead.

"Husband," she called, "I am doing as Doctor Valens instructed me. He said there is hope for our little girl." She jumped suddenly, as if she had just remembered something. "Oh! You must be hungry! I am sorry! I completely forgot about dinner. I just have to cool her down a bit, and I will be off to the kitchen," she said hurriedly.

Themis stood silently in front of his wife. Her commitment amazed him. He could not understand how she had the strength to nurse their sick daughter and still fulfill her chores.

"I am not hungry, wife," the Magistrate said gently, sitting on a small white chair by Aura's bed. "My poor angel!" he murmured, touching his daughter's hot cheek. "Your father and your mother are here, daughter. We love you!" He gave Aura a loving kiss on her forehead and felt the warmth radiating from her flushed skin.

Themis stood up slowly and took his wife by her hand, leading her to the window, away from Aura's bed. He turned to his wife, admiring the soft lines of her delicate face. He touched her beautiful face as he wiped her tears.

"Tell me, my wife. What happened?" Themis gently kissed her hands.

He noticed her hands were shaking and cold. *The poor woman has been going through a lot,* he thought, waiting for her answer.

"Upon returning home from my errands, I encountered her in a state of distress, sobbing and wailing," she murmured.

"Doctor Valens already told me that. He also mentioned that she was screaming Anandy's name. I want to know what *really* happened, wife." He studied her face, searching for answers.

"That's what happened, husband," she replied hesitantly.

Themis's expression changed to a displeased frown. His eyes never wavered from hers. "Wife..." he paused for a moment, "I know there is something more to it. I understand I made it clear that I didn't want to hear about our daughter's...*stories...dreams...*" The unease in his voice was clear.

She nodded and lowered her eyes, avoiding his. Themis held his wife's face between his hands.

She's so beautiful! Even after so many years.

"Tell me what really happened." His voice was low and gentle.

She opened her mouth but changed her mind. She lowered her gaze once more, avoiding her husband's.

"Wife, tell me what happened *now!*" Themis's voice was no longer gentle and low.

"It's...it's..." She gazed at the rough, wooden floor.

Themis clenched his fists. The walls of the white room seemed to close in on him as the temperature rose, like a boiling pot. He could feel his skin getting hot.

"How dare you have secrets from your husband? Did you forget your place, woman?" he bellowed, his voice booming like thunder.

His wife's eyes widened as she took a step back. Her teeth chattered with fear as her entire body shuddered. Themis's voice reverberated around the entire house.

With a swift and sudden movement, the door opened. Mattas and his wife were standing at the threshold.

"Oh! I hope I am not interrupting, Magistrate," the advisor said politely. "Your servant girl allowed us upstairs."

"You are not, Mattas." Themis's wife shifted her gaze away from the floor, her eyes now meeting her husband's. "We are done here. My daughter needs my attention now," she said.

A fireball had ignited in Themis' stomach, growing in intensity and making its way up to his chest.

This woman is disrespecting me in front of another man, he thought, clenching his fists tighter. He could feel the fingernails buried in his skin. He ignored the pain.

The advisor bowed his head slightly to the Magistrate's wife. "My lady, I brought my wife in order to ease your burden." Then, turning to Themis, "There is a matter that requires your attention, sir." Mattas stepped into the room, followed by his wife.

Themis's wife's face softened when she saw the older lady. She seemed relieved to have her dearest friend with her in that hour of need.

"Oh, my dear friend! I am here now for you and your little girl." The good woman embraced Themis's wife in a gentle, loving hug.

The Magistrate took a couple of steps toward the ladies. His heart raced as his blood boiled. His knuckles were white from gripping them so hard.

Mattas stood between him and the women. "Themis, my friend. Come with me. I have some important news for you." He wrapped his left arm around the Magistrate's shoulders and guided him out of the bedroom, turning to his wife and giving her a meaningful look. She nodded. The advisor closed the door behind him.

Themis ran down the stairs and sprinted to his office. His heavy steps echoed in the house. Mattas took his time walking silently behind the Magistrate. By the time he got into the office, Themis was walking up and down the room, fuming.

"Who do you think you are, Mattas?" The Magistrate jumped as Mattas closed the office door behind him. "This is not your house! It's *my* house! I am the one who gives the orders here! Do you understand, advisor?"

Mattas didn't reply. The tranquility in his eyes only served to further enrage Themis.

"How dare you enter my daughter's bedroom without my permission? Did you forget who I am? I am the Magistrate! I am the most powerful man in Green

Valleys! No one disrespects me in my own house!" Themis yelled, throwing a vase at the door behind him.

Mattas merely glanced at the shattered vase, undisturbed. His full attention was on the Magistrate.

"Why did you bring me here if you have nothing to say, advisor? Did you forget who I am?" Themis asked breathlessly.

"Perhaps *you* forgot who you really are, Themis," Mattas said calmly.

The Magistrate didn't reply. His entire body was shaking. His throat was burning from the yelling. He was confused.

Mattas observed the Magistrate. His face was emotionless. "When one asks the question you just asked me, it means he is uncertain of whom he is," the advisor replied calmly. "By belittling others and trying to put them in 'their places' or reminding them of whom he *is,* he is desperately trying to convince himself that he is that person." He paused. He gazed at Themis. "Is that the case for you, Themis? Are you uncertain of whom you are? Is that the reason you yelled at your wife and broke that vase? Are you trying to make a point? Or are you trying to hide your own doubts and insecurities, *my friend?*"

Themis stood speechless in front of his advisor. Nobody had ever talked to him in such a manner. Especially Mattas, reliable and polite Mattas.

"Perhaps you are hiding your own fears, Themis." Mattas's voice was low but firm.

The Magistrate felt like an invisible hammer had crushed him. He reached for a chair behind him and sat down, gazing at the floor.

"Fear?" he repeated. There was no longer anger or frustration in his voice, only shame.

Mattas pulled out a chair and sat next to the Magistrate. "Yes, fear," he repeated. "Let me ask you again, Magistrate. Is your behavior a way of coping with fear?"

Themis had always avoided this word. It had been a forbidden word in his father's house. It was a forbidden word in the South. This unspeakable word was also a forbidden feeling. No man should experience fear.

"Fear makes you less than a man." He could hear his late father's voice whispering these well-known words in his ear.

He could hear the old man's voice and his scornful laughter as clearly as he could hear Mattas. The realization that the voice wasn't coming from his head but from a place next to him sent a shiver down his spine. Themis glanced down at his blood-stained hands. There were some minor cuts caused by his fingernails being pressed against his skin. There was a slight burning feeling coming from them. Neither the pain nor the blood bothered him. The only thing on his mind right now was fear.

I am scared. I am lost. Fear makes its home in my heart for the first time in my life. But I dare not to say these words aloud. No soul should learn from my lips about my weaknesses. I must keep my name and my title. Themis clenched his fists again. The pain was a bit more acute than the first time. Feeling his nails buried in his flesh was a way of taking his mind off from that unspeakable word. The forbidden feeling among men in Green Valleys.

Mattas could sense the Magistrate's pride. He knew talking to him was pointless, but it was his duty as his senior advisor to give him the news.

"Magistrate," Mattas said, "I just got the first report from the men I sent in search of Anandy."

Themis's face lightened. "So? Where is my son? Did they find him?"

"Not yet, but there are witnesses who saw him walking determinedly at the borders of the City toward the South."

Themis furrowed his brow in confusion. "Why would Anandy go to the South? There is nothing for him there. It doesn't make sense."

"That's why I came here, Magistrate. As you know, there are rules among the Clans." Mattas ran his fingers worriedly through his gray hair. "One cannot send their own warriors to another Clan's lands. Therefore, I cannot send our men to the South without the permission of their leader. Besides, we would need Leader Dansa's permission to send some warriors from the City's army to the South. There are not enough warriors in your personal guard for such a quest."

Themis sighed. He knew Mattas was right. There were ancient agreements among all clans that needed to be respected to keep peace and goodwill in Green Valleys' lands. He placed his left hand under his chin and meditated on the topic for a few moments.

When he spoke, his voice was distant, as if it was coming from a dream. "Send the army to the South, advisor."

Mattas's heart skipped a beat as a wave of fear washed over him. "Themis," he called faintly, "you can't do that! The agreements made by our ancestors," he hesitated, "you cannot break them!"

Themis narrowed his eyes, and his pale lips shivered in anger. "I am the *Magistrate*, old man. I am the *Law.* I am above agreements. Send the army and bring my son back. Even if it means burning those hellish lands to the ground."

Chapter Eight

Adira

Mattas's wife delicately placed a cold washcloth on Aura's forehead. "You will come back to us. Your parents need you. *We* need you, my lovely." Her voice was full of gentle, maternal affection. She was an experienced mother and grandmother.

Standing by the window was the Magistrate's wife, staring into the night sky. "My babies always loved watching the stars and the moon." Her heart was heavy. The image of Aura crouched hopeless in a corner on the kitchen floor in a delirious state plagued her memory. Her pale, shivering lips pronouncing those horrific words still haunted her.

No! she thought, forcing the memory from her mind.

"My lovely," the advisor's wife called softly.

Themis's wife didn't reply. Her thoughts were darker than the night sky.

There was a tender touch on her back. "I know you don't want to, but you should rest, my lovely."

The younger lady turned her attention to her friend, stopping for a second to watch the latter's gentle eyes.

"Thank you for coming in an hour of need, my friend. But I would rather stay with my daughter," she said.

"I understand, my lovely," the older lady replied. "Here, have some bread and cheese with me." She reached for her big leather bag. "We need some energy if we are going to bring our girl back to us. Come. Eat with me." Mattas's wife took a beautiful loaf of bread and placed it on Aura's snack tray. The bread was brown and soft. The intoxicating aroma of freshly baked bread invaded the younger woman's nostrils. Her stomach roared a bit. Next, the older lady took from her bag a bunch of small, purple, seedless grapes. They looked soft and juicy.

The advisor's wife smiled. "And here is your favorite, my lovely!" She placed a piece of hard cheese on the tray.

Reluctantly, the Magistrate's wife took a seat by her friend's side at the small circular table in Aura's room. She attempted to curve her lips into a matching smile, but her face felt heavy and unmoving. So, she simply put a small piece of bread in her mouth. It was soft and still warm. She took a small bite of the cheese. The strong and characteristic taste of that delicacy from Green Valleys made the poor woman realize how hungry she was.

The advisor's wife took a bottle of warm milk from her bag and poured it into two small glasses.

"I just baked the bread. It is with your favorite herbs. I also got this cheese and the milk today. It came straight from the Northern Lands. It is very fresh and delicious! Come! Have more! Eat, my lovely! Eat!"

To Aura's mother's surprise, she managed to eat more than she thought was possible.

"I really don't know how I can eat on such a dreadful day." She sighed, ashamed of her appetite.

Mattas's wife gave her famous quiet laugh, shaking her belly and arms. It made her friend smile.

"You know, my lovely, I am notorious for my laughter. It is infectious!" She filled the Magistrate's wife's glass with more warm milk. "There is nothing to be ashamed of. Kids get sick. That's the course of life. She is young, and she will be fine in no time. You know, I raised five kids, and when one was sick, all of them would get sick. It was too much for this poor old lady. I am glad they are adults, and they have their own kids to keep them up at night." She winked.

Aura's mother lowered her eyes as she took a sip of the milk and nodded politely.

"At least your older son is healthy," the older lady added casually. She stared at her friend's face.

Themis's wife felt like there was a knot in her stomach. *Anandy, my boy!* she thought, fighting back tears.

The Magistrate's wife hurried to her daughter's bedside, squeezing the girl's hand. "It won't happen if I don't say it." She quietly repeated her father's words. She could almost hear his soft voice whispering these words while he held his daughter in the middle of the night after a nightmare.

"*It's fine. It won't happen if you don't say it. Keep it to yourself, and evil won't work its way to you.*" She could hear her beloved father's voice in her ears.

Aura's mother's shoulders relaxed, and her jaw unclenched. She felt a wave of warmth wash over her, creating a sense of safety and security. *Father, I can feel you here. Please, help me! Please protect my Aura from evil!* Big tears rolled down her cheeks.

The advisor's wife rushed to hug her friend. "I know, my lovely!" She kissed her forehead. "I know it's hard, but everything will be fine. Let's have some faith. There is no need to speak to me now. The look in your eyes tells me that sorrow has taken up residence in your heart." Mattas's wife guided the Magistrate's wife to the small chair by the table. "Come, lovely. Sit down and have some warm milk. I am here for you and your baby girl," she said. "There is no need to speak to me. Please, stop crying."

"I can't! I can't! It's just too much! Oh! Why? My babies!" She wept, burying her face in her hands.

"Your babies?" Mattas's wife asked. "The girl will come back to us in no time, and Anandy is..." She halted. She didn't want to upset her friend even more.

The younger lady stopped crying and lifted her head to face the older lady's gaze. "Anandy is what?"

"A–Anandy is...is...he's fine, isn't he?" Mattas's wife stuttered.

Doubt was raised in the younger lady's heart. She could almost taste something in the air as she peered suspiciously into her friend's eyes. There was an icy feeling going up her belly.

"You were the one who cried when I mentioned the boy's name. I assumed something had happened, since he is not here by his parents' and sister's side in such a dark hour. I hope he's fine and just out being the naughty boy he is."

The Magistrate's wife did not bother to answer her friend's remark.

It makes sense, but I can feel she knows more than she's saying, she thought, forcing herself to smile.

"Of course. He is fine. I am just a bit overwhelmed by the news of the day. Would you be kind enough to bring some fresh pillows for my girl and a bowl of cold water? The servants can help you with that. I should apply more cold compresses to her forehead to lower the fever. Thank you, my lovely." She tried her hardest to give an earnest, genuine smile.

With a brief nod, the older lady hurried out of the room. Themis's wife watched her leave.

"Your grandfather taught me to trust my instincts," Themis's wife whispered into Aura's ear. "My instincts are telling me that this lady is trying to gain information from me about your brother." The icy feeling was moving up to her chest. Her hands were feeling colder. "Don't worry, my darling! I know that what you saw was not the truth. It was just a bad dream. Anandy is alive, and he is fine! Remember, it won't happen if you don't say it." She touched Aura's forehead.

The tired lady gave her daughter's hand a squeeze and planted a soft kiss on her warm, rosy cheeks.

"I love you, baby. Mother will protect you and your brother from everyone." She turned to the window and saw the bright stars bringing some light to that fateful night. *Even from your father*, Aura's mother thought. The icy feeling was on her chest now. There was fear and distrust in her heart. *I can't trust anyone! Even her!* she thought, glancing at the door through which Mattas's wife had just exited. "I trusted her my entire life. She is the only mother I have ever had. She raised me!" Tears filled her eyes. "But I am a mother myself, and it is my duty to protect my children. Even if it means keeping it all inside myself." She squeezed her daughter's hand once again, thinking of Aura's last words before she fell ill.

"Anandy is dead, Mother!" Aura screamed on the floor, hugging her knees. Tears of despair bathed her face.

"What are you talking about, baby?" Her mother tried to hug Aura and help her get to her feet, but Aura slapped her hand away and screamed in a way that would haunt her mother forever.

"I saw his body destroyed by arrows! Anandy lies dead on the grass!"

That was when Aura passed out and hadn't woken up since.

"I can't fail my children!" her mother whispered.

A chill of fear mixed with disgust ran down her spine when she thought about Themis. It'd been many months since she noticed a change in her husband's behavior. Themis had been more unstable than ever. He had become quieter and more reserved and more impatient and controlling than ever.

"Themis was always insecure and somehow unstable, but he was never aggressive. He never dared raise his voice toward me," she pondered as she placed Aura's curl behind her ear. "He is no fool to treat me with violence. Themis knows who I am. I will not give up on my children and succumb to despair, as their father did."

The room felt chillier than before. The icy feeling in her chest grew bigger and now engulfed her whole body. She shivered and raised her chest to be kissed by the cold. She could feel its embrace. As if she was welcoming an old friend, she smiled and bowed her head. It'd been a long time since she experienced this pleasant feeling, and long since she left her homeland to marry Themis.

"I am stronger than pitiful men!" Her voice filled the room. "My ancestors are with me. Their spirits are guiding my path." She felt the cold emanating inward to outward. "There is no fear in my heart, for I am Adira, daughter of Allura. I am a daughter of the North, and I never walk alone!" Adira felt her mother next to her and the icy shiver from the North in her veins once again.

"Remember who you are, Aura. You are a daughter of the North. A child of Allura. You are free!"

Aura's hands moved. Her body shivered. Adira smiled.

"Yes, my child. Feel the Northern Lands in your blood. Learn who you are, for your mother forgot it for so many years!"

Aura's eyes opened. "I always wondered what your name was, Mother. Adira is such a beautiful name."

Chapter Nine

The Monster

My jaw dropped in shock, my mind unable to process what he had said. I opened my mouth, but my lips felt dry, and I struggled to find words.

"You heard me well, Aura." There was a grave look in his eyes. "You are the one who will defeat the monster. That's why you are here."

"How... I..." Words finally came to my tongue. "How can I possibly defeat someone or something? I am not a warrior! I am just a girl!"

"Aura." His face softened. "True strength is not in a limb. Power comes from within. It comes from a gentle heart. A strong and stable mind."

I was in awe. His words resonated deep inside me.

"I am from a Society where a strong limb is worthy of all honors," I said unwarily.

The man became a child of no older than eight or nine. His eyes were shiny, and a golden light surrounded him. The child smiled at me. It felt like I was touched by the sun. He spoke to me in a sweet, childish voice that I will never forget.

"What you just described is pride." The child grinned again. "It is not true power. Everyone can have access to true power if they have eyes to see and ears to hear."

I stayed silent; the words caught in my throat. I didn't want to say anything. All I wanted was to listen and learn. My eyes, ears, and heart were fully open to that entity standing in front of me.

"Monsters are real, Aura," the child said. "They are merely a reflection of our fears and insecurities. We all face monsters every single day of our lives. They are present in every doubt we have. Monsters are there when you fear what your neighbor will say about you, or when you wonder what the future holds. You can hear them in the distant echoes of your past. Even deep within your soul. You can hear them in the back of your mind, discouraging you from reaching your highest potential. From being who you really are. From unlocking your true power. Monsters exist with the sole purpose of being defeated."

The images of a dragon and a giant three-headed werewolf came to my mind. I felt silly trying to picture the monster. Deep inside, I knew this monster was not from one of my fairy-tale books. I felt my cheeks burn, and I tried to sweep those images away.

"I can tell you one thing for sure. This monster is not what you think it is, Aura." The child smiled as if he could read my mind.

"I used to read stories of monsters and fairies when I was growing up. Books were a way of escaping reality. Being somewhere else. Being someone else." I could feel the heat rising to my cheeks. I had told no one about this.

"You try to escape reality when you do not know how to live in it." The child's voice was sweet and calm.

"Don't we all need an escape from our lives?"

"No. Escaping is the opposite of living your life. How could you possibly live your life if you try to find mechanisms to escape reality?"

I did not have an answer for that. I simply stared at him. My lips were partly open, still in awe.

"The answer is not escaping when you face vicissitudes," he said.

"What is the answer, then?" I asked eagerly.

"The answer is to be fully present. Especially when you do not want to be." The light invested in his little body shone brighter.

The idea of being fully present at every moment of my life sounded like a nightmare. Why couldn't I just be someone else, living an adventure or a

love story through the pages of a book? That was safer and more pleasant than being a little bird in a cage. Being nameless. Being only a girl. A daughter. A sister.

"Being fully present? Why would I want that?"

"Because it is the only way to master yourself." His light grew even brighter. It touched my skin. It was warm. I felt my shoulders loosen. "And you will learn how to live your life and choose which path to follow."

My face lit up with a wide, genuine smile. His light caressed my skin like a soft breeze. I felt a wave of relaxation sweep over my body. I was a bit more receptive to his idea of being fully present. Perhaps it wasn't such a terrible thing.

"Learn how to live our lives? Choose a path to follow?" I asked hesitantly, my voice barely audible.

"Yes. There is no need to escape reality when you learn how to build the life you want to live." His whole body was engulfed in that light.

I uttered admiringly, "It's like the warmth of the sun radiating around us."

The child grinned. "The sun will burn your eyes if you gaze at it directly."

"You are not burning me," I replied.

"I am not the sun, Aura."

"You are light," I whispered and marveled.

"I am a friend," he said. "A good friend."

I blinked several times. It was as if I was coming back from a dream. I looked around. The pond waters were calm and still. The simple image of that pond was enough to bring calm and peace to my heart. The low and gentle music of the birds filled my ears. I sighed in delight as the fresh breeze caressed my hair and touched my skin.

"This is the life I want. This is the path I want to choose. I want to feel this peace every moment of my life." I felt warm tears rolling down my cheeks. That magnificent garden had touched my heart. The words from

that Good Friend touched my soul. I desperately needed to live in that place with him.

The light shone even brighter. There was no need for him to utter the words. I knew it in my heart.

"Not yet," I caught myself saying. "Not until I fulfill my duty."

"Duty?" He grinned. "There is no duty, Aura."

I was confused. "Isn't it my duty to defeat the monster?" I felt awkward saying that.

"No," he said softly, "duty implies an obligation. It gives the idea of something you must do. We, the Good Friends, don't impose duties on any soul. We offer a choice, and it is up to you to build your own path."

I didn't reply. The doors and windows in my mind were open to receiving such powerful teaching.

"It is your choice whether you will fight and defeat this monster." The honesty in his voice made me tremble. It was the first time in my life I had a choice. I'd spent my entire life being told what to do. I'd never needed to think or plan for myself. It was the men's job to decide. We women obeyed.

I inhaled the sweet scent of the flowers and closed my eyes, surrounded by nature. I listened as it whispered to me. The breeze rustled through my hair. The birds chirped their cheerful melodies. I felt the rays of the sun on my skin like a comforting embrace. I opened my eyes.

"I must defeat this monster if I want to experience this peace. If I want my kin to experience it." My body trembled. "It is the only way to build a life where I will no longer wish to escape." I inhaled the fresh air. It filled my lungs and being with hope. "No one will ever feel the need to escape reality."

The child nodded.

"You told me this monster is not what I think it is. Why?"

The child looked into my eyes. I trembled once again. I felt like he could see my soul.

"The monster, Aura," he said. "It is not what you think because it is an invisible monster."

I gasped. "Invisible?"

The child didn't move, his eyes fixed on me. "It lurks in everyone's hearts and minds. It feeds itself off their insecurities while it distils its venom and traps their hosts as a parasite."

"Their hosts? What do you mean?" I felt a shiver going down my spine.

"This monster worms its way into its hosts, making them believe its presence is a natural part of themselves. They lose their sense of identity. The monster latches on to its hosts, draining them of life and happiness and sowing the seeds of fear, greed, insecurity, and violence in their hearts, making them feel weak, alone, insecure, unstable, and invisible."

"Invisible?" I asked, remembering my visions. "Invisible, cold and warm, covered and exposed..." I repeated to myself.

The child became the blond man again. His deep voice confirmed my fears. "Yes, Aura. We showed you the first signs of the monster's attack."

The recollection of that awful feeling made my skin crawl, and I felt like I was going to vomit.

"I don't understand. You told me my people are opening their doors to this monster. They are welcoming it into their houses. How could anyone possibly do such a thing knowing that this monster...this parasite will suck away all their joy at living?" I asked.

"True evil cannot be seen, only felt," he said. "The ones who were touched by the monster are unaware of it. They have been living an empty life. A life without purpose. A life based on external validation. They identify themselves with what others think of them. Their values are superficial. Unfortunately, they took pride in titles, possessions, and social positions to a higher standard than true values. Your Society is not what you think it is, Aura."

I made an almost imperceptible movement of my head in agreement. I understood that. "How could a Society be based on war and powerful men subjugating nameless women? How could physical strength be a synonym for status and power? How could the sons of the leaders be their successors someday while they condemn other men of lower birth to bend to the higher men?" I caught myself saying. "I am sorry. I shouldn't have said that."

The man turned into the lady who looked like a younger version of my mom. She smiled. It was my mom's smile.

"Don't apologize for speaking from your heart. Your Society is doomed to fall to this monster, but it doesn't mean it is the end."

My blood ran cold. "To fall? Will we all die?"

"No, darling. This is not the end, as I said. It could be the beginning of a better Society. A better world where monsters won't threaten the hearts and minds of men and women." There was compassion in her voice.

Somehow, her words gave me some hope, but I still had a question to ask. "So," I said, "how can I defeat this invisible monster? How can you defeat something you can't see?"

The woman's eyes shone for a second, just like they had when I first saw her in my bedroom. She placed her both hands around my face and whispered, "You know how. You have touched it. You know how it feels. You know the signs. Watch for the signs and work against them, Aura."

"I have touched it! How?" I was confused.

Then I saw it...

The sky turned black as night. The air became chillier and heavy with sorrow. I was no longer in that magical garden. I was back in the City. As I walked toward the Main Plaza, I heard the trickling of the fountain up ahead. I looked upon the grand structure in front of me and the sculptures of the Founding Fathers of our Society that adorned the entrance. There they were. Brave men. Proud fathers and husbands on their magnificent horses. As I was examining their faces, I noticed they were real men's faces. They were no longer proud or brave. They were in pain. Tears inundated their cheeks. Their desperate cries for help filled the air and pierced my heart with despair. I could sense the terror emanating from them.

I felt something cold touching my arms, hands, and face.

What is it? I thought, touching it.

It was snowing! It had never snowed in the Central Lands before. We had rainy days, sunny days, and plenty of cloudy days! But snowy days were common only in the North.

The earth moved beneath my feet. I lost my balance and fell on my back. The sight of a creature emerging from the ground made my blood run cold, and a scream of terror escaped my lips. Its shadow covered the sky. My entire body was shaking with terror. I watched as the Fathers desperately tried to run. But they were statues. I started to run too, but I lost my balance again. I tried to hold on to something and touched the Shadow with my left hand. I froze for a second, but I forced myself to run from it. I felt like my left hand was burning. But it didn't stop me.

I ran until my legs became heavy, too heavy to take me away from that nightmare. I stopped. It was dark but warm. I looked around, and I was at home! I was at my father's office. He was sitting in his chair.

"Father! It is me! Your daughter!" I screamed.

There was no response.

"Father! Father!" I called again in vain.

I approached him carefully. His body was slumped in his chair, his eyes closed. His head was between his hands, violently pressuring his temples. I thought of touching him, but I dared not. I felt something heavy and dark surrounding me. A kind of musty smell was emanating from my father.

"Nobody respects me! I am a sad excuse for a man! I allowed this to happen! I am useless! I am less than a man!" he repeated compulsively.

"What's wrong with him?" I asked, feeling the tears rolling down my cheeks. I could sense his despair.

The woman next to me placed her hand on my shoulder. "You know the answer, Aura."

"No, please! Not him! I lost Anandy, and now him? Oh no, please!" I begged.

The woman looked at me, puzzled. "You have lost nobody. They are not yours to be lost. People come to this world and leave. That's the course of nature. Have faith, Aura. Sooner or later you will see that nobody is actually lost."

I felt darkness overtaking my body. The musty scent grew stronger.

I heard a woman calling my name. It was my mother's voice coming from a distant place. It felt like it was coming from a dream.

"My ancestors are with me! Their spirits are guiding my path. There is no fear in my heart, for I am Adira, daughter of Allura. I am a daughter of the North, and I never walk alone! Remember who you are, Aura. You are a daughter of the North. A child of Allura. You are free!"

It wasn't her usual quiet voice. There was something else in her words.

"It is power. This is true power," the Man said, standing next to me. "It is time to go back and defeat the monster, Aura."

I opened my eyes.

Chapter Ten

When Fear Gives Birth to Madness

Time seemed to slow down. Mattas's stomach twisted in shock.

"Burn the South Lands to the ground, Themis?" His voice trembled.

"You heard me well the first time, advisor. Go now and gather our best warriors. We will leave at first light," the Magistrate replied harshly.

Mattas didn't move. "Themis, please reconsider. You are about to start a war based on assumptions. There is no evidence Anandy is in the South, let alone being held captive."

"My son needs me. Do as I say, advisor!" Themis barked.

The advisor placed his hands together, gathering all his patience and wisdom. "Magistrate," he said after a few seconds, "you are *not* listening to my words. My report was about Anandy being seen going toward the South. I never implied he was there. I simply pointed out the need to seek permission from Leader Faron to search his borders and his lands. Please, be reasonable. Let me send word to him."

Themis gasped his fits until the palms of his hands bled again. "I have had enough of your impertinence, advisor!" he yelled. "Leave now before I remind you of your place. You are nobody! You are a simple advisor. Don't forget, I can easily replace you!" He could feel the warm blood on his fingers, but it didn't stop him from burying his nails deeper into his flesh.

Mattas stood still. His gray eyes sparkled as he stared deeply into Themis's.

"What are you waiting for? Get out of here!" Themis yelled louder.

The advisor remained in the same place, gazing calmly at him. There was something in his tranquility that bothered Themis. Finally, Mattas nodded politely and left the room.

Themis sighed heavily and reached for a small bottle of liquor on his desk, which was reserved for guests. But not today.

"Old bastard! Who does he think he is? I am the Magistrate! I am the Law! I am the most powerful man in Green Valleys," he muttered, pouring some of the dark liquid from the East Lands into his golden glass. The drink burned his throat and his chest.

"That's good!" He refilled his glass.

The magistrate made his way to his favorite armchair and sank into it, sighing, feeling its comforting embrace. He put his golden glass to his mouth but stopped for a moment as he saw his bloody hand.

I don't care! Themis thought. *I deserve it!* He gulped his drink. It burned again. *Good one!* He placed his golden cup on the arm of his chair. His fingers wrapped loosely around the glass.

Themis glanced at the window across from his armchair. The curtains were open. He rubbed his bloody hand on his pants, allowing his gaze to be lost in the dark sky in front of him.

"I will ride to the South in a few hours. I must prepare for battle. Whoever took Anandy from me will pay with blood," he spoke to the night.

"Then it will be your own blood, boy!" His father's voice came from the darkness as a whisper.

A shiver went down his spine. "It is not real. I must be drunk already! The old man is dead and in Hell," Themis murmured.

"You pushed your son to his own death, useless boy. You ended your bloodline. All you have got left is a useless girl who will marry a low-birth man. And he will be the next Magistrate. You destroyed our family tradition with your stubbornness and your short-sighted views. I always wished it was you who would perished in the South Lands, not your brother. He was a real man! Not you! You are less than a man," his father roared from the darkness.

Themis lowered his gaze and glanced at his hands. They were shaking. A thin line of cold sweat went down on the corner of his left eye.

"Cat got your tongue, boy?" There was an evil laughter.

Themis didn't reply. He couldn't. Fear was stronger than his will to explain himself. To say that it wasn't his intention to send Anandy away. He wanted desperately to find his son and make amends. It was a mistake he wouldn't make again if he had a second chance.

"It was your fault! You were never man enough to be Magistrate! You lack the wisdom and strength to act in the interests of our people and our family. Even when the consequences were dire, you always took the easy way out, constantly eager to please everyone and to be on good terms with other leaders. You are a pathetic little man!"

Themis's hands were shaking uncontrollably. He dropped his glass, which shattered on the floor in front of his shoes. The Magistrate couldn't move. He tried to move his limbs, but his body was frozen and unresponsive.

"Weak boy. You are a shame to your ancestors. You are a shame to me. Just end your misery once and for all!"

Themis put his hands to his face and covered his temples. He trembled as the sweat mixed with the blood from his palms touched his skin.

"Go away!" he shouted into the darkness like a frightened child.

The voice's metallic laughter filled the room. *"Child, you were my biggest disappointment!"*

Themis felt the room getting darker around him. The air was heavy with a musty smell. The smell and the room, which seemed to become darker and smaller, suffocated him.

"Nobody respects me! I am a sad excuse for a man! I allowed this to happen! I am useless! Less than a man!" Tears of despair flooded his face.

There was silence. The voice was gone. Themis felt like the sun was standing in front of him. For a second, it felt like the room was immersed in light. There was no fear, no anger, no despair. He opened his eyes and saw the silhouette of a woman standing in front of him. She engulfed him in her light. Themis felt an incredible urge to allow his eyes to close.

The Magistrate fell asleep. The light bathed him, warm and calm. He dreamed of a garden and a kind old man offering him water.

★ ★ ★ ☾ ★ ★ ★

Mattas knocked at Aura's room and was surprised to hear laughter and excited voices. His wife opened the door. She looked radiant. "Come, husband! Come! The girl woke up! She is very weak, and she needs to rest. So don't be loud!" She pulled him by his sleeve into the room.

"Well, I won't be as loud as you are, wife. I can assure you of that." Mattas smiled. "I am truly grateful to see your beautiful eyes open, my young lady. Please accept my sincere wishes for a speedy recovery."

The ladies in the room returned his pleasant expression. Mattas felt the warm feeling that comes from true love and affection. His heart warmed a little.

"I am sorry to interrupt, but it is time for us to go, wife. Our daughter sent word about our grandson being sick," the advisor said, wrapping his arm around his wife's shoulders.

His wife nodded and kissed both ladies on their foreheads.

"I am sorry, my lovelies! My daughter always relies on her old mom when her little one is sick! It is as I told you earlier, my lovely. Kids always get sick, and there is no rest for us moms!"

Mother and daughter waved their goodbyes to the older couple.

Mattas and his wife took the stairs, greeting one of the servants in the house. They wished her a good night and took the streets of the Central Lands.

The old couple walked in silence, the only sound the crunch of their shoes on the cobblestones, until they arrived at their home, only two streets away from the

Magistrate's house. They were experienced. They knew that there was an attentive pair of ears in every corner of the City.

Mattas closed their front door behind him and secured it using an extra lock. They were at home. It was safe to talk.

"How bad is it, Mattas?" his wife asked.

Mattas pressed his lips together in a thin line. "It's terrible. Themis is lost in his fear and madness. He wants to go to war against the South."

"God forbid such a tragedy!" The old lady put her right hand to her forehead.

"How was it with you? Did she tell you anything?"

She shook her head. "Nothing at all. I feel like Adira got suspicious of me. She asked me to leave the room for a moment with the excuse of getting a few supplies for Aura."

"And did you leave the room?" Mattas looked intrigued.

"Yes," she replied. "Only to eavesdrop through the door." His wife chuckled.

"What did you learn?" The advisor beamed.

"I learned Adira remembers her roots. And she will do everything she can to protect her family against Themis."

"At least we don't have to worry about Adira and Aura for now. The child of Allura will know how to handle Themis." He paused for a moment, holding his wife's hands. "I worry about us, my love. I want you to go to our youngest son's house and spend the rest of the night there."

"But it is far! At the borders of the City and the South," his wife protested.

"I will be with you for most of the journey," Mattas reassured her.

"And where are you going to, Mattas?" She raised an eyebrow.

"To the South, Janace." His face was somber.

Janace smiled. "But first, send word of warning about the Magistrate's madness."

Chapter Eleven

Rumors

Dansa was awoken by a hand shaking him, the touch rough on his arm. He opened his eyes and saw his wife's round face.

"There is one of your Little Ones outside," she said as she kept shaking his shoulder.

"Bloody hell, woman! Take your elephant's hands from me! Tell the Little One I am sleeping!" he yelled, closing his eyes.

"He brings news about Themis's family." Her stony face matched her emotionless voice.

Dansa opened his eyes wide. He was alert now.

"Why didn't you tell me that before? Go and tell him I will be downstairs in a minute." Dansa hurriedly pushed his white cotton sheets away and jumped out of his heavy, large wooden bed.

His wife didn't utter a word. She rushed out of the bedroom without looking twice at her husband.

"Argh! That woman can't understand a simple task!" he complained as he heard footsteps from his wife's room.

The Leader of the Central Lands made sure never to share the bedroom with his wife. The idea of spending a night next to her used to make him feel sick to his stomach. His loathing for his wife and two daughters wasn't a secret to them.

I would despise that whale less if she could give me a boy, but she kept giving me little useless females, he thought, storming into his wife's room, yelling. "I told you to go downstairs, woman!"

His eyes scanned the room, searching for a glimpse of his wife. There was only a corpulent gray cat casually strolling on the brown carpet.

"Even her cat is fat!" Dansa tried to scare the cat away, but it looked at him indifferently as it lazily licked its back.

"I hate this cat!" the Leader of the Central Lands grunted.

After closing the door behind him, he washed up. He grabbed a pair of light blue pants, a white shirt, and his blue jacket. He checked himself in the mirror. He smiled proudly, touching the emblem on his jacket.

"The Central Lands' coat of arms. The City and The Coin," he murmured. "My clan!"

After a few minutes, Dansa showed up in the living room, fully dressed. He went straight to his office, ignoring his family in the living room.

There was a boy waiting for him, standing by the window. His old clothes showed his low birth status.

"Hello, Little One. Do you have anything of value to me?" Dansa closed the door behind him.

The boy, who was not much older than ten, nodded eagerly.

"Yes, sir! It's the Magistrate's family. There is trouble with his children. Both children. The girl is very sick. She is in shock. Something emotional. Doctor Valens was called in to care for her." The boy pulled his jacket's dirty sleeves down to cover his wrists, which was in vain given the fact that his clothes were too small for him.

"This is good information! What about the boy? Come on, Little One! Tell me about the boy, the wife, and Themis." Dansa's eyes were shining.

The boy spoke quickly, lowering his voice. "The son is missing. He was last seen going to the South Lands. The wife is at the girl's bedside and...about the Magistrate... It seems like his body and mind are failing him, sir."

Dansa clapped his hands in delight. "Wow! What a report, Little One! Well done! That was the best report I've got in ages!" The Leader laughed.

It wasn't uncommon for leaders to have a system of spies in their own lands. Dansa's spies were kids who would hide in every corner of the city. They were everywhere, even in Themis's house as servants. Dansa's Little Ones were his eyes and ears in the City and in its borders.

The boy waited for his reward. He was aware of how valuable any information about the Magistrate was to Leader Dansa.

"The Magistrate's only son is gone, and his daughter is very ill..." He paused for a moment. He gazed at the ceiling. "I wonder how these events are connected," the Leader said to himself.

"It seems the girl fell ill on the same day the boy disappeared. I heard she even called her brother's name when she fell ill," the boy replied.

"Is it possible that she knew about it? No...it... No! It cannot be... How! How could she possibly know such a thing?" Dansa scratched his chin with his left hand and tapped on his wooden desk with the right one.

"This I don't know, sir."

"I wasn't talking to you, lad." Dansa's voice was cold and metallic. The boy blushed and murmured an apology. But Dansa smiled and gave him two gold coins.

"Here! You deserve special payment today, Little One."

The boy's eyes shone. He couldn't believe his luck. Those coins would put food on his family's table for a long time.

"Thank you, sir! Thank you!"

The boy bowed and rushed to leave the office, but Dansa called to him.

"Not so quick, Little One. I have one more task for you."

"Yes, sir. What do I have to do?"

"It is time to spread the rumors, Little One. Fly! Sing your song, little bird. Sing your song to all the corners of the City. Send word to the others in Green Valleys." Dansa broke into a grin.

"Sir?" The boy's eyes were wide. "Do you mean I should contact the other boys and girls from the other clans?"

"That's correct! I want everyone in the Society to sing this beautiful song! Spread the rumors to all clans! Go now, Little One. Sing your marvelous song, little bird! Sing it louder than the thunder, for a storm is coming to Green Valleys!" Dansa opened the door.

The boy bowed to the Leader of the Central Lands and rushed out of the office. Stopping at the living room, he bowed politely to the ladies before taking to the streets of the City. Dansa walked to the window and observed the boy running toward the shops and stores.

"That's a good place to start, Little One," Dansa whispered.

There was a knock at the door. He didn't move. Dansa was gazing at the little figure running down the street.

"Breakfast is ready, sir," his servant girl announced shyly.

Dansa didn't reply. The boy's image disappeared at the end of the street. It was time for food now.

★ ★ ★ ☾ ★ ★ ★

"Good morning, Father," the two girls greeted him at the same time.

"Your plates are already full, girls," he retorted.

The girls didn't seem to notice the criticism. They could finally eat now that their father had joined them.

"Coffee, sir?" The new servant girl standing next to him smiled.

Dansa didn't reply but simply pointed to his empty cup.

"Girl, bring more fresh bread and the apple pie," his wife said.

The girl nodded and left the room, returning immediately with a tray of bread in her left hand and an aromatic apple pie in her right hand. She placed them on the table, and all three ladies started devouring them. The servant bowed and left the dining room.

"Eat, little pigs! Eat as if it was your last meal." Dansa disgustedly watched them.

The ladies ignored him and kept working on emptying their plates.

"Girl!" his wife called impatiently.

The new servant girl came back, smiling. "Yes, madam."

"Bring the pumpkin pie now," Dansa's wife said.

The girl hesitated for a second as she saw the pie and the bread she had just brought to the table were gone. She glanced at Dansa's plate, noticing he was still having his first slice of bread.

"Do as my lovely wife said, girl," Dansa said. "My beautiful girls are still hungry. Bring more food for my beloved family."

"Of course, sir!" The girl ran back to the kitchen.

"You whales are embarrassing! Control these endless pits you call stomachs and have some etiquette! Let the food rest on the table for at least five minutes," Dansa barked as soon as the servant left the dining room.

The servant returned a few moments later holding a big tray with a fresh and crispy pumpkin pie. The cheeks of all three ladies were flushed. They were staring at their empty plates.

"Here you are, madam, sir," the girl said politely.

"Fill my cup with more coffee," Dansa said, smiling at his family. "Eat, my beauties! Your plates are empty. Eat, for today is a glorious day, and your healthy appetite makes it even more beautiful!"

Chapter Twelve

The Note

His eyes scanned the night sky in front of him. The burden in his heart weighed on him like a stone. He felt a growing unease.

"I wonder what today will bring my way," he whispered.

The previous day's events were still vivid in his mind. The outcome of his actions was still uncertain. He opened the window. The chilly night wind entered his pitch-dark bedroom. The moonlight brought some light into his chamber.

"It will be morning soon." He inhaled the cold air. "Chaos will ensue."

The moon shone brightly, shimmering in the night sky like a beacon. It felt so close. He felt the temptation to reach his hand out the window, but he resisted. To touch the moon. To feel its healing power. Its peace.

"The big, luminous full moon beaming down at me," he whispered, searching for hope in his heart. "May fortune smile on me once again."

A low and gentle knock at his door brought him away from his reflections and back to reality.

"So, it's begun," he whispered to the moon, which seemed farther away than before.

The man didn't bother to light a candle. He knew his surroundings well, a valuable lesson he'd once learned through pain. He opened the door with a soft click, the hinges barely making a sound.

There was a young warrior standing at his chamber's door, hand resting on the hilt of his sword. The lad bowed his head low as he handed him a sealed note, respect clear in his posture.

The man felt a chill down his spine when he laid eyes on the wax seal.

"Thank you. You may leave now, brother," he said from the darkness in his room.

The warrior's boots echoed on the stone floor as he bowed once again and then walked down the dark hall.

The man closed the door and felt the weight of the lock as he clicked it into place. He didn't want any inopportune interruptions. Slowly, walking to his small desk at the corner of his room, he reached for a candle, but he suddenly changed his mind and went over to his wide-open window.

He took a deep breath, feeling the cold air filling every inch of his being. Then he glanced at the seal on the note once again. Overwhelming feelings of fear and doubt invaded his heart. He didn't have to open the note to understand the gravity of its content. Another wave of unwanted feelings hit him. He closed his eyes and inhaled slowly, mentally counting to four. Pausing for two seconds. Exhaling to the count of eight. His focus was completely on his breath. For several minutes, there was no letter in his hands. There was no room or the shining moon out of his window. He felt unbound from his body. There was nothing besides his breath.

"*Stay here and now.*" He could hear a familiar voice whispering words of wisdom. "*Focus and reset. You are not your emotions or your thoughts. Remember your truth.*"

He opened his eyes. In the silence, the disturbing feelings melted away, leaving a peaceful and calm sensation in their wake. He tilted his head back to take in the sight of the bright, full moon.

"May the moon be my only witness!" He broke the seal. The note was quick and precise.

After staring at the note for a few moments, he strolled to his desk. The man lit an unused candle, and the smell of melted wax filled the room as he burned the letter and placed it on a small plate. The flames quickly consumed the thin paper.

His gaze shifted to the moon, and he contemplated his choices. "I shall wait," he whispered. "This is only the beginning of the storm." The moon seemed to have moved closer to his window. He felt as if he could touch it.

The man looked at the ashes that had once been the letter and threw the plate's contents through the window.

"I hope you are wrong, Mattas. I deeply hope your reports are wrong, my friend. Green Valleys can't afford a war right now. We can't afford it," he whispered to the moon once again.

As he watched the bright stars circling the moon like a shiny belt, the man reflected on the last part of the note.

"On the other hand, Adira's behavior is promising. Janace shall monitor her and Aura. Especially Aura. If what they reported is true, her abilities are quite impressive. They can be useful in times of uncertainty."

As he sighed into the night air, he watched the vapor from his breath rise in the moonlight. The man closed the windows, walking slowly and silently to his desk. He sank into the seat, feeling the cushioning.

"My hopes and wishes are in vain," he murmured. "Mattas's reports have been accurate over the years. Themis has been showing signs of madness. His family has been on the verge of a collapse. Involving Faron in this madness, however, could present deep and catastrophic implications." He reached for a glass of water and emptied it in one gulp. His mouth was dry from the cold.

"So it's begun," he whispered once again. "I am ready. *We* are ready. We have been ready for centuries. Let the clans divide themselves. Let the Society fall!"

He placed the glass back on the table. The man glanced at the moon once again while he slowly stood up. He put on his jacket and smiled at the moon.

"It's time, my friend. We have much to do." The slender figure slowly and silently left the room, walking into the realm of darkness.

Chapter Thirteen

By the Great River

The sun was rising, painting the sky with hues of orange and pink. Ansel was preparing for the day ahead. For those residing in the West, along the banks of the Great River, being an early riser was part of life. His veins were filled with the blood of fishermen, a heritage he was proud to carry. Fishing and the river were their lives, an expression of who they were as individuals.

Another foggy morning, he thought, opening the heavy windows in his bedroom. *Perfect fishing conditions!* The air was getting colder. Soon it would be the salmon run, a period of abundance for the Society.

"We will have plenty!" Ansel murmured, watching the gentle ripples of the Great River.

Someone knocked at the door. Ansel put on his marine-blue jacket, the last piece left of his outfit. *I am presentable now,* he thought, walking to the door and opening it.

"Good morning, Father. Mother is calling you for breakfast." Usman grinned, his teeth a beautiful contrast to his tanned skin.

The Leader of the West Lands' face lit up with a smile when he saw his eldest son.

"Good morning, son. I will be downstairs in a moment. Come on in! I need to talk to you about yesterday's council." His voice was loud, as usual.

Usman nodded and closed the door, the silence almost eerie as he trailed his father to the window.

Ansel placed a gentle hand on his son's shoulder and beamed with pride.

"My son! You are taller than I am!" The leader wondered when that had happened. He always thought of his son as a lad, not a man. Seeing Usman's muscular figure filled his heart with the satisfaction of having the most perfect offspring any man from Green Valleys could ever wish for.

His son chuckled. He was tall and well built. Despite being a warrior, Usman was religious as well, particularly dedicated to academics, which made Ansel doubly proud of his boy's achievements.

"Look at them, son." Ansel pointed at the fishermen from his big brick house, their lines glinting in the early morning mist. "The hardworking men of the West, my son." Ansel's gaze fixed on the fishermen. "Fishing has been our way of life for thousands of years. The Great River is our provider."

Usman instinctively touched the coat of arms on his chest armor. He felt a warmth, overflowing with gratitude.

"The symbol of God's goodwill toward our people," the young warrior murmured.

There was reverence in his eyes. Watching the brave fishermen sailing into the Great River was proof of God's mercy on his people.

"Usman, my son, you were in the Council yesterday in the Central Lands with me." Ansel's eyes carefully studied the young warrior's face.

"Yes, Father. I kept my eyes and ears open, as you advised."

Ansel smiled. "Good boy. You learn fast." He paused for a moment and wrapped his right arm around his son's shoulders. "Look at the river, my son."

Usman found himself immersed in the vastness and the pureness of the Great River's waters. Such a magnificent miracle from God.

"Yes, Father. Nature is the purest form of God's work." Usman's eyes were shining.

"Yes, my boy. Indeed! God's work! Purest form of work," his father repeated mechanically. "The river has been providing for us for thousands of years. Every sunrise and sunset, our men come home with their nets filled with fish." He gazed at his son's face. "Our nets are always full. The river is our blessing, for we are a faithful people. We are God's servants." Ansel's eyes shone for a second. His son missed it. Usman was in awe of the immense size of the Great River, stretching far beyond the horizon.

"God is perfect, Father!" A familiar warmth rose inside Usman, and he felt a sense of safety. As his mother used to say, it was God's love.

"Indeed, my son. God is perfect," Ansel was quick to agree. His eyes were still studying Usman's lost gaze. "But men are not. Men are deceitful. Disloyal toward their fellow beings." A wave of revulsion filled his voice.

Usman lowered his eyes. He knew it was true to some extent, but he'd rather not speak ill of his earthly brothers and sisters. Thus, he remained quiet.

Ansel could sense his son's discomfort. "You are a kind soul, Usman. Just like your mother," he said, touching Usman's face. "You have her gentle smile."

Usman grinned. He loved his mother. She was the kindest lady in the West Lands, tirelessly working to build a peaceful community. Although the West Lands, or the "Wetlands" as other clans used to call them, were considered the smallest clan in Green Valleys, they occupied a vast area, making their home on both sides of the river. The Wetlands extended throughout the entire Great River.

We are the most united people among all clans in Green Valleys, Usman thought. *The Central Lands are the smallest clan in Green Valleys. There is no mountain, forest, fields, or river in it. Why is it called the biggest clan in our Society?*

"I admire your kind heart, my son. But as my successor, you must find the strength to lead and to deal with the other leaders. We are politicians. We must play the game. You must play the game." Ansel gazed at Usman, his dark green eyes shining with expectation.

Usman's heart raced. Whenever his father reminded him of his future as the Leader of the West, he couldn't help but feel a knot in his stomach.

"I was not born to be a leader or warrior," he used to confess to his mother.

"That's God's plan, and God is never wrong, my son," she would reply with a kind smile. Every time she mentioned God, that smile would spread across her face.

The young warrior remembered that warmth, causing his expression to soften.

"Usman, you are an academic," Ansel said calmly after a pause. "I need your opinion about Themis's announcement."

"Yes, Father," Usman replied.

The Leader of the West Lands' voice was low, his speech slow and precise.

"According to the books in the Central Lands, nature is not giving enough to us." The father pointed to the river. "But my eyes and our books tell me otherwise. Now, tell me, my son, what does your mind tell you?"

Usman meditated on the question for a few moments, taking his time to make a fair judgment. "My mind and eyes tell me that Themis is not being truthful. We have plenty for ourselves and to export. God has been generous to us for centuries. There is no reason for rationing." He uttered these words with a heavy heart.

Ansel smiled sadly. "You are right, my son. It deeply hurts me to see that our Magistrate is plotting against us. I supported him in the Council because it is our duty to remain united," he said, gazing at the Great River. "It is our duty as leaders, however, to remain faithful to our people, Usman."

The young man's heart raced once again. He didn't like the way his father was conducting the conversation. "What do you mean, Father? Do you mean...treason?" He hesitated.

Ansel was still staring at the river when he finally replied. "No, my son. It is not treason if you remain faithful to your people. Our loyalty lies with these fishermen and in the Great River. May God help us all!"

★ ★ ★ ☾ ★ ★ ★

It was approaching dinnertime when Usman got home from his daily duties. His conversation with his father from the previous day still haunted him.

We can't go against the Magistrate. It will be suicide! We don't have enough warriors to go to war. I don't even want to think what would happen to us if the other clans attacked us, he thought as he walked back home with a heart full of fears and doubts.

Usman opened the front door of their brick house. An intoxicating smell hit his nostrils. His stomach roared. All his fears and doubts disappeared for a moment.

"Hum, trout," he said, following the smell to the kitchen.

His mother was making some salad and boiling some potatoes while the fish was baking. She smiled widely when she saw Usman.

"Hello, my love! Are you hungry?" She kissed both of his cheeks.

The boy smiled. "I am always hungry for your cooking, Mother."

"That makes me content! Go wash your hands and then to your father's office. He wants to talk to you. If you see your two sisters, tell them to stop fighting and come here to help me with dinner. Those two girls are always fighting over toys!" Her laughter filled the room with a warm, joyful sound.

After washing his hands, Usman went to his sisters' room to tell them to help their mother. At the sight of him, the twelve-year-old twins immediately ran to him, eager to give him a hug.

"Bear hug, Usman! Bear hug," they demanded as he squeezed both of them together in his muscular arms.

"That's enough, girls." His cheeks were flushed from the bear hug and the girls' kisses. "Now, be good daughters and go help Mother with dinner. I am starving!"

"But we want to play, brother!" the girls protested.

"As I said, I am starving. You two give me no choice but to eat both of you for dinner! Maybe I can add some herbs, and you will be as tasty as trout!" He grabbed both girls by an arm, placing them in the hallway.

"Go now and help Mother," he whispered.

The twins ran merrily down the stairs, their laughter and skipping echoing through the house. As they ran, their identical pink dresses twirled and danced. Their ponytails, which were a rich, dark brown, were bouncing from side to side as they sprinted down the stairs.

Usman shook his head, laughing at his silly little sisters. But his smile dissipated once he stopped at his father's office door. He knocked, and his father yelled for him to come in.

"Come, Usman. Come and read this note from the City." Ansel's eyes were wide. The excitement in his voice was clear.

The young man took the note, and his face turned pale when he read it. "Is it true, Father?" he asked in shock.

Ansel nodded. "I got three other notes with the same contents." He showed Usman the notes. "Themis lost his mind after learning of Anandy's disappearance and his daughter's emotional state," he replied in his usual loud tone.

"Who sent you these notes, Father?" Usman asked, still in horror.

"As you know, son, we have loyal friends beyond our lands. They help us see and hear what our eyes and ears cannot." Ansel spoke quickly.

Usman couldn't find the words to express himself, but Ansel's brain was overflowing with ideas. He couldn't stop talking.

"It was as we talked yesterday, son! Themis lost his mind a long time ago. He probably made up those numbers. He's evilly plotting against us and all the other clans! He is after our wealth! It is known everywhere that the City makes nothing. It is a waste of space with all those shops and busy streets. The wealth lies on the land and in the river! We must prepare, son!"

Usman finally spoke. His voice was faint and hesitant. "Prepare for what, Father?"

Ansel looked at him. His dark green eyes were dark, almost black. His voice was deep and harsh. Usman felt a shiver going down his spine.

"We have to prepare," Ansel repeated. "Prepare to defend our clan from those parasites! Gather our men and fortify our borders. We will not give the fruits of our labor to the City."

Chapter Fourteen

Chilly Winds

The chilly wind blew snow straight into Cato's face. He didn't mind it. His body welcomed the cold. He was built for it. The snowflakes kissed his cheeks as though they were welcoming him home. The old man smiled, exhaling the cold air slowly.

"Hello, my old friend," he whispered to the wind. It blew more snow onto his face.

His grin widened as he entered the Northern Lands. Cato dismounted his robust brown horse, gently pulling his fingers through its thick, luxurious mane and pressing his forehead against it.

"Thank you, my friend. Thank you for carrying my old body to our land. Rest now," the man whispered, feeling the horse's breath slowing. The animal slowly closed and opened its eyes. Cato smiled.

"Please, take good care of my friend," he told the stable boy who approached him.

"Yes, advisor," the boy nodded, gently guiding the horse through the snowy ground.

"Thank you, lad!" Cato looked at the snowy wonderland around him. The advisor observed the northern people carrying on with their daily tasks, caring for the animals, fulfilling their duties, and living their lives. The old man greeted the busy citizens of the North. It felt good to be home.

We befriended the cold and the snow. This is our way of life, he thought, stopping to contemplate the Mighty Mountains.

"The Mighty Mountains! The Soft White Blanket of the North," someone said next to him.

The advisor knew that voice very well. It was Erhart, the High Captain of the North. Cato looked at the warrior next to him, and his face hardened. No words needed to be uttered. They knew it was time to talk. The road from the Central Lands was not a safe place for discussion. The men walked silently toward Cato's house.

The advisor's house was only a few meters from the place where they dismounted, but both men walked slowly. They kept their chins up, allowing the snow and the cold to kiss them. They had missed their home.

Erhart and Cato found themselves in front of a medium-sized house. They stopped at the small wooden porch and stomped the snow off their boots. Cato opened the door, and both men carefully placed their boots on the doormat.

An old lady came right away, holding a silver tray. There was a teapot and two cups.

"Come on in, you two. Come have some hot tea." She enveloped Cato in a tight embrace, planting a loving kiss on his forehead. He ran his fingers through her hair, feeling the texture, and closed his eyes in bliss. He had missed the sweet scent of her hair.

"Thank you," Erhart said to Cato's wife as she placed a cup of hot herbal tea on the dining table in front of him. The old lady smiled kindly and left the men alone.

There was a moment of silence while they sipped their hot beverages. Feeling their bodies getting warmer from the tea and from the warmth emanating from the fireplace in front of them, they waited for their heads to clear.

"I brought some warm bread and fresh raspberry jam for you boys. Putting some fresh food in your stomach will help you recover faster from the long journey," the good old woman announced, bringing a big tray filled with food.

"Thank you, my love. You always read my mind. That's your gift." Cato helped her place the tray on the table. She kissed his forehead.

"Eat, boys! Eat. Meditate on the matter. Then, talk." She placed her hand on Erhart's shoulder.

"Thank you!" The High Captain bowed to the old lady. He was very fond of her and admired her wisdom.

The men followed the lady's advice and ate and drank in silence while watching the fire burning in the magnificent fireplace.

"Come, Erhart. Let's sit by the fire." Cato gestured to two armchairs. "Let's warm our feet."

Erhart took a seat by the advisor's side. He could feel his socks getting warmer. It was a custom among the northern people to take off their boots at home. They sat by the fire in silence for several moments, watching its flames and listening to its crackling.

"I believe I am ready to address the Council events, my friend." Cato spoke slowly, as if he was coming back from a dream.

"So am I, Cato." Erhart placed his arms on his lap.

"I have been to many Councils throughout my years serving as an advisor to our leaders," Cato said. His gaze fixed on the fireplace's flames. "I have seen and heard more than I would wish to..." He paused for a moment, turning his gaze to Erhart.

The captain was looking calmly at the older man. His blue eyes showed patience as he waited for the advisor to speak again.

"Erhart," Cato said, "this Council was a disaster. Its outcome represents serious implications for the five clans of Green Valleys."

Erhart nodded. He didn't reply. It was time to listen and learn.

"Conrad is a smart lad. I admire his courage and energy to go against Themis and the other leaders," Cato continued. "But I admire him even more for reading between the lines. Retreating was the wisest response."

"Indeed, Cato," Erhart agreed. "Wise is the man who picks the right battles."

"Yes, my friend. The battle against Themis and the other leaders was not the one to be picked." The advisor paused. "Not at that particular time."

Erhart nodded slowly. "We must prepare."

"And we will."

"At the right moment," the captain added.

Cato smiled at the astute remark. "We must wait for Conrad before acting. He will need our advice."

"And we will be at his service. At the service of the North," Erhart replied.

"Meanwhile," the advisor said, "we must gather our books and inspect those numbers. It is clear the numbers presented at the Council were manipulated."

"In order to serve a powerful man's interest." Erhart ran his fingers through his wavy brown hair.

"The numbers were only a distraction. Its sole purpose was to instill chaos."

"He has already succeeded." Erhart handed a note to Cato.

The old man read it and smiled sadly. "It is only the beginning..."

Cato placed both hands on his armchair and pulled himself up. He strolled in front of the fireplace and stood by the large window of his living room, spending a few moments contemplating the light snowfall. Erhart joined him in silence.

"My friend," the advisor finally said, "let's prepare our animals and our supplies. The storm and the shadow are upon Green Valleys."

"We will be prepared to defend the North." Erhart could see it as well.

"We will have extra time to prepare. Our geographical position is our advantage. We are isolated from the other clans." Cato's voice was heavy with sadness.

"Fear will consume them quickly."

Cato closed his gray eyes, exhaling slowly and softly. When he opened them, they were clear and bright. "May the Soft White Blanket protect the North once again, Erhart."

Chapter Fifteen

The East Stands Still

Gilbride was sitting in his small office, notes spread out before him on the rustic, heavy wooden desk. He could feel the wood grain beneath his fingertips. The old leader's body was bent in an arc above them. His eyes were cold, a perpetual state of lifelessness.

"I must confess I saw it coming," his eldest son said.

Gilbride looked at Gillion. *Of course you did, you fool. You saw the boy vanishing, the girl contracting that unexpected illness, and Themis falling ill. Why not see a pot of gold coming my way?* he thought, examining his son's recently acquired wrinkles. *His mother, may her soul rest in peace, gave birth to him fifty years ago. After half a century on Earth, I would expect him to open his mouth only to talk about important matters.*

Gilbride sighed tiredly and spoke in his characteristic slow whisper. "Thank you for bringing the unfortunate news to me, my son."

"What are you planning on doing, Father?" Gillion couldn't hide his impatience.

"What am I planning on doing? Please, share your suggestions with me." Gilbride's voice was slow and fatigued.

"We need a plan." Gillion adjusted the straps of his light warrior's armor, feeling the cold metal on his skin. He felt a lump in his throat when he talked to his father, and he could barely hear his own voice. Although he tried to remind himself of how old and senile his father was, Gillion was still haunted by his childhood and teen years, when his father constantly criticized every move he made. Pleasing his father was still on his mind.

That's ridiculous! I am not a lad anymore. I am already fifty years old. I have nothing to prove to this old crow, he thought, knowing in his heart that it was not true. He had much to prove to Gilbride.

The old Leader of the East Lands hid his amusement behind his tired eyes. "A plan?" he asked flatly.

"Yes, Father. Themis talked about rationing due to insufficient provisions," Gillion replied, making sure to speak loud enough that his half-deaf father would hear him.

"He did, indeed." Gilbride's gray eyes were fixed on his son's. He had grown interested in this conversation.

"Well, Father." Gillion took a chair and placed it across from Gilbride's desk. "Let's be honest here. We are doing well. I don't know what Themis meant by insufficient provisions. Insufficient to whom?" He poured some beer from a clay jar into two glasses and offered one to his father, who murmured something inaudible, taking a small sip. Gillion gulped half of the beer from his glass. His mouth was dry.

Finally, he is showing some perspicacity! the old man thought, taking a second sip.

Gillion leaned toward his father and searched for some emotion in his eyes. There was none. *Why am I wasting my time with this old crow? He's dead inside,* he thought as his father turned his attention back to the notes spread on his desk.

"Father," he tried, "I agree with Leader Conrad. There must be a mistake. I can't see a valid reason to ration our provisions. Here, check our numbers! It is fall, and we have taken two times more from the land than last year. We are not getting less; we are getting *more* from the land!"

Gilbride took the heavy book in his hands and examined the numbers. He already knew them by heart, but he wanted to know where this conversation would lead.

"Their numbers and our numbers don't match! While I understand all the politics behind your support of the Magistrate's decision to ration, I also understand that you still hold true to our people and our own interests." Gillion's eyes were shining passionately as he gesticulated over the desk.

Gilbride nodded slowly. "Yes, Gillion. My faith resides in the East." His voice was a deep rumble, lacking emotion.

"The Magistrate lied!" Gillion flailed his arms. "He has lost his mind! Our informers say he has succumbed to madness. In his delirium, he is trying to steal from us! It is time for us to defend our own interests!" He was out of breath and his bald head was sweating.

Gilbride placed the black book on his desk and reflected for a few moments. His face was blank.

"Father? What do you say?" Gillion asked impatiently. His heart was pounding. He could feel the warmth radiating from his bald head.

The Leader of the East Lands looked his eldest son in his eyes, and when he spoke, his voice was not a tired whisper. His eyes were no longer empty.

"I say you are right. You made me proud today, my son." There was a fire burning in his eyes and a deepness to his voice. He sounded and looked thirty years younger.

Gillion didn't reply. He opened his mouth to speak, but all he could hear was the sound of his own breathing. His eyes were wide with wonder. It was the first time in his life that his father had taken the time to hear his opinions or even to consider them. He had to remember to close his mouth, which was agape in complete astonishment.

"Themis hasn't been a stable man for a long time. He is a bomb about to explode. I don't believe he is the one behind this..." He paused, searching for the right word. "Deception! He is being manipulated by someone." Gilbride tapped his fingers on the back cover of the black book, the sound echoing through the room. His gaze was fixed on his son's.

"By whom?" Gillion asked weakly, still recovering from the shock of having an actual conversation with his father after so many years.

"By someone who would benefit from the chaos." Gilbride smiled. It was not a pleasant one. It was evil, mischievous, and disturbing. "Because hell will break loose among the five clans of Green Valleys soon, Gillion." Gilbride spoke in a way that made Gillion believe it was what his father had hoped would happen.

Gilbride's smile sent shivers down Gillion's spine. He had no recollection of the last time he had seen his father smiling. Actually, he had no memories of his father holding a proper conversation or even paying attention to the world around him.

It's diabolical. It is unnatural, he thought, staring at his father's expression.

Gillion gathered all the courage left in his being and opened his mouth to ask what needed to be asked. "What do you mean, Father? Who is behind this conspiracy? Who would benefit from chaos?"

"Our culprit will reveal himself, eventually." The old man kept the disturbing smile on his face. "Meanwhile, we will occupy ourselves with what matters now."

Before Gillion could ask more questions, Gilbride did something so shocking that it almost made his son pass out. The old Leader of the East Lands grasped both of his chair's arms and pulled himself up. He did it with such ease that would have made any lad envious of such vitality. Gillion covered his mouth in dismay.

It's been over thirty years since I have seen Father standing up unassisted. He was always weak! Always sick! He is walking as well as I am! What sorcery is this? Gillion thought, feeling panic growing.

Gilbride stretched his back and tilted his neck from side to side, sighing in relief. He glanced at his son. There was amusement in the old man's eyes. The leader walked around the desk without difficulty. His steps were precise and smooth.

Gilbride sat on the desk in front of Gillion. He lowered his gaze to meet his son's astonished eyes.

"What I mean, silly boy," Gilbride said jovially, "is that there are others who have already drawn the same conclusions as you did. They are plotting." Gilbride's gray eyes were shining with emotion, something Gillion had never seen. His voice was deeper still. "Fear is a ladder. When you climb the ladder of fear, you reach panic. When you reach panic, you climb a bit more, and you reach chaos. Fear leads to panic, and panic leads to chaos. That's what the future holds, Gillion."

"What does the future hold for us, Father?" The warrior felt a chill running down his back as sweat beaded on his forehead. He couldn't stop thinking about how his father's sudden change of behavior was something unnatural and evil.

Gilbride walked back to his seat. "I have lived seventy-five years. I have seen enough of men to tell you one thing, my son." He sipped some beer. "Nobody will suspect whom they underestimate." He pointed at himself. "You asked me what the future holds for the East Lands, Gillion, and I can't tell you exactly what it is, but one thing I will tell you for sure: we will secure our future. We will stand on our green fields as we have been proudly standing since our fathers came to these lands. Keeping our image as slow, submissive, harmless farmers." He grinned in that diabolical way again, making Gillion shiver.

Gillion took a few moments, his pulse racing as he tried to make sense of his father's words. His clan's words echoed in his mind.

"The East stands still." He repeated the famous words every citizen of the East Lands learned as a child.

Gilbride smiled once again. This time, it wasn't evil. It was in approval.

"The East stands still," he said. "We will stand still and watch our neighbors fight and destroy each other. Then we will come to take our spoils. That's how the East works, my son." He gazed at his son.

"That's how the East works." Gillion smiled for the first time on that chilly morning. He had finally understood his father's words.

Chapter Sixteen

The South

Mattas's back hurt, and his thighs felt tight after riding his horse for hours from the City to his son's house. After dropping Janace off, kissing his grandchildren, and hugging his son, he rode for another couple of hours to Leader Faron's house, the most luxurious home in Green Valleys.

Home to the wealthiest man in the Society, he thought, standing at the strong double wooden door.

A servant opened the door. "How may I help you, sir?" She smiled at him.

"Good morning, young lady," Mattas greeted her cordially. "I am Mattas, the Magistrate's advisor, and I have come here to discuss some important matters with Leader Faron." He pointed to the emblem in his outfit. It was the City's coat of arms: the City and the Coin. Then he pointed to the silver coin emblem on his chest, the Magistrate's advisor's emblem. "My apologies for coming unannounced. Urgent matters brought me here," he added skillfully.

The girl smiled once again, looking over his shoulder. "I will call the stable boy to get your horse. How many horses are there?"

Mattas noticed her surprise, seeing no committee of warriors, advisors, and servants with him.

"It is only me today, young lady. The Magistrate sent me on a matter that was solely entrusted to myself to discuss with Leader Faron."

"Oh, I understand." She moved to the side so that Mattas could enter the house. She got his jacket, hanging it by the door.

The girl guided him to a spacious living room. "Please, take a seat, sir," she said, pointing at a comfortable armchair. "I will let Leader Faron know you have arrived."

"Thank you." Mattas watched the girl disappearing down one of the many hallways in the famous warrior's house.

Mattas looked around discreetly, glancing at the richly decorated room. It wasn't his first time in that house, but he couldn't help but be amazed by the wealth displayed in each corner of the living room. He tried to recollect everything he knew about the leader. *I remember his mother. A woman of legendary beauty; Faron's resemblance to her is like a mirror. She was the only heir of the wealthiest family in Green Valleys.* He gazed at the painting in the center of the room, a young lady in her twenties. Long, wavy brown hair, turquoise eyes, and a spectacular smile. *The most beautiful woman in Green Valleys. Poor thing! So much wealth and beauty! And she died giving birth to her first and only child: Faron. The husband never remarried. I remember how devastated he was by her death. She was the love of his life.* Mattas glanced at Faron's father's portrait next to the lady's. A muscular, tanned warrior. A good-looking man, but nothing compared to his wife and son's beauty. He looked grave and proud in the portrait. His dark eyes were full of deception and knowledge. *When did he die? Five? Six years ago? I remember him well. A skilled warrior and a man of letters. Knowledgeable in the art of politics. And cunning. He inherited all her possessions, which belong to Faron now.*

Mattas saw the first rays of sun invading Faron's luxurious living room. *He has been up for two hours by now*, the advisor thought, recalling how the Leader of the South was famous for his peculiar habits. *It seems we will have one of the characteristic sunny, warm days of the South.* Mattas was growing tired of the constant cloudy days in the Central Lands. Faron's lands were famous for having a sunny, warm climate.

This is good! He probably finished his morning training and is finalizing his bath, which means he will be alert and relaxed at the same time. Let's hope the odds are in my favor today.

He ran his eyes along Faron's exuberant furniture. *He has a weakness of heart for beauty and very expensive tastes. Well, he is a bachelor and much younger than the other leaders. Besides, young Conrad. Faron inherited his mother's wealth. And he controls the military. And where there is the army, there is money.*

"Greetings on this beautiful new day, Honorable Advisor Mattas!" Faron saluted as he entered the room in his leader's clothes, which did not hide his muscular frame. His cheeks rose up in a broad smile, and his eyes sparkled like two precious jewels.

The legendary Faron! The fearsome warrior of magnificent beauty! Too good to be true, Mattas thought, smiling politely as he shook hands with the leader.

"Greetings, Leader Faron! My apologies for coming early in the morning without announcing myself." Mattas slightly bowed his head.

The Leader of the South Lands smiled even broader. "Don't worry about formalities, my good Mattas. As you probably know, I get up with the birds for my daily practice and my reinvigorating bath. I was on my way to eat breakfast when I was informed of your visit. Would you care to join me for some food?"

Mattas was skilled enough to know that you didn't refuse such an invitation in Green Valleys, for sharing a meal was a sacred ritual.

"Thank you, sir. It would be an honor." The advisor placed both hands on his chest, slightly bowing his head once again.

Faron wrapped his strong right arm around Mattas's shoulders and guided him to the dining room. Mattas sat on the golden chair he was directed to. The leader sat on the host's chair at the far end of the table, with the advisor on his left side. The long, heavy dining table sat on top of sophisticated tapestry. Mattas didn't have time to fully appreciate it. He was trying to keep up with Faron's energetic movements and words.

"Woman! My good fellow Mattas will join me for breakfast today. Bring your mouth-watering bread and your world-famous cherry pie. My good friend here should try your outstanding cooking," Faron announced as one of his maids was setting up the table. The young lady smiled proudly and rushed to the kitchen.

Faron's words are smooth as honey! His seductive words cast a spell, making him even more dangerous. I must choose my words cautiously, Mattas thought, smiling and nodding at his host.

After a few moments, the table was elegantly adorned with flowers, fruits, various kinds of bread, cheese, eggs, and the "world-famous cherry pie." Mattas ate a bit of each, constantly paying compliments to the food and the beautiful table presentation. Faron looked pleased and held a light-hearted conversation about his favorites on the table, explaining how fresh and hand-picked the ingredients in his dishes were. The advisor followed the conversation by asking a few questions and showing his undivided attention to the leader's narrative. Finally, there was a moment of silence.

This is the moment! Mattas thought, observing Faron sipping his coffee from a white cup with a golden line encircling it.

"I am much thankful for this feast! You spoke fairly about the girl's cooking. It is divine! Thank you once again for the kind invitation," he said, raising his glass of water to the warrior, who smiled at him.

"While I wish I could carry on with our delightful conversation, I must admit that this is no social visit, as you already know, sir," Mattas continued. "The matter which brought me to the great South is sad."

"I hope this matter doesn't involve death, Mattas." Faron's eyebrows furrowed and his lips pursed with concern.

Mattas lowered his voice. "We are not quite certain whether it involves death or life, sir."

Faron leaned closer and whispered, "Please, tell me how I can be of assistance."

Mattas paused for a moment to gather his thoughts and choose the right words. "I came here on behalf of the Magistrate, intending to request your help on a matter of great importance."

"Of course. Tell me how I can help," Faron said.

Be wise, Mattas, the advisor thought, *choose your words well and play the game.*

Mattas placed his glass on the table and lowered his voice. "Sir, you understand that this is a very delicate subject for the Magistrate, and he would prefer it to remain between us."

Faron leaned back in his chair, his hands clasped together, and gave a quiet reply. "There is honor among us warriors. We are not gossiping old ladies, Mattas," he said. "You have my word. I will keep the matter private. I will do my best to put all my resources and the South's at the Magistrate's service," he added, keeping a serious face.

"I am glad to hear that and so will the Magistrate. There was a sudden turn of events in the Magistrate's house. His daughter fell ill and is under the care of her mother."

"I am deeply sorry to hear about the girl. My sincere wishes for good health to her," Faron said in a sympathetic tone.

"Much appreciated, sir," the advisor replied. "However, this is not the matter that brings me here." He chose his next words carefully because the future of Green Valleys depended on it. "What brought me here was Anandy's fate." He finally said it.

"His fate? What do you mean, Mattas?" Faron looked puzzled.

"Anandy is currently missing. He was last seen walking toward the South. I would ask your permission to lead a search group, hoping to find the boy," Mattas explained.

"I will be by your side, leading the searches, Mattas," Faron said resolutely. "Will Magistrate Themis join us?"

"His daughter's illness has prevented the Magistrate from joining us. He entrusted both of us with this valuable mission, since he assured me you would gallantly offer to join the search group," Mattas replied.

Faron nodded, and his voice echoed through the room as he called to his servant. "Woman! Send word to High Captain Callan to come for once." Turning to Mattas, he spoke in a reassuring tone. "We will track down Anandy if he is in the South, Mattas. I assure you this much. Nothing happens in my lands that I don't know about. I am very fond of the boy, since he spent so many years in the

Army Camp. We will find him and take him home, Mattas!" There was honesty in Faron's words and kindness in his smile.

Mattas raised his glass in a silent toast to Faron.

I pray you are right. Our future hangs in the balance. Curing Themis's madness depends on it, he thought, forcing himself to give the warrior his best smile.

Chapter Seventeen

Listen and See with Your Heart

Themis tossed around, feeling the softness of the mattress under his body. He was covered with two thick blankets.

I am soaked, he thought. His shirt was glued to his back. "Why am I in bed? Who brought me here? I fell asleep in the office..." he murmured, trying to push the blankets away. It was cold. He tried to move, but there was a dull pain in his neck and knees.

"Am I sick?" He was confused. "Wife! Wife!" he yelled.

Adira came hurriedly after a few seconds. Doctor Valens came into the room shortly after her.

"Good to see you awaken, Magistrate," the doctor said politely.

Themis's mouth hung open in bewilderment. "What's happened?" he asked, astonished, staring at his wife and at Valens.

Adira handed him a glass of water and helped him sit down. "I will help you bathe and get changed. Your fever is gone now." She placed her soft hand on Themis's forehead.

Valens nodded. "Magistrate, you have been sick for a few days," he said, taking a chair next to Themis's bed.

"For a few days?" Themis repeated mechanically. He didn't remember falling ill. His last memories were of being in the office. He had heard his father's voice, and there was a silhouette. *A woman's silhouette. She was shining as if she was the sun itself,* he thought perplexedly. *It must have been a dream,* he thought, trying to convince himself, although he knew deep inside that it was as real as the chair Doctor Valens was sitting on.

"It's been five days, Themis," Adira said softly. "You and Aura fell ill on the same day. I went to your office early in the morning to call you to see our daughter, but I found you burning with fever and delirious. So I called for Doctor Valens to attend to you." She smiled tiredly at him.

Themis's head hurt. He couldn't believe his ears. "You said five days, wife?" he asked faintly.

Adira nodded and helped him with another sip of water while Doctor Valens checked his temperature and performed a physical exam.

Although Themis had questions, he was weak, too weak even to speak or to demand an explanation. His kids were in his thoughts. His heart was heavy with sorrow and shame.

"I am so sorry to have been a burden to you in the past few days, wife. Please, go attend to our daughter. She needs you," the Magistrate said.

Adira's tired face lightened. "Oh, Themis! You don't know?" She rushed out of the room.

The Magistrate was confused. "What's wrong? Why did she leave so abruptly?"

Valens smiled too, which was odd, given his serious demeanor. Themis raised an eyebrow at such a sight, but he didn't make any comment.

A few moments later, Adira showed up at the door, holding Aura's hand. Themis's heart raced. His lips shivered. He wanted to smile, but he feared it was a dream or a nightmare. He feared something horrible would happen and he would find himself panting in his dark bedroom, soaked in sweat, calling for his ill daughter.

"My mind must be playing tricks on me! Am I dreaming? Is that you, daughter?" Themis asked, his eyes sparkling in the light as he blinked several times.

Aura smiled. Themis's heart melted. It was his little girl standing in front of him.

"Yes! It is you! I know your beautiful smile, girl!" There were tears in his eyes. "You look thinner and pale, but you are still my little girl." He finally allowed himself to feel some happiness.

Valens offered his chair to Aura and helped her sit down. The girl kissed her father's forehead. "You also look thinner and pale, Father."

Themis laughed quietly, pressing his daughter's hand against his chest. "You are a vision of Heaven, my daughter." He tried to hold back his emotions, but a single stubborn tear made its way down his left cheek. The Magistrate didn't bother to wipe it. He held his girl's little hand against his chest, feeling the warmth and softness of her skin. Feeling the life inside her.

Adira was standing behind Aura, watching that beautiful moment between father and daughter. She also had tears in her eyes. Her heart was heavy. *Please, Themis! Please, fight and come back to your family*, she thought, placing her hands around the girl's shoulders.

Themis grabbed his wife's hands and kissed them. "Thank you! Thank you for taking care of our daughter," he murmured.

Adira's eyes lit up in response to the unexpected show of affection. She couldn't shake the unease. She felt a mix of emotions, ranging from affection to apprehension, when she thought of her husband. Adira loved him, but she feared his instability. She feared for her family.

"Well," Doctor Valens cleared his throat, "I am sorry to interrupt, sir and ladies, but I believe it would be prudent for the Magistrate and the girl to eat and rest. After all, you are still recovering, girl."

Adira nodded politely. "Yes, Doctor Valens. Janace, please take Aura to her room and help her get ready for lunch," she said as Mattas's wife entered the room.

Doctor Valens frowned as he heard the ladies' names, but he kept his thoughts to himself, since it wouldn't be prudent to correct the Magistrate's wife in front of Themis. The doctor forgave the Magistrate's wife's blunder, taking it as a side effect of sleep deprivation. He acknowledged the lady had been under too much stress, taking care of her ill daughter and husband.

The older lady smiled broadly at Themis. "Praised be the Lord for your recovery, Magistrate."

Mattas! The South...the soldiers...Anandy! Themis thought, trying to control himself and not jump out of bed. He simply returned her gaze. *All of this can wait until after lunch. I need my strength if I am going to burn those Hellish Lands to the ground.*

"Come, child. Come. Let's choose a beautiful dress for you today. How about that flowered blue one you love so much? Oh! Let's fix those curls as well! I am thinking of a new hairstyle today. I believe you will love it." The old lady laughed in her characteristic way as Aura giggled.

Themis smiled at his daughter's childish laughter. He hadn't seen her laugh like this since she was very young. His girl had always been a shy little bird in a cage.

She seems at peace. Things must be good.

"I must bid my farewell, Magistrate," Valens said. "I will return in the evening." Then, turning to Adira, he added, "A warm bath, a dry change of clothes, and a hearty meal will help the Magistrate and the girl restore their strength. Keep the windows open for fresh air and change his sheets and blankets. Call me if needed."

"Thank you, Doctor Valens," Themis said as he watched Valens leave the room and close the door behind him.

"I will be back in a moment to help you." Adira rushed to prepare her husband's bath.

She was about to leave the room, but Themis held her arm. "Wife," he murmured, "I must ask you. What happened during my absence?"

"First a bath. Then, food. After that, we can talk. There is much to be talked about, Themis," Adira said, gently freeing her arm from her husband's grip.

Themis watched in dismay as Adira silently left the room, closing the door behind her.

She called me by my name! She also called the other two women by their names! That's not right!

Themis couldn't get out of his mind the way she had talked to him in front of Mattas and his wife. He could see her face clearly in his mind. She had twisted her lips in disgust. Her voice was as cold as a blade. Her nose was up with pride.

"*Let it all go,*" Themis heard a soft whisper telling him.

Themis's body tensed. *It is the voice of my dream!*

"The venerable old man from my dream in the garden! That's his voice!" he whispered, closing his eyes. He could feel the soft grass underneath his feet and the warmth of the sun above his head.

"*Only true forgiveness heals. Forgive and you will be healed, child.*" Those were the words the elderly had told the Magistrate in that garden, handing him a glass of water.

"*Drink it and you will feel better, my friend.*" The man had smiled at him. For a second, Themis was transported back to that heavenly garden. He could see the tall, ancient trees. He could hear the birds singing. The taste of that miraculous water was vivid in his mind and heart.

He went to the window and with difficulty opened the heavy lock. Themis felt the fresh air of the morning. He elevated his eyes to the blue skies and felt his face being kissed by the sun. Birds were singing a beautiful and peaceful song in a tree in front of his bedroom. Themis felt peaceful for the first time in a long time.

"Nature heals, child." The elder's voice was speaking from a place behind him.

The Magistrate nodded, agreeing with that ancient wisdom. He took a deep breath and inhaled all the aromas of nature, exhaling heavily with a sigh as if he was releasing all the darkness inside him.

"I need guidance and wisdom, Venerable Elder. I am lost. Hope has abandoned me, and despair made its home in my heart," Themis said as he looked at the blue skies.

"Listen and see with your heart. We will walk with you, child," the skies whispered to him as a tear of happiness and pain rolled down the Magistrate's face.

Chapter Eighteen

Duty

Callan, the High Captain of the South Lands and Faron's most trusted advisor, was standing in the opulent room, frowning.

"It has been five days and no sign of the boy, sir." His voice was low and harsh.

Faron didn't reply. He was sitting in his spectacular dining room, sipping a glass of water. He had just finished his breakfast with Mattas.

The advisor observed both warriors intently, noting how different they were. Callan was the bigger man, but reportedly less skillful than Faron. The captain had a hard face and the hot blood so characteristic of warriors. Faron, on the other hand, was the epitome of beauty. All Five Clans regarded him with admiration, remarking on his striking good looks. Although he could have any woman in the Society, he was still a bachelor. Faron's charismatic personality and gentle demeanor made him a beloved figure among his peers. His charisma and intelligence helped him stand out among other politicians and build strong relationships with the other leaders.

The last five days living in the same quarters with Faron had helped Mattas draw a better opinion of the Leader of the South.

A magnificent warrior and a master in the art of stoicism. Faron is a powerful politician and a wealthy man, the advisor thought, observing the young leader's sober manners. *That's what makes him a very dangerous man*, he concluded.

Callan's right hand was placed on the pommel of his sword in the scabbard attached to his belt. His left hand was on his left thigh, close to his hidden dagger. His shoulders were tense. He gazed at Faron, awaiting a reply, but his attention was on every corner of the room. The High Captain was always alert. Always ready for action. Ready for battle.

A valuable yet dangerous man to have around, Mattas thought, noticing the captain had clenched his jaw. *Callan is growing impatient. He is not the type of man who can be ignored.*

It was like Faron could sense his captain's feelings without having to look at him. "Thank you for your report, Captain Callan. You may leave now."

Callan's face softened. He bowed politely to Mattas and Faron, silently making his way out of the room. After several moments of silence and reflection, Faron finally spoke. His voice was deep, and his renowned turquoise eyes looked darker.

"My good Mattas," the famous warrior began, "my sincere apologies to you and to the Magistrate. I have failed in my duties as a leader and a friend. After five days of searching every corner of the South and questioning every citizen, we failed to find our beloved Anandy. I am sorry!" He lowered his eyes.

There is sorrow and guilt in his voice, Mattas thought, searching for any signs of deception in Faron's face. There was none.

"Leader Faron, please do not blame yourself. I am a witness to your goodwill. Unfortunately, the odds were not in our favor this time. After five days, I believe it is time for me to return to the City and inform the Magistrate of my failure," Mattas said humbly. "I am immensely grateful for your hospitality and your willingness to assist the Magistrate's family in such stressful matters." The advisor slowly stood up from his chair. "I must go now and make the arrangements for my return."

"Our failure, my friend Mattas," Faron said, standing up from his chair. "It is also my duty to inform the Magistrate of *my* failure. I will join you on your journey to the City to present my apologies myself."

Mattas was caught by surprise. *No good omens will come from this journey. Persuading him not to go will raise suspicion. All I can do is try to gain time to alert Janace,* the advisor thought, nodding.

"I very much appreciate your offer, sir. I will take this opportunity and visit my son on the borders of the Central and the South Lands before my return to the

City. I wish to spend the morning with my two grandchildren as I plan to begin my journey after I eat lunch at my son's house," Mattas replied politely. "I also believe it will give you some time to plan for your journey, Leader Faron."

"That's wise, my friend Mattas! It's imperative that I make some arrangements before my departure." After a pause, the warrior grinned. His face lightened. "And it is imperative for you to spend time with your grandchildren. Please, allow me to send a couple of toys to them. As you know, the South Lands have the best artisans in Green Valleys. I will also send a bottle of our best wine for you and your son to enjoy over lunch today," he said in a tone that indicated he wouldn't accept no as an answer.

Mattas smiled at such a kind gesture. After all, he was a grandfather and a father. His journey to the South was rushed due to Themis's mental instability, which prevented the advisor from bringing gifts, as he always did whenever he visited his children and his grandchildren, who were too many to count on his fingers.

"Although I don't deserve such kindness, I am deeply grateful to you, Leader Faron. I must prepare for my journey. I will meet you on the Temple's road. Farewell for now, sir." Mattas shook hands with the Leader.

"I will call the woman to make the arrangements for the toys and the wine. Farewell, my friend." Faron left for the kitchen.

The advisor watched the Leader giving instructions to his servants, asking them to pick the absolute best from his winery. The South was not only famous for its Army Camp and its military. The Last War took place when Green Valleys was created, as it was now. One big clan, home to five clans where the Magistrate was the Law. It was a long time ago. Hundreds, maybe thousands of years ago. Nobody was certain about it. All the registers from before the Last War were destroyed. That part of the history of what was called Green Valleys was erased. Since then, the South had become much more than a synonym for war and weaponry. The Iron Mountains provided the best iron in the region. The most skilled artisans and blacksmiths were in these lands. Because of its warm weather, the South was home to the best vines in Green Valleys. The unique, bold flavor of the wine from these lands was deeply appreciated everywhere.

Mattas was thinking about the Last War, the erased part of Green Valleys' history, lost in thought, pondering all that had once been. All that wasn't. And all that would be if things hadn't happened the way they did. His head was filled with the hidden, dark past when he found himself at his son's door.

Mattas dismounted and knocked. A young woman opened it after a few seconds. She grinned when she saw him.

"Greetings, Father!" She kissed him on both cheeks. Mattas's daughter-in-law treated him as a father, for it was the custom in Green Valleys.

"Greetings, daughter!" Mattas hugged her.

The lady fixed her long, straight red hair behind her ears as a little boy came running toward Mattas, almost knocking down his mother.

"Papa!" The little boy jumped on him.

"Hello, my little one!" Mattas brushed the boy's red hair away from his forehead and kissed it.

"Papa! Papa!" A younger girl with even redder hair came trotting, carefully avoiding her mother.

Mattas easily picked her up. With both kids in his arms, he squeezed and kissed them. The little ones giggled.

"I wish I had your strength, Father!" The woman sighed. "I could never pick both of them up at the same time!"

Mattas smiled, kissing his grandchildren once again.

"Come on, kids! That's enough! Let Papa come into the house. He must be tired from the ride!" the lady said.

The kids agreed reluctantly, holding his hands and pulling him into the house.

"All right, little bunnies! Leave Papa alone!" A young man came from the living room. "Welcome back, Father!"

"Thank you, my son!" Mattas hugged him. "Leader Faron was kind enough to send toys for the kids, and a bottle of his best wine for you."

"That's very kind of him," his son replied. "Why don't you help your mother bring the toys and the wine?" he told his kids.

The woman nodded, and the kids ran outside, giggling and skipping.

"There is a note for you, Father," his son said gravely. "It is in the office."

Mattas nodded, rushing to his son's small office. There was a note from Janace on the desk. He broke his family's seal and eagerly read it. He was livid.

Themis woke up after five days of fever! Mattas thought as he burned the paper. The advisor had managed to keep in regular communication with his wife through his employer's reliable army of spies. So it was not new to him that Themis had fallen ill on the night of his departure. Doctor Valens attributed his condition to the same mysterious illness that had afflicted Aura, but little did he know it was due to the Magistrate's madness.

Adira had requested Janace's help and informed her of Aura's recovery. Since then, Janace had regained Adira's trust, being Mattas's eyes and ears in the Magistrate's house.

All seemed good and promising with Themis's sudden illness. Having him out of the way for a few days and having Adira relying on Janace while I was in the South searching for Anandy bought me enough time, Mattas thought, watching the flames on the small plate in front of him. *But I failed to find him! I fear for Anandy's life. And now I must face the Magistrate with Faron by my side. No good omens will come from this matter!*

Mattas sighed. He got out a pen and two sheets of paper and wrote two notes, one to Janace and the other to the man he reported to.

The advisor returned to the living room to join his son and his family for lunch. Mattas looked at his grandchildren happily riding their wooden horses. The old man smiled.

"Let's hope Faron's sugar-coated manners will impress the Magistrate in the same way he impresses children with his gifts," he murmured.

Chapter Nineteen

Ghosts from the Past

Dansa stared intensely at the girl's face, searching for lies. "Are you certain about this, Little One?"

"I am, sir," the timid girl replied, rubbing her tiny white hands on her old yellow dress.

She is not lying, Dansa thought, sipping some warm tea. *Unexpected news, indeed.* He took another sip of his warm herbal tea, hoping it would soothe his concerns.

"What a way to end a perfect week!" He caught himself saying it out loud while he glanced out the window.

Noticing that the girl was still there, the Leader of the Central Lands got a couple of silver coins from his pocket and gave them to her.

"Well done, Little One. You brought me valuable news. Take these coins and get some food for your family." He handed them to her.

"Thank you, sir! Thank you!" Her smile could not hide her happiness.

She has a sweet smile, he thought, getting a third coin.

"Here, Little One. Get yourself a new dress," he said.

"Oh, sir! Thank you!" The girl smiled broader.

"Go! Sing your sorrowful song across Green Valleys. May the Five Clans hear about the fall of Themis," Dansa said somberly.

The girl's smile vanished. There was darkness in the Leader's voice. The girl nodded and rushed out of the office. Something in the old man's voice scared her.

"Go, Little One! Sing your song, my little bird!" he whispered to himself, watching her leave the office, carefully closing the door behind her.

Dansa took a long sip of his herbal tea until the last drop. His distracted gaze swept his office furniture as he tapped his fingers on his light wooden desk.

"Oh, damn you, Themis!" he murmured, trying to think of what to do next.

After five days of fulfilling the Magistrate's duties and his own as the Leader of the Central Lands, he felt confident in his capability to take the seat of the most powerful man in Green Valleys. In the Magistrate's absence and his son's, the power went to the Leader of the Central Lands.

Power. Full power over these lands. The power to create and end laws. Power to do as I please, he thought.

"Themis fell ill, and his only son is missing. It is my right!" he whispered, staring at the empty teacup in front of him. "Themis was always weak. Madness is his family curse. It killed his brother, his father, and all the men in his family. They are cursed! It is only a matter of time before he is dead as well."

The Leader of the Central Lands looked at the papers on his table. "Bills, decrees, laws, proposals, requests... It is my duty now to do a better job. Green Valleys need a reliable leader and Magistrate. For far too long has the cursed Magistrate's family been drowning our Society in their madness." He placed his hands on the table with the palms facing up. "It is better this way," he said, gazing at his own hands.

Dansa sighed. His neck felt tight. His shoulders felt heavy. Reclining in his chair, he distractedly ran his eyes over his office. His lost gaze stopped at the large window across from his desk. He noticed it was open. Walking toward it, he could feel the chilly air.

"What a gorgeous evening!" he said, admiring the bright stars and the moon.

Dansa's eyes marveled at the bright evening. His gaze was lost in the contemplation of the stars and the bright moon. His mind took him to a different time, a different life. A time when he was not Dansa, the Leader of the Central Lands, but was simply Dansa, a shy and quiet young man in the South Lands' Army Camp. The son of a great leader and destined to be a great leader himself someday.

It was on nights like this that he used to slide out of the big dormitory that he shared with other young cadets and peek out of the hall windows to see the moon and the stars. On most nights, his best friend was with him. Life in the Hellish Lands was not that hard because they had each other. Since their first years of life, they were inseparable. If you wanted to find one, you had to look for the other. They were always playing and running together. Getting into trouble together. Fighting together. Studying and training together. They were always together.

"We will be side by side until our last breath! Forever together!" they used to swear to each other under the moonlight.

I am lost without you. I have been lost for so many years. You were my happy place. You and I were everything! Dansa thought as the moon's light bathed his face.

"I survived those Hellish Lands because of you," he whispered, feeling his heart pressured in his chest.

He placed his hand there. "It is still here. The pain is still here after so many years," Leader Dansa murmured.

There was a heavy knock on the door. Dansa was transported back to the present day, leaving behind his young and naïve self.

"Husband, dinner is served," his wife said in her characteristic impatient way.

"I will be with you in a moment," he replied faintly.

The door closed. His wife had left. Dansa stood by the window. He closed his eyes, and a tear rolled down his left cheek. "I miss you, my dear friend! Life is lonely without you! Be at peace!" he whispered to the moon and stars.

Dansa opened his eyes. He wiped away his tear, closing the window. He glanced once again at the dark sky and sighed heavily.

"It's time to go back to the present and forget the ghosts from the past," he silently told himself, opening the door.

He walked down to the dining room to join his family for dinner. His wife was waiting for him at the entrance of the dining room. Her face was grave, and she murmured, "Husband, there is a man looking for you. He is in the living room."

"Who is he?" Dansa asked, wondering who would have the audacity to visit him unannounced at dinnertime.

"I have never seen him before. He forced his way in, despite me telling him to wait outside. I am worried about the girls. Should I contact the warriors to come at once?" She bit her lower lip.

"He *forced his way in*?" Dansa asked in disbelief. "Who would dare do such a thing in my house?"

"He doesn't seem to be a warrior, husband. As I told you, I have never seen his face before," she whispered.

"Send word to the warriors and send the girls to your bedroom. Follow them and lock the door behind you," Dansa instructed.

His wife nodded and left. Stopping at the dining room door, she looked at her husband as he entered the living room.

Be careful, Dansa, she thought as she commanded the servants to take her daughters to her room. *I have a knot in my stomach,* she thought, instructing the servant to call the warriors. The lady locked the door in her bedroom and waited for her husband to return.

He seems to be a commoner, Dansa thought, walking toward the man.

"Greetings, Leader Dansa." The man smiled politely, revealing perfect white teeth in contrast to his straight black hair and black eyes. His skin was pale.

"Who is this man who forces his way into my house?" Dansa asked impatiently.

"My apologies to you and to your honorable lady, sir!" the man replied respectfully. "I came here to deliver a very important note, sir." The man bowed exaggeratedly at Dansa and handed him a black envelope.

"Thank you, sir! I will be on my way now." The man bowed once again, and before Dansa could say a word, he vanished through the front door.

The man is fast! Dansa thought, staring at the unusual black envelope in his hands. *I have never seen this one,* he thought, examining the unknown seal and the unusual type of paper.

"It feels rough," he said as he touched the black paper. "What an unusual color! I have seen white and yellow paper, but never black!"

"We came to your assistance, sir," a young warrior said, followed by two others. They were part of Dansa's personal guard.

"All is good," Dansa replied. He was gazing at the black envelope.

★ ★ ★ ☾ ★ ★ ★

Dansa's wife was in her room with her daughters. The lady was doing her best to comfort her girls by hugging and reassuring them that their father had the situation under control.

"Is Father fine?" the oldest girl asked.

"He is," the mother whispered.

"I am hungry, Mother! Will we starve for the rest of the night?" the younger one complained.

"I don't know how you can think of food! I am sick to my stomach worrying about Father and the dangers of having such a wicked man under our roof! What could have happened to us?" The oldest one placed her right hand on her forehead, rolling her eyes dramatically.

"The wicked man wouldn't do anything to us because Father wouldn't let him." The youngest one wrinkled her nose at her sister's face.

The oldest one assented, and they returned to their prayers. The mother could not help but smile as she heard her daughters talking about their father.

The prayers stopped abruptly. There was a knock at the door. The ladies did not dare say a word.

"Wife! Girls! It's me!" Dansa said from the other side of the door.

The girls ran to the door, opened it, and jumped on their father, who almost lost his balance and fell.

"I was so concerned about you!" the youngest one said.

"No! *I* was concerned about you! She was hungry!" the oldest one retorted.

"I am fine, girls! It's safe to go downstairs and eat your dinner. My poor girls must be starving! Go now and eat!" Dansa said as the girls wasted no time running to the dining room.

"I am glad you are fine, husband," his wife said awkwardly.

"Thank you, wife." He looked tired and pale.

"What is it?" The woman pointed to the half-opened letter her husband was holding.

Dansa glanced at the letter, then placed his gaze on his wife. "This...this is a proposition."

"Who sent you this proposition?" She raised an eyebrow.

"I don't know." He shrugged. "But whoever this person is, he has ill motives that I am not inclined to comply with." His voice cracked slightly.

Chapter Twenty

The Guests

Themis was uneasy. He moved uncomfortably in the armchair in his bedroom. He rubbed his sweaty hands. His mind was racing with unwanted thoughts.

It's almost dinnertime. I haven't had the chance to talk to my wife or my daughter in private. I must know what happened while I was sick and ask about Anandy. His hands were shaking. He felt his skin getting cold and chills in his limbs.

"Let it all go." The old man's voice whispered in his ears.

I can't! I must know! It is my family! I am the Magistrate! Themis could hear his voice screaming inside his head.

"Let it all go," the voice repeated.

"I can't! My head is full! It hurts! Why is my head feeling so heavy? It is just...too heavy for my neck to sustain..." he moaned in pain.

"*You can do it! Breathe in slowly. Breathe out even slower. Come back to your breath. Come back to yourself.*" The voice was coming from inside his head now.

Themis closed his eyes and took the first breath. It was clumsy and too fast. He got dizzy.

"I must try again!" he told himself. "I must come back to myself, as the Venerable Elder advised."

The second try was better. He tried to inhale deeper and slower, but he rushed his exhale.

I will try again! Counting might help! Themis thought.

The Magistrate inhaled: *1, 2, 3, 4. That's enough!* Themis thought, exhaling: *1, 2, 3, 4, 5, 6, 7, 8.*

He opened his eyes and noticed that his heart wasn't beating as fast as before. Themis closed his eyes once again, repeating the process three more times.

When next he opened his eyes, he felt warm. He felt balanced.

The door opened. It was Adira. She stopped at the door.

"You look much better, Themis." She smiled tiredly.

"Thank you, wife," Themis murmured.

"Dinner will be served in a moment," she announced.

"That's good! I am starving!" Themis said jovially.

Adira chuckled. Themis could not help but admire her beautiful smile.

"Wife," he called, "we need to talk."

"I know. There is much to talk about, Themis," Adira replied calmly.

Themis opened his mouth to speak, but he stopped. He frowned. His lips were partly open in surprise.

Horses? Voices? he thought.

"Do we have visitors?" he asked Adira.

"Yes, we do. Mattas returned from the South from his quest to find our son. Leader Faron insisted on accompanying him on his way back to greet you," she explained dully.

"What did you just say? Mattas returned from his quest to find Anandy? Which quest? Who sent him?" Themis squeezed the arm of his chair.

"You did, Themis." She was no longer smiling. There was no emotion in her voice.

"I did not send him on a quest to find Anandy! I sent him to..." He stopped, biting his lower lip.

"You sent him to start a war against our most valuable ally. You sent him on a suicide mission to attack the South. They are war, Themis. They are *the military*. You did so based on your own assumptions." Adira pressed her lips together.

"How do you know this much, wife?" Themis narrowed his eyes.

"I know what is there to be known, *husband.* You were bedridden for days, and *I was* the one in charge of many things. Including helping Mattas clean up your mess." She raised her chin and an eyebrow.

Themis's astonishment prevented him from speaking. Although his mouth was open, words refused to come out. He was in complete disbelief.

Who does this woman think she is? A woman is in a charge of cleaning up my mess? She calls me by my name like she is my peer, Themis thought as revolting thoughts and sensations dominated his body and mind.

"Themis," Adira called softly, noticing the change in her husband's behavior, "we will welcome our visitors and thank them for their efforts."

"Who are *you* to command me, woman?" Themis asked. His voice was full of disdain, cutting through the air like a razor.

"I am Adira. Child of Allura. Daughter of the North. I am from the purest and highest blood lineage in Green Valleys. The blood of our founders runs in my veins," she said solemnly.

Themis felt his blood run cold. He had never witnessed a woman speaking in such a way. There was power in her voice.

"Now, I ask *you,* Magistrate," she continued, "who are *you* to defy *me*?" Her eyes burned with a kind of fire that Themis had never seen in his life.

Themis remained silent. His eyes were wide with shock as he gazed at his wife. Cold shivers travelled through his body.

"I will send a servant to help you downstairs. Don't make our visitors wait," she said, walking to the door.

As she closed the door behind her, leaving an astounded Themis behind, she sternly warned, "And I advise you caution in your words tonight, Magistrate."

★ ★ ★ ☾ ★ ★ ★

Within a few minutes, the Magistrate found himself sitting in the dining room with his wife on his right and his daughter on his left, waiting for their guests. The shock of his conversation with Adira was still vivid in his mind. He was uncertain of what to do. It wasn't right to let a woman talk to a man in that way. But he would deal with her later. It was the time to be a host. Hosting another leader was not only a courtesy or social activity — it was also political. Especially when your guest was the wealthy and powerful Faron of the South Lands.

"I am very glad to see you sitting in good health, Magistrate." Mattas greeted him politely.

Traitor! You were conspiring behind my back with my wife! That dirty witch! Themis thought as he tried his best to nod cordially at his advisor.

"You are a sight for sore eyes, my dear Magistrate!" Faron said merrily.

"Welcome to my house, Leader Faron!" Themis greeted the leader.

"Thank you for welcoming my little intrusion." There was a pleasant smile on the warrior's face. "Greetings, honorable lady!" The Leader of the South Lands bowed.

"Greetings, Leader Faron!" Adira replied.

"Please, allow me to apologize for my arrival coinciding with dinnertime. To make up for my indiscretion, I brought a box containing thirty bottles of our best wine for your appraisal, Magistrate Themis," Faron said. He stopped for a second, then swiveled to face Adira and resumed speaking. "And for you, honorable Lady, I brought our finest delicacies." Faron offered an enormous basket filled with grapes, olives, nuts, and pies.

"That's very kind of you."

"I hope this token of my sincere apology will make up for my interruption of your meal, my lady."

It seems the affable Faron has brought an army of gifts to my house, Themis thought, struggling to keep a neutral face.

"And for this lovely girl," Faron said as he turned to Aura, "I brought the most beautiful flowers of the South Lands. Please, my lovely young lady, accept these flowers as my wishes for a speedy recovery." He walked toward Aura, holding an exquisite colorful bouquet.

"Mountain flowers!" Aura exclaimed. "They are my favorite!"

"I know. That's why I picked them myself, especially for *you,*" Faron said, looking into Aura's eyes and giving her a different smile.

"Thank you, sir," the girl murmured shyly, lowering her eyes.

As Faron handed her the bouquet, his fingers intentionally touched hers, and he caressed her left hand for a second. The others didn't see it because it was a planned move by Faron. But Aura blushed as she looked at him and saw those penetrating turquoise eyes staring intensively and meaningfully at her. There was something in his smile that made her cheeks burn even more.

I feel like my hand is burning, she thought, avoiding Faron's eyes.

"Thank you for the flowers, sir," Aura murmured.

"My pleasure, young lady," Faron said, smiling pleasantly at her and her parents.

It seems like our seductive Leader Faron came here for something more than duty, Mattas thought, observing the awkward interaction between Aura and the warrior. *He is playing a dangerous game here. And it will be even more dangerous if he wins.* Mattas frowned as he raised his glass to follow the toast proposed by Faron to celebrate the return to health of Themis and Aura.

The warrior's eyes were fixed on Aura like two greedy sapphires. There was hunger in his red lips. Hunger for something beyond his possessions.

It is worse than I thought! The man is playing his seduction game, Mattas thought, trembling at how the subtle scene in front of him unfolded.

The advisor's eyes scanned every face at the dinner table. The Magistrate was lost in his thoughts. Adira and Janace were apparently busy taking small bites of their food.

Mattas turned his gaze to Aura and saw her rubbing her hands. The girl did not notice his eyes on her as she was secretly glancing at Faron. Mattas saw her pupils dilate and her cheeks flush.

The advisor felt the hair on the back of his neck stand up. *What a terrifying ordeal! What have I done by bringing Faron here?* he thought, trying to regain his composure while keeping a pleasant smile on his lips.

Chapter Twenty-One

Answers

The dinner passed like a dream. The food was delicious, and the conversation was light and pleasant. Themis spoke and ate very little. His body felt weak and weary. But he still felt obliged to fulfill his duties as host.

Everyone's plates were empty. The chocolate cake and the fine strawberry pastries served as dessert were almost over. The conversation seemed to fade away.

Themis cleared his throat. "Thank you for the cooking, ladies." His voice was almost a whisper. It was time to wrap up the social visit. *Time for some explanations.*

"We are glad you enjoyed it, Magistrate," Janace replied cheerfully.

Themis tipped his head in agreement with the old lady's remark, but he was studying his guests with keen eyes.

"Gentlemen, would you care for some digestif liqueur in my office?" Themis inquired, standing up from his chair. His moves were slow. Every step was a struggle. He felt as if there was no energy left in his body.

"It would be my pleasure to try one of the famous digestives from the City, my good Magistrate!" Faron exclaimed as he also stood up from his chair. "Thank you, my dear ladies! This feast was memorable!" he added.

"Oh, sir!" Janace said, smiling broadly at the warrior. "If I knew you would gift us with your magnificent visit tonight, I would have cooked a few more dishes."

"You are very welcome in our house, Leader Faron. Thank you for your gentle words," Adira added.

"Your kindness and your grace shall not be forgotten, my dear ladies," Faron said, slightly bowing.

Aura remained quiet, nodding politely at Faron as he left the table.

"Thank you, ladies!" Mattas said, excusing himself from the table and following the other men to Themis's office.

The ladies waited until the men had left, then the sound of plates clinking filled the room as they hurried to clean up the table and do the dishes.

"I will start washing these," Adira announced, piling up six soup bowls. "And you girls bring the rest to the kitchen. Thank God we have three sinks! One for each of us! Otherwise, we would be done with all these dishes by morning. The three servant girls had to leave in a hurry as soon as dinner was done so they could tend to their sick mother. Thankfully, their help made the cooking and serving process go much smoother. Oh, my! So much work to do! I hope their mother is not severely ill. Do you remember how she used to help babysit Aura, Janace? Oh! Such a lovely lady! I am so fond of her." Adira sighed.

Janace didn't reply to Adira's question at first. She was focused on something that seemed more important to her.

"Girls? Yes! Finally, someone acknowledged my proper age," Janace bubbled, collecting all the spoons and placing them in a big serving bowl. "Of course, I remember that lovely lady. Her girls are the sweetest. Very hard-working young ladies. Do they still sleep here from time to time?"

"Yes, they do. Only if the workload is heavy. Otherwise, they go home to sleep with their old mother," Adira replied, disappearing into the kitchen.

"Old mother!" Janace interjected. "I wouldn't like if my children referred to me as 'old!'" She turned to Aura, adding, "After all, I am a girl!" She winked at her and took her load to the kitchen.

Aura giggled. She loved Janace's good cheer. Having her around was a way of brightening those confusing days when her mother behaved and looked so different.

Mother doesn't talk to me. I have so many questions, the girl thought, stacking the plates. *Mother said we had to wait for Father to recover. Then we could talk.*

Father is fine now. Why doesn't she tell me about Allura? Who is she? What about the North? And... Anandy... Where is he? How can Mother be so calm knowing he is gone?

Janace interrupted Aura's thoughts. "Where should we put these beauties?" The old lady was back from the kitchen. Aura hadn't heard her steps. Janace was holding the vase with the flowers Faron had brought for Aura.

Aura remained silent, her eyes fixed on the floor. She could feel her heart pounding. Her hand still felt like it was scorching, like a flame had touched it. She felt something warm growing inside her. She couldn't explain what it was, but it felt confusing and unpleasant.

"Lovely?" Janace called her, handing her the vase.

"Well," Aura began, "I believe they will adorn our living room," and placed them on the coffee table in the living room. "They are so beautiful! I love them!" She grinned, smelling the intoxicating floral aroma.

"Indeed! They are gorgeous," Janace agreed. "Just as Faron is! Isn't he a dream?" The old lady winked, chuckling. Her whole body shook like a bowl of jelly.

Aura lowered her eyes, and her cheeks flushed violently. She didn't know what to say, so she just took the stacked plates to the kitchen.

You don't have to utter the words, lovely. It is all written on your face, the old lady thought, watching the girl vanish into the kitchen.

Aura placed the plates in the sink next to her mother's. She turned on the water and started working on washing them.

"Finally! I thought I would have to bring those plates myself!" Adira said. She was smiling.

Aura looked over her shoulder to check if Janace was around. "Mother, we have to talk," she whispered.

"It is not the right moment." Adira's voice was low. She focused intently on the plates in front of her, the clinking of the cutlery ringing in her ears.

"It is *never* the right moment, Mother! What are you waiting for? I need answers!" Aura retorted. The warm feeling inside her was still there.

Adira stopped scrubbing the soup bowl. She gazed at the soapy water in front of her.

"Now that I have got your attention, Mother," Aura said, "tell me why Leader Faron and Mattas are here." Aura touched her left hand. The skin felt hot to the touch.

Aura saw tears in Adira's eyes as her mother turned her gaze to her. The Magistrate's wife closed her eyes for a second, taking a deep breath.

"Let's go for a walk in the garden." She dried her hands with a small cloth.

Aura nodded, ashamed of making her mother cry. Adira wrapped an arm around her daughter's waist.

"Let's get our coats. It is a beautiful and chilly fall evening." Adira guided her daughter to the living room.

"Are you going somewhere, lovelies?" Janace asked, wiping the dining table with a wet cloth.

"Yes, Janace. We will go for a walk in the garden. Aura and I need to talk," Adira said.

"Indeed. Enjoy your walk!" Janace said, her eyes twinkling.

"She knows more than she says," Aura mentioned as they stepped into their garden.

"Janace and Mattas have been valuable friends and allies in times of need. They are trustworthy, Aura." Adira raised her chest to inhale the chilly air.

"Our garden is fabulous! Nature is sacred, daughter." Adira walked toward their cherry tree and touched it reverently. "There is so much wisdom and power. Unfortunately, this knowledge is almost lost."

Aura observed her mother as she walked through the garden. Every step she took and every move she made was meaningful. There was purpose and grace in her being. Aura had been to that garden millions of times. She had grown up surrounded by those flowers and sat down by that cherry tree many times. But this time, it was different. There was something mystical, something powerful in that garden.

"Come, Aura. Touch it." Adira pointed to the cherry tree. "Feel it."

The girl raised her left hand. It had felt hot and tender since Faron touched it. Aura hesitantly placed the hand on the cherry tree's trunk. She felt a cool sensation going through her fingers, travelling through her hand, forearm, upper arm, shoulder, and chest. Then this pleasant feeling went down her core, arms, and legs. Her whole body was immersed in cool and calm. Aura closed her eyes. She was in the garden of her dreams. That beautiful garden. The warmth of the sun kissed her skin, and the softness of the grass massaged her bare feet.

"I am back!" she murmured as tears rolled down her cheeks. "I have been dreaming of coming back for days! It is Heaven!"

"Nature heals, daughter," Adira whispered.

Aura opened her eyes. She was back in her family's garden. Adira was standing in front of her. She studied the tree intently, feeling the roughness of its bark.

"Nature means everything in the place I come from, daughter." Adira gazed at the tree. There was a dreaming smile on her lips.

"You called yourself a daughter of the North. I always thought you were from the Central Lands." Aura was looking at her mother's face under the moonlight. *Mother is glowing!* she thought, observing Adira's shiny skin. Her blue eyes were bright as two little stars. She had never looked more beautiful.

"I am from the North. That is where I was born. I grew up there. I came to the City when I was around your age to marry your father." Adira's gaze was now placed on Aura.

"How didn't I know that? How do I know so little about you? You are my mother!" Adira's words took Aura aback. She felt betrayed. Sad. Unworthy of her mother's love. She was confused. It was as if she lived in a bubble of lies or hidden truths.

"I am a woman. Women are nameless and powerless. It does not matter who we used to be or who we are. We are born to be a man's daughter and a man's sister. Then we grow up to be a man's wife, and, hopefully, a man's mother," Adira replied bitterly.

Aura felt a wave of sadness invading her body. She felt pain, too. It was her mother's pain and her own. Two oppressed, nameless women from Green Valleys. A mother and a daughter who were strangers to one another.

"I feel like I don't know you anymore. Everything is so different now. You have a name. A place you came from. A history! You are talking about nature with so much wisdom." Aura's voice quivered with emotion, and tears formed rivers down her cheeks. "I really don't know who you are!"

"This is who I am, Aura. This is the first time you can see me for who I really am." Adira hugged her daughter tight and caressed her hair.

"And who am I, Mother? I am so confused!" Aura cried copiously. The confusion. The betrayal. The secrecy. They were scarring her heart deeply. Her entire world was turned upside down.

"You are Aura! You are the daughter of Adira. A child of Allura. You are a daughter of the North. The wisdom and power of our ancestors run in your veins." Adira held her daughter's face in her hands. "This ancient power gave you the most valuable gift of all. A gift I was blind enough to deny for so many years!" She closed her eyes and a tear rolled down her right cheek. "I was *forced* to deny!" She opened her eyes. Aura read shame in them.

"What gift is it, Mother?" Aura asked.

"It's the sight. You have the gift of sight. This is a powerful gift, daughter. Use it wisely!" Adira wiped away her tear.

Aura could not believe her ears. "Sight?"

"Yes! I am sorry! I lost my way. Confusion blurred my mind. I am no longer that weak woman, for I know who I am." Adira kissed Aura's forehead. "It is time for you to learn the truth."

"Yes. It is time for you to give me answers," Aura agreed. "First, tell me why Leader Faron and Mattas are here."

Adira sighed, lowering her eyes. "They are here because of Anandy."

"But... I saw... I saw...him...in my vision... He..." Aura couldn't utter the words.

"I know what you saw, Aura." Adira's voice trembled with emotion.

"You do? How?" Aura was confused. She remembered little from the events that followed her vision.

"When I got home, I found you on the kitchen floor. You were mumbling things." Adira touched the tree's trunk once again as if trying to absorb some of its strength. "You said you saw Anandy lying dead on the grass." Her voice was faint.

"Yes! Yes! Oh, Anandy!" Aura was shaking. Tears came back to her eyes.

"My darling!" Adira took her daughter in her arms. "Please, don't cry! You saw him hurt. It does not mean he is gone."

"What do you mean?" Aura stopped crying and raised her chin to look at her mother's face.

"There is hope for Anandy! That's why Faron and Mattas are here," Adira said, smiling through her tears.

"What do you know, Mother?" Aura was wiping her own tears with the backs of her hands.

"On the night you fell ill, your father lost his mind. He commanded Mattas to gather an army and attack the South," Adira murmured.

"Oh, my! Attack the South? Why?" Aura covered her mouth with her hands.

"Anandy vanished shortly after the Council. Your father and Mattas sent a handful of their most reliable men to search for your brother. According to the reports, Anandy was last seen going toward the South Lands," Adira explained.

"Yes! The bells! I heard the bells in my vision! They attacked him on the road," Aura trembled.

"Attacked?" Adira raised an eyebrow. "Who attacked him, Aura?" Her voice was shaky.

"I don't know. I couldn't see their faces. There was a shadow and darkness," Aura said, running her fingers through her blond curls.

Adira sighed once again. "That's concerning. I didn't know that." She placed her left hand on her chest.

"Mother, please tell me what happened after Father commanded the attack," Aura pledged.

Adira placed her right hand on the top of the left, on her chest. "Mattas took Janace to their son's house on the border of the Central and the South Lands. Then the advisor travelled alone to seek Faron's help to search for your brother."

"And how do you know all these things, Mother?" Aura frowned at Adira.

"Because Themis fell ill on the same night he had ordered the attack. I was the one who received Mattas's note addressed to your father the following morning. Mattas hoped he could persuade Themis to give up on the attack. His visit to the South was his way to form an alliance with Faron. And, hopefully, show your father that he doesn't offer a threat to him or to Anandy. Mattas also tried to buy us some time and to start the searches for your brother." Adira paused for a moment. "I know all these things because I opened the note. Since then, I have been keeping in constant communication with Mattas."

"You opened a letter addressed to Father?" Shock overcame Aura. "Mother! We can't do that!"

"I know! I am not proud of that, but I don't regret it." Adira gathered the right words. "Your father has been unstable lately. Could you just imagine the implications of attacking the South? They are the military! Faron is a powerful man."

Aura didn't reply at first. She was reflecting on what her mother had just told her. After a few moments of silence, her face lightened. "They found Anandy! That's why they are here!" She clapped happily.

"According to Mattas's latest note, he, Faron and Captain Callan were searching for Anandy with some of the most valuable warriors in the South." Adira looked at the stars. "I wish with all my heart that they had found Anandy, my darling. A sense of calm assurance that your brother is alive fills my heart. I can't make sense of it, but I can feel it like a whisper inside me." Adira smiled. It was the most beautiful and purest sight. It was a smile of a mother full of love and hope.

Chapter Twenty-Two

The Proposal

Mattas took a seat next to Faron and watched as Themis walked slowly toward his desk, sitting down in his chair. His face betrayed him for a second, showing a glimpse of pain.

Even the simplest movements are a struggle for him, the advisor thought.

There was a moment of silence. As was customary, they waited expectantly for the host to take the lead and begin the conversation.

"Thank you for your visit, gentlemen," Themis said, serving some liqueur to his guests. His voice was harsh and low.

"Thank you for taking us to your dining table, Magistrate." Faron's features, which were usually beaming, had become taut and strained.

"Thank you, sir," Mattas said quietly, taking the small glass offered to him.

Themis glared at his advisor for a second. There were flames in his eyes.

It seems I wasn't forgiven for my disobedience, Mattas thought, watching the Magistrate raising his glass and drinking the liqueur in one gulp. Faron and Mattas repeated the gesture.

"Well, I assume tonight's visit wasn't about pleasantries." Themis placed his empty glass on his desk.

"Indeed, sir. Duty brought us here," the warrior replied. Worry clouded his bright turquoise eyes a darker hue.

Themis looked, confused, at both men. "Could you be more specific, Leader Faron?"

"We humbly came to your presence to inform you of our failure, sir," Faron replied. His voice was heavy with shame and sorrow.

"I beg your pardon?" Themis's eyes were on Mattas, who remained silent.

"After five days searching every corner of the South Lands, we failed to find Anandy, sir," Faron said.

"Searching for Anandy in the South Lands?" Themis raised his eyebrows.

Faron glanced confusedly at Mattas, who remained silent. "Yes, Magistrate. I led the searches with our good friend Mattas. Callan, the High Captain of the South, and my senior advisor, joined us," he added. "He selected ten of our best men to join us."

"So your best men failed to find my son?" Themis filled his glass once again with liqueur.

There is a slight tremor in his hands, Mattas thought.

"Yes, sir," Faron replied, gazing at Themis.

"So, my son vanished." Themis gulped from his glass. As he tried to refill it for the third time, he dropped the glass on his desk.

"Let me help you, sir." Mattas subtly took the bottle from Themis, wiping the liqueur from the desk with his handkerchief.

"Thank you, my *friend.*" The Magistrate gave a steely glare.

"It is my duty to be of assistance, even in unorthodox ways, sir," Mattas replied.

"I see." Themis blinked twice, showing vulnerability.

Faron remained sitting, silently observing the two men for a second. "Magistrate," he said, "my men found something."

There it is! Mattas thought, closing his eyes to take a deep breath.

"Is it about my son, Leader Faron?" Themis asked impatiently.

"I am afraid it is." The Leader of the South Lands placed an object wrapped in a piece of white cloth on the desk.

Themis was about to take it, his fingers almost touching it, when an icy feeling suddenly ran down his spine. He held his breath as fear filled his eyes. "Blood!" the Magistrate whispered. He gazed at the small object in front of him for a moment.

Then placed his eyes on both men across his desk. They avoided his gaze. Themis gathered his courage and unwrapped the object.

There was silence.

"Anandy's golden pocketknife!" Themis exclaimed in terror.

"Yes, sir. We found it in the bushes on the side of the road in the borders between the City and the South Lands. Hidden in the surroundings of the temple," Faron said, keeping his gaze lowered.

"Anandy?" Themis murmured. His attention remained completely locked on the pocketknife, his eyes still firmly glued to it.

"We found signs of a fight. There was blood. *Lots* of blood. No one was found in the field, dead or alive."

Themis didn't reply. He didn't bother to look at the men sitting across from his desk. He was gazing at the small, bloody object in his hands, hoping it would talk to him and tell him what happened to his only son.

"We believe Anandy was ambushed on the road." Faron spoke in a soft tone.

"No sign of my son?" Themis raised his chin. His dark eyes met Faron's turquoise eyes. The Magistrate's lips were shivering.

"I am sorry, Magistrate." Faron lowered his eyes once again.

"My son is... H–he is..." Themis gasped.

"We can't say for sure, Themis," Mattas interjected. "As Leader Faron mentioned, we found only the knife. We have hopes Anandy escaped *alive.*" His gray eyes were shining with hope.

Themis felt like he was in a dream. He held the pocketknife close to his chest and squeezed its handle.

"Magistrate, we will not give up. I will not give up. I will find Anandy! Remember, there is hope!" The advisor placed his hands on the desk, pressing his fingertips onto the wood.

"Why didn't he come home?" Themis blinked several times, as if he had just woken up.

"I beg your pardon, sir?" Leader Faron leaned closer.

"If Anandy is alive, why didn't he come home? Where is he?" Themis placed his red eyes on Mattas's.

"We don't know, sir. There are various plausible scenarios. He might be hiding. Maybe he is hurt and recovering somewhere... We can't tell for sure," the advisor reasoned.

"My son is dead!" Themis squeezed the pocketknife harder against his chest.

Mattas raised his voice. "No, sir! There *is* hope! We will keep searching for Anandy! He must be somewhere!"

"Thank you for your service and your friendship, good Mattas. You did all you could." Themis's voice was faint.

How can you give up on your son so easily? Mattas thought as he stared at the Magistrate in disbelief. "There is more to be done! I can do more!"

"If it helps, I can put at your service all the South Land's armies to search for Anandy in every corner of Green Valleys, sir. Just say the word, and my armies are yours," Faron announced.

"I am deeply thankful for your generous offer, Leader Faron." Themis's eyes were empty.

Mattas felt a shiver going down his spine. He moved uncomfortably in his chair. The room suddenly felt colder, and darkness seemed to seep in.

It is a musty smell! Why is it so cold here? The windows are closed, the advisor thought, looking around to check the doors and windows. Mattas felt like a headache was setting in. He gave his head a little shake and tried to focus on the conversation.

"It is my duty as one of the Five Leaders to put my resources in the hands of the Magistrate. Please, accept my offer. I insist, sir."

"That's such a generous offer, Leader Faron." Themis placed the pocketknife on the desk and looked at the warrior. His attention was on him now. He was no longer grieving or lost in despair. He was back to discuss important matters.

"It is a sincere offer, sir."

"The duty of a leader does not include offering the military to help the Magistrate on a personal quest," Themis declared, his fingers interlaced on the desk. He was no longer trembling. He was focused.

"Indeed," Faron agreed. "But I would like to offer it as a gift, perhaps."

"And why do I deserve such a generous gift, Leader Faron?" Themis wondered, placing his right hand under his chin. His dark eyes were suspicious.

No! It is not the moment for that, Faron! Don't do it! Mattas thought, watching the events unfolding in front of his incredulous eyes.

Faron didn't reply. He blushed and lowered his eyes.

"It is my daughter, isn't it?" Themis hissed.

"It is not the right moment for that, sir," Faron murmured, gazing at the floor.

"I am no fool, Faron! I saw how you looked at her and how you brought her flowers," Themis spat, clenching his fists on the desk.

The warrior remained silent, uncomfortably running his fingers through his wavy brown hair.

"You come to my home uninvited to bring me the news no father would want to hear, and you have the audacity to flirt with my daughter under my nose?" Themis was breathing fire. He clenched his fists tighter.

Mattas thought of intervening, but he was unsure how he could be of any help.

"I did not come here to flirt with your daughter, sir." Faron endured Themis's furious gaze. "I came here out of duty to inform you of our failure."

"How do you explain your frivolous behavior? How do you explain your gift to my daughter?" Themis punched the desk with the bottom of his right hand.

"Leader Faron is famous for offering generous gifts, Magistrate. He had told me of his intention not to come here empty-handed. It was under my recommendation that he brought flowers to the girl. There was no ill intent from him," Mattas finally intervened, noticing a thin line of blood staining Themis's fingers.

Themis didn't seem to hear his advisor's words. He glared at the warrior, his eyes blazing with rage.

"It is true, sir. I simply brought gifts to the ladies in this house out of courtesy," Faron explained calmly.

"And out of courtesy, you flirted with my precious daughter? Do you take her for a low-birth tanned woman from the South Lands?" Themis snapped.

"Themis!" Mattas interjected. "It is not wise to offend the good women from the South. They are Leader Faron's people."

The Magistrate ignored his advisor's advice. "I am waiting for your response, Faron."

The Leader of the South Lands leaned toward the Magistrate, his muscular arms flexing as he placed his large hands on the desk. His face and his manners were undisturbed. "I came here as a friend, Magistrate. I advise you to be cautious when you talk about my people. Do not take me as an enemy."

A stoic man, Mattas thought, observing Faron's cold, controlled manners.

"I brought gifts out of courtesy, as I mentioned before." Faron's voice was low. "I did not intend to offend you or your daughter. I can assure you I had no ill intentions toward the girl, for it was the first time I had ever seen her." He reclined back in his chair.

Faron opened his mouth to talk more, but he quickly changed his mind. Themis was staring at him.

"I meant to have a conversation about this matter with you at a later date. Circumstances, however, have made their appearance today. I must confess that your daughter's beauty stoked me in a way that was unexpected to me." Faron looked around the room, searching for the right words.

"It did?" Themis said scornfully.

"Yes, it did," Faron replied, ignoring the tone. "I always thought of myself as an unmarried warrior. But, after meeting your daughter, I have changed my mind." He paused and inhaled deeply. "I wish to marry your daughter, sir."

No good omens will come from this! Mattas thought, using all his willpower to sit still.

"To marry my daughter, Leader Faron?" Themis couldn't hide his surprise.

"Yes, sir. Your daughter's beauty is famous in Green Valleys. I could witness that it is not only her beauty that makes her so remarkable. She is a gentle flower. I can see virtue and goodness in her pure heart. It would honor me to call her my wife. Please, accept my proposal of marriage and all my resources as the leader of the second-biggest clan in Green Valleys. I am the wealthiest of men and the best warrior alive. I offer myself as a husband, and I pledge to honor and respect your daughter and to give you grandchildren that will fill your life with joy," Faron said.

"My daughter is only twenty years old. I assume you are in your late twenties, Leader Faron?" Themis asked.

"I am twenty-nine years old, sir. I am no longer a lad," Faron replied.

"Indeed, you are no lad," Themis observed.

"Yes, only a man will give you what a boy can't, sir." Faron's eyes were shining.

"And what is it, Leader Faron?" Themis raised an eyebrow.

"A grandson to continue our bloodlines. A boy to become the Leader of the South Lands and the Magistrate." Faron's eyes sparkled as his lips curved into a dazzling smile.

"*You ended our bloodline*." Themis heard his father's voice whisper in his ears.

The Magistrate felt a strange contradictory sensation — hot and cold simultaneously. His hands were clammy and icy.

"*You are useless. You killed your own son*," the voice hissed.

Themis felt a dull throbbing at the back of his head. He was confused. The room seemed to swallow him. The Magistrate brought his hands up to cover his ears. Mattas could see expectation in Faron's eyes. The Leader of the South was waiting for an answer.

"I believe it is time for the Magistrate to return to his chambers. It was his first day on his feet," Mattas chimed in eagerly. "I am sure the Magistrate is honored to have such a proposition from you, Leader Faron. He will meditate upon it, sir."

"Of course, my good Mattas," Faron replied. "Have a good night, gentlemen."

"You as well, Leader Faron. My wife will guide you to the guest room," Mattas said, walking the warrior to the door and closing it behind him.

"Themis," the advisor called softly, "would you allow me to walk you to your bedroom, sir?"

"A grandson...to be the next Magistrate..." Themis felt like his voice was distant, as if it was coming from a dream.

"The next Magistrate will be Anandy, sir." Mattas walked toward the desk, placing his hand on the back of the guest's chair.

"*Anandy is gone, Themis. You killed him*," the voice said.

"He's gone, Mattas. My son is gone. I am left with a daughter who is at the age of marrying someone." The Magistrate's eyes were red and empty.

"No, Themis. There is a possibility that Anandy is still alive. We cannot give up on him. Let's send our own men to search for Anandy. Let's use our contacts. We don't have to accept Leader Faron's proposition." Mattas's heart was racing.

"My daughter needs a husband and a son soon," Themis said.

"The girl doesn't have to go through that, Themis. Please, listen to me. Let's find your son!" Mattas put his hand to his mouth. The musty smell was unbearable.

The Magistrate looked out the window and saw the moon.

"*Listen with your heart*," the venerable old man's voice told him.

"I am too tired. I cannot," Themis murmured.

"*Listen to your heart, and you will find the answer*," the voice repeated.

"I cannot..." Themis mumbled once again.

"I beg your pardon, Themis?" Mattas leaned forward, trying to hear him better.

"I cannot... I am too tired... I cannot..." Themis repeated.

The old man's voice was gone.

Chapter Twenty-Three

The Shadow

Aura smiled, admiring her mother's peaceful expression. "Your face shines more than the moon and the stars, Mother!"

Adira wrapped her arms around Aura's shoulders. Placing a loose curl behind her daughter's ear, she kissed the girl's forehead.

"I am scared, Mother," Aura whispered.

"So am I, Aura... But we must be brave. Be brave for our family. Be brave for ourselves." Adira hugged her tighter.

Aura opened her mouth, but words refused to come out. She wanted to tell her mother about her visions, about the garden, about the monster...about everything.

Not now. I am tired. There is much to think about, Aura thought, looking over her mother's shoulder. The stars were shining. *A bright ceiling of stars.* She recalled the title of a story from her old fairy-tale book.

Nature gifts us every moment of our lives. Each evening, we get a new ceiling to look at. On some magical nights, Nature gives us a bright ceiling of stars. But it is not any night sky. It is a magical one. It is a portal to take us to a world full of magic and beauty. A world where there is no sorrow or shame. This is the world of stars. A world that is a fairy tale itself. A perfect world... Aura still knew the first paragraph of the story by heart. She knew most of the stories in that book by heart. *A perfect book filled with perfect stories,* she thought, sighing.

"I wish our lives could be like a shining star," Aura murmured.

"Who said they can't be?" Adira wore a knowing smile.

"How could it possibly be when we face so many vicissitudes? There is so much sorrow in our lives! Endless conundrums and dangers!" Aura's light blue eyes were shining with tears.

"My baby!" Adira wiped them away.

"I sometimes wonder why we have to face such misfortune, Mother." Aura's voice trembled as a wave of sorrow and fear crashed over her.

"While it is true that misfortune and vicissitudes are part of our lives, it does not mean they are more powerful than our light, Aura," Adira whispered.

Aura looked inquisitively at her mother.

"Stars shine even on the darkest nights. Although we cannot see them, they are there." Adira pointed at the sky. "They are up there, shining. Darkness cannot take your light away, my little star."

"I wish it was true, Mother." Aura lifted her head and looked at the clear night sky.

"It is true if you choose to believe it." Adira took her daughter's hands and gently touched her face, guiding her gaze to meet hers.

"Do I have a choice?" Aura asked as her gaze met her mother's.

"We always have a choice. I choose to keep shining in the darkest of hours. What do you choose, Aura?" Adira's voice was grave and deep.

Adira quietly placed her golden braid on her left shoulder. Looking into the older woman's blue eyes, the girl saw light and kindness.

So different from Father. Aura thought of Themis's black hair and his cold, dark eyes.

Aura inhaled the chilly evening air. She looked at the magnificent cherry tree, the majestic moon, and the countless shiny stars. *The bright ceiling of stars.*

"I choose to shine with you, Mother. I choose to shine and defy the darkness." Aura felt a warm feeling growing inside her. Her hands were shaking with excitement. She could feel it coming.

★ ★ ★ ☾ ★ ★ ★

It felt like it was daytime, for there was light as radiant as the sun itself. Instinctively, I sheltered my eyes with my hands.

"Hello, Aura," he said.

"I know your voice," I replied, lowering my hands and opening my eyes. The light diminished. I saw a silhouette of a man. I blinked a few times so my eyes would adjust to the bright light.

The man from the Garden was standing in front of me, wearing the same garments. I was no longer wearing my warm fall dress. I was wearing a light, long, white dress. My loose curls fell freely down my back. I was barefoot, just as I had been in the Garden. Same dress. Same hairstyle. And bare feet. I was just myself.

"You came to me?" I whispered in disbelief.

"Yes, I came to you in an hour of need," he replied.

I nodded. I knew it. I could feel it. Looking at his serene face, I felt as if words were unnecessary. We could understand each other in the silence of our hearts.

"Are you ready?" He offered his right hand to me. He was smiling.

"I am." I placed my hand in his. I smiled back at him, feeling the warmth of his hand. After the initial tingling sensation, a pleasant, warm feeling traveled from his fingers into mine.

He gently guided me through the garden. I looked around, searching for Mother, knowing that she was no longer there. It was only us, the man and me.

As we walked, I saw the dry leaves falling from the trees and decaying under my bare feet. The flowers were dying. The grass was dry. The garden was dying. I uttered no word. I simply walked hand in hand with him. The fire was burning inside me, keeping me warm. So warm!

There was no fear in my heart. I walked confidently into the garden, knowing what was waiting for me. I could feel it in my core. It was there, waiting to meet me.

"Here we are." The Man's face was somber. There was sadness in his eyes.

I stood silently in front of him. I could feel his sadness in my heart.

"Look, Aura." He pointed at my house.

I hesitated for a moment. "Do I really have to see it?" I murmured, shutting my eyes.

"Yes. You must see it. Open your eyes, Aura." The Man's voice was gentle but firm.

I opened my eyes, and I saw it! Oh! I saw it! I tried to face the urge to turn my face away and run, but I knew it was pointless. I knew I had to see it. I had to face it.

"Do you see it, Aura?" His eyes were on me.

"I see it." My voice sounded distant and faint.

I could see it. I saw a shadow over my house. It was coming from Father's office.

"It's done, then. The Monster got my father." I could barely recognize my voice.

The Man didn't reply. He stood next to me, watching the shadow and watching me.

"Is it over for him?" My voice was shaky. I glared at the shadow.

He spoke no words, but his eyes spoke to my soul.

"I will not allow it to take my father!" I hissed.

The Man didn't reply, just stared.

"I will kill this thing! Before it takes my father away, I will kill it. I cannot afford to lose anybody else!" I said.

The Man remained silent.

"It is just the beginning, isn't it? This...this...monster came for my people. It will take us one by one!" The fire inside me was growing stronger. The warmth was no longer pleasurable. It was unbearable.

"Anger and despair will take you nowhere, Aura," he spoke slowly.

My heart was racing. I was panting and sweating profusely. The fire was burning my skin. How could I stand in a dying garden, watching that monster burying its teeth in my beloved father? How could I stand next to this unknown man and watch the shadow taking over my house?

"Why don't you help him?" I cried. The fire's heat was consuming me from the inside out.

"I cannot help the ones who are deaf to my advice."

"He is not deaf! He is sick! He needs help!" I yelled.

"A doctor cannot treat a patient who does not wish to be healed." The calmness and kindness in his voice made the fire in my core burn even harder.

"You didn't try! You are lying! You are trying to deceive me! You... You do not exist! You are only in my head!" I yelled. My skin was burning. I felt fire consuming my flesh.

"Aura, please. Do not push us away!" There was deep sorrow in the Man's eyes.

"I... I...am burning!" I screamed in terror as I looked at my arms and legs. The flames were fully consuming my body. I was a fireball, screaming and crying in a dying garden.

The Man closed his eyes and raised his hands. He whispered a few incomprehensible words. I fell to the cold grass.

"Do not allow anger and despair to take over your being, child." I heard the Man's voice in my head.

★ ★ ★ ☾ ★ ★ ★

Aura felt powerful arms carrying her up the stairs. There was a grassy smell coming from those arms. There was warmth, but not the burning fire she had felt earlier.

"What is happening?" Aura murmured, trying to open her eyes.

"Your mother asked me to take you to your bedroom," the male voice told her, gently placing her in bed.

"What is happening?" Aura was confused.

"She is coming with the advisor's wife to care for you," he told her, taking his arms away.

"Oh... I am burning." Aura shivered. Tears rolled down her cheeks.

"You will be fine, girl." There was kindness in his voice.

"I am Aura. Call me Aura," she said, finally opening her eyes. She saw Faron leaning toward her at her bedside.

"You will be fine, *Aura.*" The warrior's voice was low and gentle.

Aura didn't reply. She was in shock. She couldn't believe her recklessness.

"Oh! I thought it was a dream! My apologies, Leader Faron!" Her voice was weak but rushed.

"Please, call me Faron." He fixed his eyes on hers.

"Thank you for bringing me here, sir. I can hear my mother coming upstairs. I appreciate your kindness, and I do not want to trouble you late at night," Aura said, trying to avoid his piercing gaze.

"It is no trouble, *Aura.* Please, I am no *sir* to you. I am simply Faron, and you are simply Aura. That is what we should be to each other, my star." The warrior's voice turned into a secretive whisper.

Aura felt a shiver going down her spine.

His eyes. His smile. There is something...what is it? Aura thought, studying his face.

Faron suddenly leaned closer. Aura's heart was beating faster than it ever had in her entire life. He gently took her hand and kissed it respectfully.

"Goodnight, Aura. I will see you in the morning, my star." Faron left the room.

Aura watched him leave as she rubbed her hand, speechless. Her head filled with strange emotions and thoughts.

"Thank you, Leader Faron! Thank you so much for your help! Please, go to sleep now. You must be tired!" Janace said, rushing into the bedroom. "Oh, my! I knew you needed some time to recover, lovely! Do not worry! I am here! Your mother is boiling some water for tea!" The old lady closed the door and opened Aura's closet, searching for the girl's nightgown.

"You're drenched in sweat! Oh, poor little one! You passed out in the garden! You must have a fever! Come! Come! Let me help dry you and change you into something warm. Your mother is coming with tea for you!" Janace said.

Aura didn't reply. She was so deeply entrenched in her thoughts that she was unaware of her surroundings.

"Are you sick again, lovely? You look as white as a ghost!" the old woman stated.

He called me Aura... He kissed my hand, she thought, rubbing her hand.

Janace observed the girl for a second. "Did you hurt your hand when you fainted, lovely?"

"No... I feel like my hand is burning... It feels like I placed it in boiling water," Aura replied.

His lips felt like fire on my skin, she thought, watching Janace delicately drying her sweaty arms with a soft towel. *His lips are soft and his manners are gentle.*

"I will close the window, child," Janace announced.

Aura nodded and watched Mattas's wife walking toward the window.

"The stars look so bright and beautiful today!" the old woman said, stopping for a moment to contemplate the dark skies.

Aura suddenly smiled. *He called me 'my star,'* she thought, rubbing her hand, feeling the warmth growing inside her once again.

Chapter Twenty-Four

Sing Your Own Song

Dansa watched as the horizon turned a brilliant orange with streaks of pink and purple. The first rays of the sun were breaking into the dark curtain of the night. A single seagull gliding through the air caught the leader's eye. Its wings flapped in a steady beat as it soared gracefully into the distance, fading away into the horizon.

I envy you, seagull, he thought, closing his tired eyes for a moment. It had been a sleepless night for him. The house was quiet and asleep.

"I envy your freedom," Dansa murmured, opening his eyes.

Soon, every soul in Green Valleys would get ready for the day. *Another day,* he thought bitterly.

The Leader of the Central Lands motioned to open the window, but he changed his mind at the last minute. Hesitantly, Dansa walked back to his desk. He glared at the black envelope folded in half.

Bad omens, he thought as his agitation grew.

A knock at the door abruptly brought him back from his thoughts. Dansa reluctantly walked over.

Nothing good comes this early in the morning, he thought, glancing one last time at the note before opening the door.

"My apologies for the intrusion at such an early hour, sir." The young warrior standing in front of Dansa quavered, cleaning the sweat off his forehead.

"Did you find him?" The Leader could read fear on the boy's face.

"No, sir." The warrior lowered his eyes.

"What did you say, warrior?" Dansa raged.

"We haven't found him, sir," the warrior replied.

"How could you possibly not find him? You had an entire night to search for him." Dansa was livid.

"We did search for him, sir. But the scoundrel vanished," the young man explained hurriedly.

"Get our best warriors and search each hole of the Central Lands. Come back after you find him." Dansa narrowed his eyes.

"Yes, sir!" the warrior said.

"You may leave now," Dansa grunted.

The warrior nodded and left hurriedly, yelling orders to the other warriors in the living room, disappearing through the front door.

"Bloody hell!" Dansa slammed the door behind him and grabbed the note once again.

"Husband? Are you all right?" his wife asked as she opened the office door, rubbing her eyes.

"Go back to sleep, woman!" Dansa spat.

"What is this commotion about?" Her eyes were wide open now.

"Go back to sleep! Don't make me repeat it a third time, woman!" her husband growled.

The woman didn't move. "It is about last night, isn't it? It is about this note," she said, pointing at the envelope in Dansa's hands.

The Leader didn't reply. His eyes were fixed on the letter.

"How bad is the damage, husband?" she asked boldly.

Dansa put the note down on the desk. "It is a terrible ordeal, wife. It could cost me *everything*!"

His wife closed the door behind her. She resolutely extended her open hand to her husband. "Give me the note."

Dansa shook his head. "You don't give me orders. Go! Do woman things!"

"I *am* doing woman things, husband," she replied. "I am taking care of my family and my husband. It is my duty as a woman and a wife."

Her husband glared at the note as if it was a disgusting animal. It was difficult for other people to understand Leader Dansa's motives or even his intentions. He was a walking puzzle. Dansa was playing his own little games. However, his wife could read his feelings better than anybody else. She could read the fear in his eyes — a rare and frightening sight.

"Husband," she called softly, "I know you better than anybody else." She took two steps toward him. Dansa looked at her suspiciously. "When you accepted to marry me, we told each other all our secrets." She lowered her eyes. "And we have our own secrets ourselves as a family. Secrets...we created... Secrets...we learned to love."

"Yes," he said. "I know who you are. You know who I am." It was the first time in many moons they had looked at each other eye to eye.

"We know each other's deepest and darkest secrets." There was no pride in her voice. "Trust me, as I trusted you when I was still a girl."

Dansa reluctantly gave the black envelope to her. A gasp escaped the woman's lips as she read the contents of the note.

"Oh! This is plain blackmail!" There was horror on her face. "How is it possible?"

The Leader of the Central Lands didn't reply. He placed a hand on his forehead and ran his fingers through his straight brown hair. His gaze was lost in the air.

"Who sent you this note?"

"The scoundrel said a stranger had given it to him to be handed to me last night," Dansa said faintly.

"A stranger..." his wife repeated, "a foreigner, maybe... What did the warriors learn from his interrogation?"

"Nothing." He shrugged.

"Nothing?" she repeated in disbelief.

"He vanished." Dansa collapsed on the chair, both hands pressing the sides of his head.

"But...but...how can someone just vanish?" She was dumbfounded.

"Because he wasn't a commoner, wife. We believed he was a nobody. He played the game. He played too well," Dansa replied.

"He made us believe he was not a threat. It was all planned!" His wife took a seat across the desk.

"He played us!" Dansa hissed.

"He did!" She placed her hands on her lap, rocking her body forward and backward as if she was trying to soothe herself.

"Whoever sent him," Dansa murmured, "is a powerful man."

"Burn the letter! No soul should learn its contents. Especially Themis! If he does..." she put a hand to her chest, "it will be our end! His wrath! Oh! It will be our fall!"

Dansa watched as his wife got a candle from the side table and lit it with trembling hands.

"We shall not talk about this note or this proposition!" she demanded, placing the letter close to the flame. "Let's burn this cursed note!"

Dansa had a sudden change of heart. He grabbed the note from his wife's hands and placed it back in the black envelope.

"They know what I did," he said calmly. "But who are they?" He felt his reasoning mind was coming back to him.

The woman watched him in dismay. "What are you doing? Just burn it!"

"No." Dansa's voice was low. "I need to keep this note safe. I need it for the future." He placed his tired red eyes on his wife. "The man behind this note will not stop until I am ruined."

"You are the leader of the biggest clan in Green Valleys! You are powerful. No one else has the resources you have. You have your Little Ones to be your eyes and ears on the streets. They can sing any song you want. You are Dansa from the Central Lands!" There was passion in his wife's voice.

"Themis is more powerful. He is the Magistrate," Dansa whispered.

"Themis is a broken man. You are a whole man! You are the most powerful man in Green Valleys now. Use this power now!" The woman's face was shining.

"What are you trying to say?" he asked.

"Get your army of Little Ones and send them to sing your beautiful song! Do not take the blame for your actions! Blame someone else!" Her eyes were still shining.

"But...this man... He knows my crime! He will accuse me. Themis will learn what I did." Dansa looked at the envelope in his hands. "His proposition is...it is...ill!"

"You will not abide by his terms, husband. You are the one who plays the bigger role now. Call your Little Ones and let them sing, Dansa!" There was a wicked smile on her face.

Chapter Twenty-Five

For the Greatness of the East Lands

Gillion kept his head down as he stepped into the hallway. He felt the weight of his head, full of concerns, would make it impossible for him to elevate his gaze. The wooden columns seemed to be obstacles in his way. He zigzagged around them. The latest developments from the Central Lands were disturbing.

"What do you have for me today, son?" Gilbride said, taking a sip of his herbal tea. He could hear his son's heavy steps in the distance.

"Recent developments in the Central Lands," Gillion replied, rubbing his bald scalp.

"I am listening." The old leader took another sip.

"The girl's recovery was followed by the Magistrate's. Although not fully recovered, it is reported he stands on his feet now," Gillion said, making steady hand movements. The Leader's son was renowned for his grand and exaggerated hand gestures.

"As expected. What else do you know, son?" Gilbride seemed indifferent.

"It seems the Magistrate had informally accepted the death of his firstborn." Gillion hesitated for a second.

"How so?" Gilbride placed the empty cup on his dining table. "Accepted the death of his only son?"

"After days of searches in the South Lands, Leader Faron's men found the boy's golden pocketknife, a present from the Magistrate to his son. And there was blood on it," Gillion said hurriedly.

"Interesting." Gilbride ran his fingers over the rim of his empty cup.

"There is something else, Father." Gillion rubbed his shaved face.

"I assume it must be quite intriguing," the Leader of the East said, observing his son's nervous behavior.

"Indeed, Father. I must confess I didn't see it coming." Gillion rubbed his chin once again.

"I am still listening." Gilbride's voice was emotionless.

"Leader Faron insisted on joining advisor Mattas on his journey to the Central Lands to inform Themis of their discovery." Gillion was now rubbing his right cheek.

Gilbride remained motionless, not uttering a single word, gazing at the empty cup.

"During his visit, Leader Faron proposed marriage to the Magistrate's daughter," Gillion said, lowering his eyes, ashamed of not being able to see it coming.

"Ha! *This* is unexpected!" Gilbride's laughter filled all corners of his rustic dining room.

"Forgive me, Father. But I cannot see how it can amuse you." Gillion's eyebrows furrowed in confusion.

"It amuses me to see a man's cleverness." Gilbride was smiling.

"Indeed, Father. Leader Faron's cleverness put him a step ahead of all of us," Gillion agreed.

"Perhaps it did...or perhaps it put him a step behind us..." the old man said.

"I am afraid I do not follow your reasoning, Father." Gillion scratched his bald head once again.

"Take a seat, son." Gilbride pointed to a chair. "Be a good boy and serve both of us some tea. We need to keep our nerves in check in order to plot our next move."

"Of course, Father." Gillion handed the teacup to the old man and filled one for himself.

"Leader Faron's proposal was a brilliant move. Perhaps a bit rushed." Gilbride sipped from his cup.

"Agreed. I would not expect such a rushed proposal. Clearly, the girl will attract suitors from all corners of Green Valleys." Gillion held his cup between his hands, blowing on the hot brown liquid inside before carefully taking his first sip.

"Faron is no fool. He must have had his reasons to rush it. Perhaps circumstances forced him to take such a precipitous decision," Gilbride said, taking a long sip.

Gillion observed his father's calm and calculated manners. *An old crow,* he thought.

"What do you think our next move should be, Gillion?" the old man asked, placing his cold gray eyes on him.

"Well," Gillion pondered his options for a moment, "I believe the East should present a suitor."

"And who would this suitor be? It must be someone who would benefit us entirely. Faron is lucky enough to be young, handsome, and single." Gilbride kept his gaze on his son.

"My youngest son is single..." The younger man hesitated.

"Ha! Your youngest?" Gilbride's guttural laughter resonated throughout the large dining room.

"I beg your pardon, Father?" Gillion clenched his jaw.

"Oh, you silly boy! Your youngest is only twenty years old! How can that little rabbit-face compete with a man like Faron?" Gilbride replied.

Gillion felt his blood boiling. *This old crow!* he thought, fighting the urge to jump down his father's throat.

"Forgive my frankness, my son. But we should be rational. We need someone who can present a fair competition against Faron. Do you have anyone in mind?"

"No." Gillion struggled as he tried to regain control of his emotions.

There was a moment of silence. The younger man had his gaze fixed on the teacup in front of him. His mind was a jumble of chaotic thoughts and doubts.

I know Father is testing me. That old crow does not trust his own shadow. I will be the Leader of the East Lands one day. I must gain his trust if I want to learn his political secrets, he thought, searching his father's gray, emotionless eyes for any traces of emotion. There were none. *This man is a riddle! It is impossible to know what he is thinking. I must learn his secrets!* Gillion thought, amazed at Gilbride's self-control.

"Father," Gillion called hesitantly, "do *you* have a suitor in mind?" He had to know.

Gilbride was pleased. "I have something more profitable for us than a suitor, son." He placed his half-empty teacup on the wooden table.

"What could be better than a suitor, Father?" Gillion's eyes widened in puzzlement.

The Leader of the East Lands reached for his teacup and drank the dregs in one gulp. He gently placed it back on the table and looked into his son's eyes.

"A puppet!" His eyes were shining in a sinister way.

Gillion had to blink a few times to be certain that he was not dreaming. "A puppet? Did I hear you right, Father?"

"Yes, you heard me right, son. The East will have a puppet as the Magistrate." There was amusement in the old man's eyes.

"Forgive me for not following your reasoning, Father." The son placed his teacup on the table.

"There is nothing to forgive, my son." Gilbride grinned. "Being enigmatic is my curse."

Gillion studied Gilbride's face closely, nodding in agreement. He was trying to contain the feeling of anticipation bubbling up inside him.

"Son, let me ask you a question," Gilbride said.

"Yes, Father."

"Do you remember our lands' words and what they mean?"

Gillion did not hesitate. "'The East stands still' means we never interfere in other clans' businesses. We keep our distance as harmless farmers."

"Indeed, son! Indeed!" The old man ran his fingers over the wooden table as if he was meditating on something. "We truly maintain our image of harmless farmers, but it does not mean we do not interfere."

The son leaned toward the table between himself and his father. "Do we interfere in other clans' affairs, Father? How so?" he asked in a low tone.

"Of course we do, silly boy!" Gilbride laughed out loud.

Gillion lowered his eyes, feeling his cheeks burn.

"Gillion, there is much for you to learn about politics," Gilbride said, wiping a tear of amusement from his face. "The ways of the East are secretive. We observe. We spy. We plot. And we take action behind the curtains. To the world, we are harmless farmers, when in reality we are treacherous snakes." There was a calm to his voice.

Gillion mouth was agape in disbelief. His father's words were going against everything he had learned. Actually, the past few days had challenged Gillion's knowledge on many matters.

"Often, as leaders, we must do things we are not proud of," Gilbride said gravely. "However, we must do things to protect our people. It is all for the greatness of the East Lands!"

"What did you do, Father?" Gillion narrowed his eyes. His mouth was dry. His heart was pounding.

"I did what I had to do to protect the interests of our clan," Gilbride said dully.

"I fear asking you about your crimes, Father." Gillion's lips trembled.

"Leaders do not commit crimes. While we resort to less than orthodox ways of dealing with a crisis, you cannot say they are criminal actions." Gilbride reclined in his chair, tapping his fingers on the wooden table.

Gillion nodded slowly, trying to read between the lines.

"Take the example of Themis's son," the Leader said casually.

"What about him?" Gillion raised an eyebrow.

"His disappearance was quite convenient to us because it put Themis in an unfavorable situation." Gilbride stopped tapping on the table, placing his hand under his chin.

"Forgive me, Father. I cannot see how the boy's misfortune would be to our benefit." Gillion frowned, thinking hard to understand his father's enigmatic ways.

"You lack perspective, son. Let me break it down for you. The Magistrate's family is notorious for being cursed with madness. Themis has been showing signs of instability and a lack of righteous judgment in his actions. As a leader, it was my duty to show my support for his decisions, even the rushed ones." He poured some water in a glass. "Son, Themis's decisions were leading us to an abyss of famine and misery."

Gillion gave a slight tilt of his head in acknowledgement.

"While the boy's misfortune is a sad deed, it benefits us because it unveils his father's inability to keep his seat as the Magistrate of Green Valleys." Gilbride gulped the water from his class. "Eventually, the boy would have shown the same signs of madness, and we would be stuck with a new generation of madmen as our Magistrates."

"Father! What are you trying to say?" Gillion gasped, his hand instinctively flying to cover his mouth.

"I am saying it will benefit Green Valleys if the Magistrate's family is out of power. Having a reliable Magistrate would be the best option for us." Gilbride's voice dropped to a low, raspy whisper.

"If Faron marries the girl, he will be the next Magistrate." Gillion scratched his shaved face.

"Faron can marry the girl, but he will not be the next Magistrate if we take Themis down." Gilbride's eyes were shining. He twisted his face into a malicious grin.

"You are talking about treason!" Gillion's voice came out as a squeak.

"You lack perspective, son," his father said.

"Give me some perspective, Father," he replied in his own deep voice.

"You call it treason; I call it saving Green Valleys from the Magistrate's madness. First, he talks about rationing our provisions. What will he do next? Take away our fields?"

"And this puppet would be the new Magistrate?"

"Finally, some perspective, my son." Gilbride smiled.

"Who would betray Themis? Who would risk exile or death to take down the Magistrate of Green Valleys? Why would anyone do that?"

"Someone who hides a secret so terrible, it would mean exile or death. What would a dead man choose when destruction is the only choice?"

Chapter Twenty-Six

The Suitor

The sun was at its brightest as Usman ran his daily inspection around the Great River. The sentinels greeted the young warrior as he walked among them, breathing their boredom into the air. He had positioned each warrior at a "vulnerable point." According to his father, it was vital to protect the river from Themis and his army of thieves.

Nothing out of the ordinary, he thought. *Father's idea to fortify our borders and get the warriors ready for battle was rushed. I doubt Themis would attack us,* he pondered, walking among the streets of the West Lands.

"Usman!" his father called.

The son turned around to face his father, who raised a hand, signaling him to stop walking.

"Greetings, Father," he replied cordially, coming to a full stop.

The Leader smiled at his son, patting Usman on his left shoulder.

"If I didn't know you better, I would think you were avoiding my presence, son."

Usman didn't reply. He had spent the last few days avoiding being in the same quarters as his father, which included working long hours in the Central Building as a way of being late for meals and waking up earlier for his daily physical exercises, preventing him from sharing the breakfast table with his father.

"I have wonderful news, son!" The Leader of the West Lands rubbed his hands in excitement.

These words sent shivers down the young warrior's spine. *What would be "wonderful news" when we are preparing for a potential invasion?* Usman thought, doing his best to grin politely.

Ansel didn't expect his son to reply. "I received a few notes from our loyal friends."

You mean your spies, Usman thought as he simply stood in front of Ansel, looking at him. The grin had vanished from his face.

"According to the reports, it seems the girl and the Magistrate have recovered from their illnesses." The Leader of the East Lands was smiling.

"God is merciful!" Usman allowed himself an honest smile. "Great news, indeed, Father!" The young warrior had been praying for their good health since his last conversation with his father.

"Indeed, son! God's miracle!" Ansel gazed at his son's face. "Walk with me, son." He wrapped an arm around his son's shoulder.

The men walked around the Great River. Despite the sun above their heads, the chilly winds made them tuck their chins in. Fall was making its presence known. The fishermen were busy with the salmon run. They ran into a group of fishermen landing with their nets filled with salmon.

"What a blessed fishing day, my friends!" Ansel greeted the men.

"It certainly is, sir! The Great River has been generous to us!" the oldest one replied, pointing to the fat fish in his nets.

"Beautiful, my friend! Beautiful!" Ansel said, examining the man's nets. "Go to the Central Building for the division! The five biggest fish are yours to feast on with your family tonight. Tell the warriors it is my gift to you, my friend!"

The fisherman bowed. "Thank you, sir!"

Ansel and Usman watched the men heading toward the Central Building to give their share to the Central Lands.

"You see, son," Ansel said, "it is important to take good care of our people, for there is no West Lands without its people."

"Yes, Father. Our people are our wealth." Usman nodded, repeating the famous words of the West Lands.

"They truly are our wealth," Ansel said. "It is time to take better care of them."

Usman looked at his father. There was confusion in his eyes. "How can we take better care of our people?"

"It is time to expand our clan and make it more powerful." Ansel spoke gravely.

"Expand our clan? Make it more powerful? I cannot understand your words, Father. Our clan developed around the Great River. Our lands are vast, and the river is our provider. We already are powerful and large, if that is what you are trying to say."

"You speak truly, my son. Our lands are vast. Our geographical size is extensive, yet economically we are considered as the least among the clans in Green Valleys." There was disgust in Ansel's voice.

The warrior nodded. He knew how the other clans perceived the West Lands. "You know they speak wrongly about us, Father. We are big and prosperous."

"Indeed, son. However, our judgment of ourselves has little value in the Central Lands. You see, son...there was an unexpected turn of events...and I would like to discuss it with you." Ansel spoke slowly, choosing his words carefully.

"Of course, Father. I will do my best to be of assistance," Usman replied humbly.

"I know you will, son." Ansel smiled, but there was sadness in his eyes. "It seems the Magistrate's son is dead."

Usman lowered his head, closed his eyes, and murmured a prayer. "May God keep his soul. May his family find comfort in their hearts," he said frankly.

"May God keep his soul!" Ansel repeated, awkwardly bowing his head. His eyes never left his son's face.

"I believe it would be prudent to attend the funeral and to pay our respects to the Magistrate's family," Usman said, trying to regain control of his emotions. Hearing about death always had a profound effect on him. Although he was around Anandy's age, Usman had never had a proper conversation with him. But it didn't stop him from feeling sorrow over his fellow warrior's premature death.

"Yes, son. We will pay our respects to the Magistrate's family!" Ansel spoke fast and excitedly. There was no longer sadness in his eyes.

“I will make the arrangements for our departure,” Usman said as he motioned to leave.

“This conversation is not over, son,” Ansel said.

“I am sorry, Father.” His son blushed.

“You see, there is a very important detail to be discussed.”

“Yes, Father.”

Ansel looked at the Great River and at the white clouds in the sky as if he was searching for the right words.

“Usman...you see, son... The Magistrate’s only son died. Themis is left with a daughter in the age of getting married...”

“Father!” Usman interjected. “Now I understand! That’s your way of growing our clan? Proposing marriage to the Magistrate’s daughter?” His pulse picked up, and his cheeks were burning.

“Why not? People revere the girl's beauty in all Five Clans! She is praised for being kind and respectful. And you... Oh! Just look at yourself!” Ansel held his son’s both shoulders. “You are a handsome young man! You turn the heads of all girls in the West Lands!”

“Father! Do not talk frivolously about the girls in our clan,” Usman reprimanded.

“I am simply stating the truth! Our girls are very respectful and honest. But it does not stop them from appreciating your beauty.” Ansel’s eyes glinted with malicious glee.

Usman bit his tongue. He knew it was not right to go against his father or to correct his behavior.

I should not have reprimanded him. He is my father. It is my duty to respect him, the young man thought, turning his gaze to the Great River.

Ansel placed a hand on his son’s face. “Usman. You are indeed a kind soul! I believe you and Themis’s girl will be a match made in heaven. Just think about it, son! The girl will attract suitors from all clans. It would be better for everyone if you were the one who will marry her. You would be a just and honorable Magistrate.”

Usman read pride and ambition on Ansel's face. His heart ached to see how strong his father's earthly passions were.

"My destiny is not to become a Magistrate. I am not equipped to be a leader. I was born to serve," Usman whispered.

"So, serve Green Valleys as their Magistrate. Themis's nonsense is hurting our people. It is hurting our lands! I believe it is God's will to end that madman's bloodline!" Ansel spat on the ground.

The warrior looked at him, terrorized. *How can he talk about God in such a wicked way?*

"Father," Usman said after a few moments of silence, "as you said, the girl will attract suitors. Maybe she already has."

"Well," Ansel said, "Faron has already proposed marriage to her."

"Leader Faron proposed to her? And you are suggesting I compete with him!" Usman's eyes were wide open.

"Why not?" There was indifference in Ansel's voice.

"Father, we are talking about Leader Faron. He is the wealthiest of men. He is the Leader of the South Lands. His beauty is legendary. His skills in war are beyond this world! He is not human!" Usman lowered his eyes, regretting his words.

It was not right to say Leader Faron is not human, Usman thought, but it was too late to explain himself. *I should think more before allowing my emotions to control my tongue,* he reprimanded.

"Ha! Do not be childish! Faron is just a man. Themis has not accepted his proposal yet. So, we stand a chance."

"What makes you think I stand a chance against Faron?" There was doubt and sadness in Usman's voice. He didn't want to be part of these evil political games. He didn't want to have to compete with anyone for marriage. It was wrong to propose to a lady merely out of ambition.

"Marriage is the foundation of a family. It is an act of true love. A love so powerful that it will be the source of new lives!" He could hear his mother's words in his mind.

Ansel took two steps closer to his son and gazed at Usman's light green eyes for a few moments.

"Faron might have beauty, power, skills, and wealth. But he does not possess your kindness of heart and your high morals, son. Your generosity is unparalleled, like a beacon of hope in the darkness. You are decent. You are loyal. Your faithfulness and devotion to God are commendable. Your worth is beyond this material world, son. Come to the Central Lands with me and show these men what being worthy means."

Chapter Twenty-Seven

The Hidden Library

The man walked slowly. His mind was on the last note he had received from Mattas. The walls around him stood high and mighty. He ran his fingers over their rough surface. He could feel their energy, the power through his fingertips buzzing and vibrating. A wave of warmth flowed through his veins, a pleasant tingle. He felt the grandeur of the magnificent building as he breathed in its energy. The silent hallway stood majestically ahead of him. He exhaled heavily and entered it. His mind was back at the here and now. The bright room was empty.

I never walk alone, he thought.

He entered the room and stopped in front of a column. He touched it, closing his eyes. "You have been sustaining this mighty room for thousands of years. Thank you!" he whispered, bowing in reverence.

"Welcome, brother!"

The man opened his eyes. An elderly woman was standing in front of him, smiling in a way that warmed his heart.

"Thank you, sister!" the man murmured.

"I have prepared a desk for you." The woman opened a heavy wooden door without difficulty. "After you, brother."

"Thank you, sister." The man entered the room and heard the woman closing the door behind him. He inhaled deeply, closing his eyes.

It has been several years since my last visit, he thought.

"But not a thing has changed since then, brother," she replied.

The man opened his eyes and smiled at her. No words were needed. When she smiled back at him, her teeth glistened like pearls. She fixed a gray curl behind her left ear and silently guided him through the immense room. Her white dress gently swept the brown floor as her long curls danced freely around her slim back.

"Here we are." She pointed at a table by the window.

He looked through the window and saw the blustery afternoon waving good-bye. *The sun is going down and soon the moon will rise,* he thought, looking into the lady's eyes.

"Your friend will watch and guide you tonight." He heard her voice, but her lips were not moving.

After so many years, you still remember our little games, sister, he thought.

"And so do you, brother." Her voice was in his head.

The man closed his eyes. He could see a tiny, skinny girl standing in front of him. Her pink dress moved graciously as she fixed her blond curls behind her ears.

"You still remember me!" Her childish voice was full of excitement.

"How could I forget my only sister?" he replied.

"And how could I forget my only brother?" the girl replied, looking at the tall, thin boy standing in front of her.

The girl walked toward him. She kissed his right cheek as she wrapped her arms around his neck. The boy melted into his sister's hug. All his worries and sorrows disappeared. Life became simple, as it was in their childhood years. She smelled like home. She smelled like peace.

He opened his eyes and saw the elderly lady standing in front of him. Both had tears in their eyes.

"I miss you, sister," he whispered, kissing her wrinkled hands. "I came here seeking guidance and knowledge. Please, Keeper of the Hidden Library, share your gift with me!"

"I, the Keeper of the Hidden Library, grant you your wish." She offered her hand.

He placed his hand on hers and felt a chill coming through his fingers and up to his arm. She smiled.

"Come with me, seeker. I grant you access to the Hidden Library! Walk through these halls. Read the forbidden books. And drink from the Fountain of Ancient Wisdom!" Her voice was as powerful as the gusty winds of that afternoon.

Then the curtain of reality fell, giving place to a bright light. It temporarily blinded him, as if a shiny white wall was standing in front of him. Slowly, the light faded away. He found himself standing in an enormous room. He noticed the pure, white walls around him towering up to a point where he was unable to glimpse the ceiling.

The walls touch the sky, he thought, remembering his mother's words.

He saw heavy books piled up on the floor. The piles surrounded him. There were books of all shapes, sizes, and lengths. Their covers held drawings and words. In certain books, the words were in different languages, still unknown in Green Valleys. Some were as old as time itself, while others were as new as a baby coming out of their mother's womb. And some books were still to be written.

"The Hidden Library!" he exclaimed.

The woman in front of him nodded. The light emanating from her illuminated the entire room. Her white dress shone like the sun on a summer day; her white teeth sparkled like precious gems in the light. When she spoke, her voice sounded like the wind.

"Welcome to the Hidden Library, Daman. Brother of Indra. Child of Allura!"

Daman bowed. "You have my gratitude, Indra. The Keeper of the Hidden Library. Child of Allura!"

"What is it you seek, Daman?" The walls seemed to vibrate with every word Indra pronounced.

"I seek knowledge and guidance on a terrible matter, Indra." His voice trembled.

Indra remained silent for several moments. Her eyes scanned Daman's soul. He could feel them scanning his memories. His emotions. His thoughts. His motives.

When she finally spoke, her voice resonated in the room like a storm.

"Your reasons are noble, brother. Nevertheless, I am afraid you are not the one for this task. You chose exile. You retreated. Now you rule from the shadows of death."

Daman closed his eyes, inhaling deeply. "I am aware of it, sister," he said, opening his eyes. "It was my choice, and I do not repent it. Circumstances, however, arose in a way that now challenges my decision."

Indra looked at him with compassion. "Brother," she said in her normal tone, "are you certain of what you wish?"

"Yes, Indra." There was no hesitation in his voice.

"We do not interfere in these matters." The light emanating from her shone stronger.

"This is not a mundane matter of men playing the game of power. It is a matter beyond our understanding." Vapor came from his mouth as he spoke. He could feel the cold coming in waves. He welcomed it.

Indra didn't reply. She kept her light blue eyes placed on her brother.

"Sister, I understand the implications of my wish. However, I cannot retreat in times of need." He paused for a second. He ran his eyes over the room. "You can feel *it* as well. It is already here." Although his lips did not move, Indra heard his voice loud and clear in her head.

"Yes, Daman. Evil was released in Green Valleys," she replied.

"Show me the Ancient Texts of Allura. I pledge to you, my sister! Share with me our Mother's knowledge, for she once defeated evil!"

The Keeper of the Hidden Library remained silent. Her tall, slender figure was motionless, observing her brother.

"It is time to fight, sister. It is time to use our gifts to save everything that is good and pure in this world." He felt the cold growing inside him. It was stronger, colder than the chilly winds caressing his skin.

"Our Mother shared her gifts with men. They betrayed her. They killed our Mother and erased her name from History." There were tears in Indra's eyes. "They took away everything from Allura's daughters. We are nameless. We are forgotten."

Daman put his right hand to his chest and lowered his head. "Men like me, sister. It is a source of shame for me."

Indra placed her cold hands on her brother's. The cold did not bother Daman. It was also inside him.

"Do not be ashamed of others' sins, brother. You have been living an honorable life."

"An honorable life demands I act when evil approaches our neighbors, sister. A good man cannot sit still and watch his fellow beings perish." Daman lowered his light blue eyes and ran his fingers worriedly through his gray straight hair. "Please, my sister! I implore you to help me fight evil. This is our duty as Children of Allura. It is time for Allura's legacy to make itself known."

Chapter Twenty-Eight

The Ways of the North

Conrad rested his tired head on the back of the leather armchair and closed his eyes, exhaling heavily, sinking into it.

"There is too much in my head and not enough space," he whispered as his eye caught a few dry leaves moving rhythmically in the wind.

"It is like a dance, isn't it, Conrad?" It was Cato's wife. She had a smile on her face and a tray in her hands.

"Yes. It is a rare winter's dance." Conrad got up and helped the old lady to place the heavy tray on the table.

"Here, Conrad. Have some warm tea and these cheese biscuits. Cato bought some fresh herbs from the East after the Council in the Central Lands. I hope they will last a while!" the woman said, pouring some tea into Conrad's cup and filling his plate with two biscuits, grapes, wild berries, and olives. "Eat, my boy! You look thinner every day!"

The Leader of the North gently kissed the old lady's hand.

"You are the true treasure of these lands!" he said, devouring the biscuits. "Oh, my dear lady! How does your cooking get better whenever I come to visit?" He winked at her, sipping the tea.

"You are a joy to have at home, my boy!" The lady gently caressed his straight blond hair and kissed his forehead. "Cato is here," she said. The front door opened slowly.

"I will let you boys talk. Do not dare to leave without finishing your plate, Conrad!" she said.

Cato chuckled at his wife's remark, taking off his boots. He kissed her forehead and gently touched her hand as she walked past him. Conrad observed the older couple and smiled.

This is true love. It is still alive after so many years together.

"Greetings, Conrad!"

"Greetings, Cato." Conrad got up slowly, holding on to the table for support. He grunted with pain.

"Do not bother with formalities. Please, sit down. You do not seem fit today." The advisor took a seat on the opposite side of the table.

"The journey...the Council...and the aftermath... Well, it has been quite a heavy load for me! I must confess I was not prepared for its repercussions," the young leader murmured.

"Indeed!" The advisor's face hardened. "That was certainly an unexpected turn of events."

Conrad nodded and stared out the window. He was still watching the leaves dancing to the wind's music.

"We must talk, Cato. Erhart is outside. I can hear his footsteps. I took the liberty of inviting him to join us."

"Of course, Conrad. It was a wise decision."

"Greetings, Cato and Conrad," Erhart said. He was at the door, hanging up his heavy winter jacket.

"Please, take a seat! I brought another cup of tea and more food for you, Erhart!" The advisor's wife showed up carrying another tray. The captain helped her place the teacup and the food on the table. "Eat, my dear Erhart! Eat. Then, talk!"

The three men assented, and they started working on their food. The only noise was the wind outside. After several minutes, the food was gone. The teacups were empty. Their stomachs were full. It was time to empty their heads.

"Come, gentlemen. Come to the fireplace, please." Cato pointed to two armchairs.

The three men took their seats by the fireplace, watching the flames as they carefully chose their words.

"I believe," Cato started, "we should talk about the Magistrate's decision to accept his son's death."

Conrad felt a chill of fear run down his spine. He didn't want to have this conversation, but it was necessary. It was time to talk about the skeletons in the closet.

"Indeed," Erhart agreed. "Leader Faron's proposal was unexpected. The other clans should present their suitors soon."

"The West will present Usman, Leader Ansel's only son, as a suitor. There is no word from the East, though. It seems they have no champion to present," Cato pointed out.

There was a moment of silence. Conrad was still staring at the flames in the fireplace.

"I wonder," Erhart said, gazing at Cato, who nodded, "well, I wonder if the North will present a suitor as well." Both men were looking at Conrad.

The Leader of the North laughed. He placed his hand on his ribs, laughing again. Then he turned his attention to the captain and the advisor.

"Conrad," Cato called softly, "what do you think?"

"What do I think about what?" The Leader was still smiling.

"What do you think about the North presenting a suitor to Themis's daughter?" he asked awkwardly.

Conrad spent a few moments observing the advisor, studying the older man's face. "You mean when will *I* propose to Themis's daughter?"

There was silence. Neither of the men replied. There was no need for that.

"Cato and Erhart, I believe there are matters of importance to be discussed today. Marriage is not one of them," Conrad replied. He was no longer smiling.

"I beg to differ, Conrad," Erhart said. "This marriage would have serious implications for the future of Green Valleys. The man who marries Themis's daughter will be the next Magistrate. Therefore, he will be the most powerful man in Green Valleys."

"You speak wisely, Erhart," Conrad said. "This marriage is a matter of importance. But you failed to mention that it is practically settled Faron will have his proposal accepted by Themis." Conrad gazed at both men. "Faron is the one who has the most to offer. He is the best suitor. This is certain." He paused for a second, standing up with difficulty. He walked toward the window. "However, the question is: will this marriage benefit him?"

The other men exchanged a look. There was fear in their eyes. They didn't reply.

"We know it will not." Conrad's eyes were shining. "Faron is wasting his time. Ansel is wasting his and his son's time. Gilbride is the only one not wasting time on marriage proposals. The old leader must be planning a silent attack." His back was facing the wall. The sun's light illuminated his thin figure. "Another question can be raised, though. When will the North act?"

Cato stood up slowly from his armchair. "Conrad, are you certain it is the right time to act?"

The young leader turned his gaze once again to the fireplace and watched the bright yellow-reddish flames performing a delicate but deadly dance. It was a captivating spectacle. Conrad took two steps toward it. The warmth emanating from the fire was soothing. Slowly, the pain in his head dissipated. The thoughts and emotions weighing on it gradually made their way out of his mind. He took a deep breath, closing his eyes. The flames were still dancing in the darkness of his closed eyes.

"No. It is not the right time." Conrad opened his eyes. "Although I cannot sit still and watch in terror the outcome of this sour business, I must remember my duty as a servant of the North," he said, turning to both men. His face was heavy with grief. "We should wait until the final, crucial element is added to the puzzle, my friends. *Then,* the North will make its appearance once again in the Central Lands. Until then, we wait for the puzzle to complete itself."

"Conrad," he said softly, "this is the right approach." He touched the leader's left shoulder.

Conrad didn't reply. He simply smiled at the advisor. The captain's eyebrows lifted in approval as he gave a slight nod.

"It is settled!" Erhart said. "The North will not interfere."

"For now," Cato replied quietly.

"The North will be ready when the time comes, Conrad," Erhart said confidently.

Conrad nodded. *Will I be ready when the time comes?* he thought, feeling a wave of pain through his right rib. He rubbed it discreetly.

"Conrad, you are doing the best you can." Cato could read the young man's troubled face.

"Conrad," Erhart said, "your own essence is your best advisor. Trust in yourself. Trust in your good judgment and keep working toward the path of honesty and goodness. These are the ways of the North."

"The ways of the North," Cato repeated gravely as he looked through the big window above the fireplace. "Keep faithful to the ways of the North, and the answer you are seeking will come to you."

"The ways of the North," Conrad repeated as he was transported to another time and another life, when he was a little boy. A time when his father belonged to the Realm of Living. A time when his father used to tell Conrad the old stories of the great deeds of the North.

"Our people's history is rich! We are different, for we are open to the world around us. Our world is not inside of us. It is around us. The world is every tree, leaf, and branch you see. It is every living being you see. Big or small. Menacing or meek. Alike or not. The world is the mountains. The river. The fields. The forests. The known and the unknown. Protect the world around us! Fight for everything that is good and pure in this world, my son! These are the ways of the North."

His father's voice echoed in his ears, like he was standing right beside him. Conrad shivered, exhaling the cold air. There was vapor coming from his mouth. He felt his skin freezing as he stood by the fireplace in Cato's house.

Then he finally understood his father's words.

"It is time," the Leader of the North said, facing the High Captain and the advisor. "We must see him." He shivered again as the cold air emanated from his lips.

Chapter Twenty-Nine

I No Longer Walk Alone

Morning light entered the white room. Its rays delicately took the darkness away, bringing the hope of a new day filled with possibilities.

Standing by the window, Aura watched as the sky was painted pink, orange, and yellow.

"It is beautiful!" she murmured, putting two fingers to her forehead. She applied some pressure, hoping it would take the pain away.

"A sleepless night brings unbearable headaches." She remembered her mother's voice echoing from childhood days when sleeping was something too terrifying to do.

Aura closed her eyes, taking a deep breath, a wave of feelings invading her.

I don't know what to do, she thought, burying her face in her hands. She wept bitterly. Her chest hurt, her head, and her soul. The pain was dominating her being.

"What is wrong with me?" she whispered. "I feel so lost! My father...the Man from the Garden...the monster...Anandy...Mother...and...and Faron..." She felt her heart race, and that warm feeling grew inside her. After a few moments, Aura's forehead was covered in sweat.

What is wrong with me? I feel like my skin is on fire! she thought, reaching for a hand towel on her little white desk. Her fingers trembled, and her hand accidentally bumped into a glass. As it shattered on the floor, Aura felt like something inside her also broke into a thousand pieces. As she prepared to get on her knees to clean, a light tap at the door made her freeze.

Giving a last glance at the shattered glass, Aura wiped her tears and opened the door as she tried to draw a smile on her face.

"Are you feeling sick, lovely?" Janace asked, standing at the door. She was wearing her nightgown.

"I am fine. I dropped a glass...and...I–I am sorry I woke you up," Aura murmured.

"Oh, my! You have been crying, lovely!" Janace stepped into the room, closing the door behind her.

"No, no, no... I am fine, thank you." Aura instinctively touched her cheeks, trying to cover the signs of tears.

"Aura," the old woman said kindly, "I have known you since you were in your mother's womb. There is no reason to be ashamed of your feelings." She wrapped her arms around the girl's back, caressed her hair, and kissed her forehead.

Aura melted in that hug. It felt warm, cozy, and safe. The girl could feel something emanating from the old lady. She was uncertain what it was, but it felt right.

"I–I...oh! I am so lost! I don't know what to do!" Aura placed her head on Janace's shoulder and cried.

"Oh, my little girl! You are not lost! I am here! Please, talk to me. Let me help you find your way," the older woman whispered.

"I don't know how. Nobody can help me. I am doomed!" There was despair in Aura's voice.

"Nonsense! There is no such thing as being doomed." Janace wiped the girl's tears away. "Come! Sit here with me. Talk to me." She pointed to the two white chairs on which she had sat with Adira days before.

Aura assented and took a seat next to Janace, carefully avoiding the shattered glass on the floor.

"Do not worry about the glass, lovely! We will take care of it later! Your feelings are the priority now!" She pointed to the floor. "This little mess can wait."

"Thank you...oh... I feel my skin burning..." Aura wiped some sweat from her forehead.

Janace sat quietly for a few moments, examining the girl's face. She pressed her lips together. Without a word, she stood in front of Aura and placed her hands on the girl's face. She gazed at Aura, who felt a chill going down from her cheeks to her chest, her core, arms, and legs. It was a cool sensation. Then it became colder. Aura shivered. Janace smiled, satisfied.

"You know, Aura," Janace's words sounded like they were coming from a distant place, "we sometimes get too much inside of us. Too much! Often, they are things we do not need. In the absence of knowledge of what to do with them, we simply cling to them, when in reality, we should keep inside of us only what is good for us."

"How can I do that? It sounds impossible to keep only what is good inside of us when there is so much evil in the world." Aura lowered her gaze.

"Oh, my sweet Aura! I am old enough to know that there are always ways to do things in life. Let me show you the ways of the place I come from."

"The ways of the place you come from?" Aura stopped crying. "Are you from the North as well? Just like Mother?"

"Yes. Mattas and I were born and raised in the Northern Lands. Just like Adira."

"Oh!" Aura gasped.

"Yes, child. I know, we are Adira's friends and we are your friends." Janace touched the girl's hands. There was cold emanating from her hands, soothing the growing fire inside of Aura.

"Please, help me, Janace!" Aura whispered.

"First step," Janace said as she was standing up, "a bath!"

"A bath?"

"Yes. I will get everything ready for your bath. Meanwhile, clean up the shattered glass and choose a beautiful fresh dress for today."

Janace returned, the sound of her footsteps echoing through the room, and carefully guided Aura to the washroom. The room was steamy. The bathtub was full of hot, steaming water. A soothing scent came from the warm water. Aura inhaled deeply. The room was filled with that delicate, sweet smell that created a feeling of peace and tranquility.

"A warm bath for you, Aura," Janace said.

"Will a bath really help me?" The girl raised an eyebrow, glancing at the bathtub.

The advisor's wife laughed quietly. "Water cleans everything! Even our sorrows!" she replied after a few moments.

"How?"

"As you get undressed, visualize your clothes as the weight you unnecessarily carry in your heart."

Aura hesitated for a second, waiting for Janace to leave. The old lady didn't move.

"I wiped your butt many times when you were a child. There is nothing in you I have not seen before." The older woman laughed once again.

Aura also laughed, removing her clothes.

"Once you step into the bathtub, imagine the water is washing away your sorrows. Feel the warmth equalizing your soul's temperature. Close your eyes. Take your time. *Believe* in the power of nature! Once you get dressed, feel the fabric on your body. Smell the fresh clothes on your skin. Feel the freshness and cleanliness inside you." Janace collected Aura's sweaty clothes from the floor. "You removed the heaviness from inside of you," she said, pointing to the clothes in her hands. "Now, start a new day fresh!" She closed the door behind her.

Aura inhaled deeply, stepping into the bathtub. She exhaled heavily once she sat in the water, feeling its warmth against her skin.

"I believe in the power of nature," she whispered, closing her eyes. "The water is washing away my sorrows. It is equalizing my soul's temperature. It is healing me."

Aura felt her muscles relaxing. Her breathing was getting regulated. It was warm, not hot. She felt it would be right to close her eyes. And so she did.

The fresh smell of grass invaded my nostrils. I opened my eyes. I was in the Garden.

"I am back!" I exclaimed, inhaling all the distinct scents around me. The soft fresh grass under my feet and the warm sun kissing my skin made me feel refreshed. I looked around in search of him, and there he was! He was in the same spot by the pond.

I wanted to run into his arms and ask for forgiveness, but I couldn't. I was ashamed of my lack of faith. I closed my eyes and turned my back to the pond and to the Garden.

"I am glad you came, Aura," the Man said.

I didn't turn to face him. The shame was too much to bear. I simply remained silent.

"There is no need to feel ashamed. You are human, and emotions are part of human nature." His voice was kind.

"Please forgive my ignorance." Tears inundated my face.

"There is nothing to forgive, Aura." He offered me his hand. "Walk with me, please." I placed my hand in his, and he guided me through the Garden. It differed greatly from my dead garden back home. The bright sun above our heads brought life and hope.

My heart ached as memories of my home and all the sorrows dwelling in it came to my mind.

"Do not fear the future, Aura." He squeezed my hand gently. "There is always hope when you believe."

I could feel his eyes on me, but I didn't dare to look at him.

"Do you believe?" he asked.

"I want to believe." I glanced at the ancient tree next to me. I could almost hear it whispering words of wisdom. "But I fear what the future holds. I fear for my family, for Green Valleys...and for myself." My eyes met his for the first time. "There is something wrong with me," I whispered.

The Man didn't reply. He looked deep into my eyes. I knew he was searching my soul. This realization didn't bother me. I wanted it. I needed it. I had to understand what was happening to me. The guilt and shame were consuming my being.

"I am lost...confused... There is too much inside of me...feelings...thoughts... doubts... I...I ...feel like I am burning!" I cried.

"Burning?"

"There is this fire growing inside me. It starts here." I pointed to my belly. "It burns my skin. It burns me from the inside out."

"When did you first feel this burning fire inside you, Aura?" The weight of his stare was tangible.

"In our last meeting. In my dead garden."

"No," the Man said calmly. "That was not the first time, was it?"

"Yes!" I replied. There was certainty in my voice and in my heart. "I have never felt this burning feeling before. It was..." I stopped talking abruptly. I felt my heart racing again. My hands were shaking. My terrified gaze met his. "No! It cannot be!" I whispered.

The Man nodded. "Yes, Aura. Say it."

I hesitated. I did not want to say it out loud. His eyes were fixed on me. He was waiting for me to utter the words.

"You must say it out loud," he said, as if he could read my mind.

"I–I... It was..." I closed my eyes for a moment in search of strength, and when I opened them, I found it in his kind smile. The most beautiful smile I had ever seen. Watching his face somehow gave me confidence and strength. A gentle breeze blew the scent of roses directly to my face. The wind played with my curls. The warmth of the grass irradiated energy into the soles of my feet. I looked into his eyes and said those fearful words.

"The first time I felt the fire was when Faron touched my hand." It shocked me to hear these words coming out of my mouth.

"And you felt again in your house."

"Yes... I felt again in my house's garden when I turned against you...and...and...again...when Faron kissed my hand..." I touched it. The burning sensation was still there. I lowered my eyes, ashamed.

"Do not worry, child! It is gone now," he whispered, kissing my hands and forehead.

I closed my eyes and sighed, feeling the relief of a gigantic weight taken from my head. I felt a sense of lightness when I realized the fatigue in my neck had dissipated. Some unknown species of bird of a rich blue hue sang their beautiful song. Peace and contentment filled the air.

"My head and body feel so light and fresh!" I whispered.

"It makes me happy to hear these words, Aura."

"What is this fire?" I asked.

The Man could read hesitation, shame, guilt, and fear on my face. I knew they were there. I knew he could see them.

"Aura," he said, "this feeling, which you call fire, is just energy. It is misused and misplaced energy."

"Energy?"

"Yes, child. Every living being is the recipient of energy. You, among other people, are capable of feeling their energy. Sometimes there is a kind of shock when you touch someone or something holding great levels of energy inside them. The outcome of this encounter can be a pleasant or an unpleasant sensation, such as fire."

"So, you mean whenever Faron touches me, I can feel his energy?" I was confused.

"Yes. What you feel is a mix of your energy and his."

"Does this fire come from him?" My heart raced. I trembled at the memory of his intense turquoise eyes looking right at me. I could see his beautiful lips drawn into an enigmatic smile. The image of his face was clear in my mind.

"This fire also comes from you, Aura." He looked at me affectionately. There was something else in his eyes: a pinch of sadness. "You are very sensitive. You carry too much of your own energy, and of others. All this misplaced and misused energy is causing you so much pain." He took my hands. "Listen to me carefully, please."

"Yes." I nodded.

"It is a must that you learn how to control your own energy. Once you master it, nothing and nobody else will destabilize your energy ever again."

"How can I master it? Please, teach me! I do not wish to have this fire growing inside of me any longer!"

The Man grinned. I could sense he had been waiting to answer this question for a long time. "This is a long and hard process, Aura."

"Yes! I will try hard to learn it!"

"I am certain you will. A few people have mastered this skill." He looked at the pond, pondering.

I followed his gaze to the crystal blue waters of the pond. The warm breeze peacefully created ripples, which reflected the sunlight. On the other side of the pond, I could see a family of ducks, two adults and two little ones. I smiled. My gaze traveled to another corner of the pond, where two majestic swans bowed their heads together, making a heart with their heads and necks.

"This is a vision of Heaven. There is no other place like this one. This beauty is unique and captivating," I murmured. I looked up at the sky and saw a flock of migrating birds in a V formation.

"All places are a vision of Heaven if you allow your eyes to search for their beauty and uniqueness." He stood next to me to watch the migrant birds. "Remember, Aura. There is beauty in every place and in everyone. Just open your heart to it."

"Will you teach me?" I asked once again. I could not control my excitement.

"I will open the door for you. However, you must walk the path yourself." He turned his gaze back to me.

"Alone?" My hands shook slightly.

"Once you walk the path, you will never walk alone!" The Man took my hands again.

The moment our fingers entwined, a wave of energy traveled from his warm hands into my cold ones. The calmness and power emanating from him were almost palpable. I could feel his energy. It did not burn me. It did not make me uneasy. The Man's energy simply met mine. I could sense some of my energy leaving my core through my arms, hands, and my fingertips. There was a moment of greeting, acknowledgment, and communion between us. It was powerful yet peaceful.

"Allow your people to teach you how to walk the path, Aura." His voice was like a whisper in the wind.

"My people?"

"Remember your roots. Walk the path with your ancestors. Let them teach you their ways." His voice was like rustling grass.

"Their ways?" Janace's words came to mind. Had she ever said these words to me?

"But remember, Aura. There are dangers on this journey. Sometimes the danger resides inside you." The Man turned into the young version of Mother.

I smiled when I saw her sweet eyes and hugged her tight.

"Follow your heart wisely, my child." Her voice was soft and gentle, filled with wisdom and understanding.

"I will," I whispered.

"Walk the path of your ancestors. Learn the ways. Master your skills. Master your mind. And only then you will defeat the monster." She shivered. Vapor came out from her mouth.

I shivered as the snow touched my skin. She smiled enigmatically. She looked at where the pond once was. I followed her gaze. Was I imagining things? I blinked several times. It was real! I was standing by the Mighty Mountains of the Northern Lands. Although I had never been there, I knew these mountains. They were in books. I had heard about them. How beautiful they were! Their peaks were covered by a white blanket, as if a caring mother whose only wish was to protect her precious children had gently placed it there. The peaks were like a row of arrow tips. Mist covered the foothills.

I blinked in dismay, watching the misty curtain open in front of my incredulous eyes. I could not help but smile, for I saw them with me. Thousands of them standing by my side. Men and women. Children and the elderly, dressed in fur. Some carried farming tools. Others were riding powerful northern horses, the famous beasts whose long hair and muscular bodies contrasted with their peaceful nature. There was peace and nobility in the way they moved. These were no ordinary horses. Those noble creatures stood by my side too. Their gaze met mine. There was pureness of heart and love in their eyes. I felt my heart fill as I allowed myself to be lost in their dark eyes. I shivered once again. The sound of a trumpet echoed among the Mighty Mountains.

Then I saw a dignified image of a tall, slender woman in the center of her people. Her long, wavy blond hair fell free and rebellious down to her hips. There was a sort of rare beauty in her face. She was dressed in a warm white heavy fabric dress. Her long white fur cloak gently touched the fresh snow underneath her boots. The tall woman was staring at me, and her gray eyes met mine. There was ancient wisdom in them. I could feel her energy. I shivered. I felt like I was stroked by a bow coming straight to my chest and reverberating through every cell in my body.

"The power!" I whispered, watching a white light emanate from her.

She smiled, and the world around me froze. For a second, there was only the lady and me. I heard her voice inside my head. Her lips were not moving. Nevertheless, her voice was clear and soft as the fresh snow kissing the ground for the first time.

"Welcome, daughter!" She spoke inside my mind.

I dared not reply. I could not move or think. My body was frozen in amazement.

"Follow your mothers, your fathers, your brothers, and sisters. Allow your heart to embrace the old ways." She turned her gaze to the thousands of northerners standing around me.

I could feel their warmth. I could feel their energy. Their power. I no longer walked alone. My people were with me. She was with me.

★ ★ ★ ☾ ★ ★ ★

Aura opened her eyes, feeling the Ancient Power in every inch of her body.

"I no longer walk alone. My people are with me. She is with me," Aura said out loud.

"Allura," the woman's voice whispered in Aura's mind.

"Allura is with me!" Aura whispered back as she saw Allura standing in front of her.

"Walk with me, daughter," Allura whispered. The power in her voice was almost palpable. Her rebellious long wavy hair adorned her head like a crown. Her fur cloak was that of a queen.

"Allura walks with me," Aura murmured.

Chapter Thirty

Feel the Power

After what seemed like hours, a brand-new Aura emerged from the warm water. As she stepped out of the cast iron enamel-coated bathtub, her nostrils were hit by the intoxicating sweet fragrance of oils Janace had poured into the water. Her consciousness was back in the washroom. Aura sniffed her hands and arms and smiled while visions of the Garden echoed in her mind. She wrapped herself in a fluffy white towel as she thoroughly dried her dampened hair.

"My head is finally empty!" Aura whispered, cleaning the steam from the large oval mirror.

She carefully buttoned her long-sleeved light pink dress that had some floral details on the skirt. It was one of her favorite dresses. The pink resembled the color of the mountain flowers, the ones she loved the best. Although the fabric was heavier than her usual dresses, which better suited the chilly fall weather, it felt fresh and soft on her skin. After tying the laces of her black boots, she spent a few moments watching her reflection in the mirror. The girl smiling at her from the mirror was at peace. There was confidence in her eyes. As she fixed her curls, the majestic image of Allura came to her mind.

"We are so much alike!" she murmured, touching her white little face. She ran her fingers through her golden curls.

A knock at the door brought Aura back from her meditations.

"Are you all done, lovely?" Janace smiled.

"Yes, I am. I feel much better! The bath helped me! Thank you!" Aura grinned.

"Perfect! I told you so!" Janace replied playfully. "Everyone is still sleeping, since it is very early in the morning. The servant is in the kitchen. I can ask her to prepare a quick breakfast for you, lovely."

"Oh, that is fine! I am not hungry! I can wait for everyone else and share the table with them." Aura stepped out of the washroom. "I will go to the garden for a bit. The fresh morning air will be good for me. I just want to sit under the cherry tree and listen to the birds singing their beautiful songs!"

"That is a wonderful idea, lovely! Get some fresh air! It is time for you to put some color on these white cheeks." Janace kissed them affectionately. "I will call the servant to clean up the washroom while I prepare some delicious bread with my secret spices."

"Oh! That would be lovely. I am afraid I would eat two slices today!" Aura chuckled and kissed Janace's forehead as she happily skipped down the hallway.

Oh, my! My little lovely has finally found her path! Janace thought.

As Aura walked down the hallway, she ran her fingers along the cold white walls. She stopped for a moment at the top of the staircase. Memories from her first time in the Garden were vivid in her mind. She held the rustic, heavy wooden handrail and started descending the stairs. As she stepped on the wooden stairs, her breathing was regulated. She was at peace.

Once she entered the large living room, she stopped by the coffee table to inhale the colorful bouquet of mountain flowers she had carefully placed in a long glass vase.

Reminiscences from the Garden, she thought, stepping into her home garden.

Aura took in a deep breath of the crisp, chilly morning air. She could smell the grass. The earth. The last flowers of the season.

"Find beauty in every detail, everything, and everyone." She could hear the Man's voice in her head.

Yes. Beauty is everywhere, she thought.

She lifted her chin and gazed at the blue sky, allowing the warmth of the sun to kiss her face. Aura closed her eyes. She could hear the birds' beautiful, melodic song with her heart. She touched her cheeks and felt their softness and coolness.

Once she opened her eyes, her heart almost stopped as she saw Faron standing in front of her. There was a beautiful smile on his face.

"Oh! I didn't know you were here, sir." Aura blushed.

"I am sorry! I didn't want to disturb you. You seemed to be having a perfect moment." Faron's smile was brighter, more genuine than the ones he had given her the night before. "I was standing here admiring you."

"Oh!" Aura blushed violently. She turned her face away from him. "Have a good day, sir," she murmured, turning on her heels and walking away from him as calmly as she could.

Once Aura was far from the house, she turned left to the corner where the cherry tree stood. She exhaled heavily.

Oh! I can't believe he was here in the garden! He was watching me!

"Aura."

She almost lost her balance when she heard Faron's voice.

"Good morning, sir," she replied politely.

"Please, call me Faron." He walked toward her and stood by her side under the cherry tree.

Aura didn't know what to say, so she just nodded politely.

"Please forgive my intrusion. I didn't mean to offend you or to spy on you." Faron lowered his eyes and rubbed his forehead. "I was standing watching you because it was so beautiful. I had never witnessed someone having this kind of connection with nature. It was touching." He smiled shyly. "Please, forgive me." He slightly lowered his head.

"There is nothing to forgive, Leader Faron." Aura caught herself repeating the Man's words. "It makes me happy to give you a moment of beauty and peace."

Faron looked at her, confused at first. For a second, she could feel he was caught off-guard. But he quickly regained his composure.

"I hoped you would remember our brief conversation last night. I asked you to call me Faron, Aura." He struggled to look into her eyes.

Aura felt her whole body shaking when he said her name again.

"Yes, I remember last night." She inhaled deeply. "Faron."

Faron hesitated for a second, then he grinned, showing off his pristine white teeth.

His ways are different today, Aura thought, examining the warrior's face. *There is something different in his eyes and the way he grins at me. Even his words sound different.* Faron's lips were pale, and his pupils were dilated.

"You remember, my star," he whispered in that secretive way once again.

Aura smiled. Those two words had a sort of power over her. They made her feel warm inside. Slowly, she turned her gaze from the warrior to the cherry tree and touched it. The energy reverberated from its thick, large trunk to her pale hands. She closed her eyes. She saw some purple lines dancing in front of her. Those lines traveled from the trunk to her fingers and arms, involving her whole body. There was serenity. For a moment, she forgot about Faron and everything else. The tree was nourishing her. Strengthening her.

Aura inhaled deeply, and as she exhaled, she opened her eyes. Faron was standing in front of her. His lips were slightly curved in a soft, subtle smile.

"What are you doing, Aura? What sort of magic is it? I have no words to describe the light emanating from your whole body when you close your eyes and enter this state of heavenly peace. Your face is glowing, my star!" Faron's voice was low and passionate.

"There is no magic, Faron." Saying his name no longer sounded odd. "This is nature."

Faron looked at the cherry tree, then back to Aura. "It is a tree. Where does the magic come from?"

"It comes from you, Faron. It comes from me. It comes from all of us," she whispered.

The Leader placed his hands on hers. She felt the urge to take her hands away, but she didn't. It was a test. She had to know if the fire would burn her again. The events in the Garden. The Man's teachings. The Mighty Mountains. The northern horses. Her people. Allura. They were real. She walked with them now. She was walking her own path toward self-mastery. Toward confidence. To find her own purpose. To defeat the monster. Aura allowed his fingers to entwine with hers. His hand was warm. There was no fire this time. The touch of his hand was pleasant. It didn't hurt or burn her skin. Her blue eyes met his turquoise eyes. She smiled at him. Faron smiled back, and Aura felt the world lighten up.

Impulsively, Aura placed Faron's hand on the cherry tree's trunk.

"Close your eyes, Faron. Feel the power of nature with your heart."

The warrior didn't hesitate. He closed his eyes, allowing himself, for the first time in his life, to be vulnerable to a power that didn't come from him. The old rough trunk felt cold against his hand.

"Take a deep breath and feel the power, Faron," Aura whispered.

He felt like her voice was coming from a distant place, perhaps from a dream. He inhaled deeply and exhaled slowly, as he used to do before combat. His warrior's mind knew how to calm his man's body. He repeated the process, this time slower. He emptied his mind and focused on the tree. He could hear his father's voice from the past.

"Be one with the sword, Faron. Feel its handle. Its power. Feel the power, son! This is your power! You are the most powerful man alive! You are a god!" Faron's fingers trembled for a second as he felt a spark coming from the trunk. It was warm. Its energy was almost palpable. It was coming from that tree straight to his skin. The warrior smiled as a warm, loving wave invaded his heart.

I have never felt this way before, he thought. The energy spread to every corner of his body. He felt his heart melting.

"Feel the power, son. It is your power!" his late father's voice whispered as the wind blew his wavy brown hair into his face.

Faron opened his eyes and saw Aura standing in front of him. Her eyes were shining.

She is so innocent and pure. She has the heart of an angel and a beauty of a goddess, he thought, smiling at her.

"Did you feel it, Faron?" There were so many emotions in her eyes.

"I did, Aura," he replied softly.

Aura's eyes were filled with tears. Her heart was filled with love and gratitude.

"I must tell you something, Aura." Faron took her hands.

"Yes, Faron."

"I presented a formal marriage proposal to your father last night," he said, feeling an unusual unease growing inside him.

"Oh! You did?" Aura unwittingly squeezed his hands. Her heart was racing.

"Yes, I did." He gently kissed her hands. "My plan was to do it after a few days, given the Magistrate's delicate health and yours. However, your father took my behavior toward you as frivolous. I could not risk losing you for a misunderstanding. Thus, I rushed the proposal."

Aura tried to force herself to speak, but words did not come.

"I want to ask you, Aura." Faron glanced at the cherry tree. "I want to ask you, under this magical symbol of nature, to marry me. I presented a proposal to your father as a formality. However, my heart goes with you! I want *you* to accept me as your husband."

Aura thought her heart would explode. She opened her mouth, but once again, she was unable to utter the words.

Faron sighed. "I am aware of my reputation. I am aware of how others talk about my appearance. My skills as a warrior. And even my wealth. Nevertheless, Aura, I can offer you much more than that. I can offer you my eternal love and faithfulness. I can offer you a home filled with children. I can give you a family. A home. And, above all, you will always be Aura to me, and I will always be Faron to you."

The Leader of the South touched Aura's face and placed a curl behind her right ear. She felt the warmth of his palm on her cheek. His lips were slightly parted. His eyes were full of emotions. His voice was a soft whisper.

"Marry me and make me the happiest man in Green Valleys. I want my days to be filled with magic and love, just as this day is." He drew her closer to him. He could smell the oils on Aura's skin.

"I–I do not know what to say, Faron." Aura hesitated.

"Say yes, my star." He was now a few inches closer, gazing at her lips.

Aura was drawn to him. She knew she should walk away from him, but there was something about the warrior that attracted her. She did not know what it was, but it felt like she could not fight it.

"There are dangers on this journey. Sometimes the danger resides inside of you." The Man's voice brought Aura back to herself.

She delicately released her hands from Faron's and took several steps backward.

"This is a very serious matter. I am afraid I can't give you an answer now," she said.

Faron could feel confidence and calm in her voice.

"Certainly, Aura. I am sorry for my impulsiveness. Please meditate on this matter. I must return to the South Lands soon, but if you send word, I will come for you at once." He smiled. "My heart will stay with you, for it has belonged to you since the first moment I laid my eyes on you."

"I must help with breakfast now. Enjoy the garden, Faron." Aura made her way back inside.

She will be my wife in a few months. She loves me. I can see it on her face. I can feel it in the way she touches me, he thought, watching her leave.

"Feel the power, Faron. Step into it and embrace your greatness." The wind brought the former Leader of the South's voice back to the warrior's ears.

Yes, Father. I feel it, Faron thought, glancing at the cherry tree. The smile on his face was no longer shy or innocent. Malice was in his eyes. A thirst for power was on his lips.

Chapter Thirty-One

Time to Retreat

As Janace watched the events in the garden unfold, her heart pounded uncontrollably.

Do not betray me now, old friend, she thought, touching her chest.

The old lady walked silently away from the small kitchen window.

"I will be back in a moment, lovely. Do you think you can finish it without me?" She pointed at the ingredients on the kitchen table.

"Yes, madam," the servant replied. "The bread is baking, and the pie is cooling down. There are just some fruits, cheese, and olives to arrange on trays." The girl pointed at the kitchen table.

"Oh, you are a treasure of a girl!" Janace kissed her forehead. "Don't forget to have your breakfast!"

The thin girl giggled and hugged the old lady.

The advisor's wife made her way to the living room and stopped for a second to check if Aura had returned from the garden. After making sure nobody was around, she made her way upstairs to the first guestroom in front of the staircase, next to Aura's room.

Janace opened the heavy wooden door, trying to be as silent as possible. The heavy red curtains were wide open. The large, tall bed was unmade. Mattas was standing by the only large window.

The advisor didn't turn to face her. His gaze was lost in the blue sky. Janace stopped by the nightstand and poured water from the jug into a glass. She silently walked toward Mattas and handed him the glass as she joined him in contemplation of the sky. The advisor smiled at his wife. Fatigue was written in his eyes. Not physical, though, but a different, deep-rooted type of fatigue. She didn't like what she saw. He accepted the glass and sipped from it, then sighed, placing his gaze back on the sky. The old couple stood side by side as they watched the beginning of a new day.

Although Themis's house was in the Central Lands, famous for being a busy commercial center, his dwellings were in the quietest part of the City. He lived several streets behind the stores and trading shops on the top of a small hill. Being the only house on the hill on the farthest point of the City, the Magistrate's family could enjoy more privacy and were blessed with a larger portion of land. Their dazzling house was the largest in the City. There were three large bedrooms for the family and three medium guestrooms on the upper level. There were three small rooms for servants on the lower level. The housework was divided between three female servants. Aura and Adira were responsible for shopping and some light cooking or cleaning. There was a stable boy as well, and two male servants were in charge of heavy work. Two gardeners had the duty to preserve the large and picturesque house garden. Two warriors were always at the service of the family. With such a large staff, it was no wonder that it was almost impossible to keep matters private.

"There is a pair of ears and eyes in every corner of the City." Mattas's words echoed in Janace's mind.

And I am one of them, she thought, feeling the warm touch of her husband's hand on hers. The old lady smiled with the same warm feeling she felt years ago filling her heart. The feeling was there whenever Mattas touched her. Even after several moons.

"I feel the same, Janace," Mattas whispered, giving a little squeeze to her hand. "My love for you has only grown stronger over the course of these almost four decades together."

"I love you, Mattas. I am grateful for sharing all these years with you. I am grateful for our children and our work together."

Mattas turned his tired gaze to Janace once again. The fatigue was still on his face. There was also worry and sorrow. Her heart ached as she saw the lines on her husband's face.

"Be brave, Mattas," she murmured. "We need strength and clarity of mind to deal with the crisis ahead of us."

The advisor nodded as he turned his gaze to the blue skies and watched the busy birds flying in the sky.

"Early mornings are busy with our flying friends," he whispered. "It is the crucial time to make arrangements for the day."

"And a balanced mind for the day ahead of us," Janace pointed out.

Mattas nodded.

"Are you ready?"

"Yes, I am ready." Mattas's green eyes looked lighter and brighter.

"Talk to me."

Mattas put his right hand to his shaved right cheek and scratched it. "As we foresaw, Faron proposed last night," he said calmly.

"And Themis?"

"Themis is troubled." Mattas took a sip of water. "The madness is making its home in his mind and in his heart." The advisor paused for a minute to take another sip. "In his despair, he accepted Anandy's death. The idea of having a grandson to take his seat as the Magistrate seduced him."

"Seduced by Faron's sweet promises," Janace stated pensively.

Mattas nodded. "Faron was forced to present his marriage proposal to Themis."

"Forced?" There was a frown on Janace's forehead.

"Themis made unreasonable accusations against Faron."

Janace raised an eyebrow.

"Themis believed Faron's flowers, and his behavior toward Aura, were simply an attempt to flirt."

"Oh, my!" Janace covered her mouth with her hands. "Faron is determined to marry our Aura."

"And she is open to his advances."

"Indeed," Janace agreed as she remembered watching the girl and the warrior in the garden. "However, there is no naiveté in her nature anymore."

As Mattas proclaimed, "She has been guided," a smile spread across his face. "You reopened the door for her."

Janace chuckled. Her connection with Mattas was a rare gift, which she deeply enjoyed. Often, there was no need for words. It was possible to know what the other was thinking. He could say the words in her head and do the things she had planned to do.

"Talk to me, Janace," Mattas said.

"Aura has been struggling with the burden of her gift. As you know, it is not unnatural for someone like her to face confusion and pain due to lack of knowledge."

"Indeed," Mattas agreed. "She needs training."

"And guidance." Janace smiled sadly. "Her physical illness reflects her ignorance."

"The body suffers when the mind is ignorant." Mattas repeated the well-known words from the North.

"I indeed reopened the door closed by her. But that is not enough. Her surroundings and her emotions are harming her fragile being." There were tears in Janace's eyes.

Mattas's face softened as he wiped them away. "I understand, Janace," he whispered. "We must reunite her with her own people."

"It would not be wise for her to leave right now."

"Janace." Mattas took his wife's hands. "Themis's instability and Adira's conflicted feelings put Aura in this situation."

"Please, Mattas," Janace pledged. "Do not blame Adira. You know she was too young when she married Themis. She was so in love with him."

"She did everything to please him." Mattas gently caressed her hands. "She even forgot our ways and cast away her daughter's gifts. *Our* gifts, Janace."

The good woman lowered her eyes. Even though Janace had been taking care of Adira since the moment her mother passed away during childbirth, she was unable to cultivate the ideals of the North in Adira's heart.

"You were like a mother to her," Mattas said, as if he could read her mind.

"And you have been a father to her since hers died a couple of months after her wedding," Janace replied.

"Still, she allowed herself to get lost in Themis's madness." Mattas pressed his lips together.

"But she has been finding the ways of the North again, Mattas."

"Indeed, but it is risky for Aura to be in the middle of this turmoil." Mattas breathed heavily. "And now we have Faron!"

Janace nodded sadly. She turned to the window and beheld a lonely gull as it coasted through the crystal blue of that sunny morning.

"What about Anandy?" she asked distractedly.

Mattas inhaled deeply, watching the lonely gull taking to the skies. "Themis gave up on him. He considers him to be lost."

"No one is ours to be truly lost," Janace said faintly.

Mattas turned his gaze to Janace. "We all enter and leave this world, as it is the coursc of nature."

"Did you send word to him?" she asked.

"I did."

This time, Janace was the one who could read her husband's thoughts. She closed her eyes as she exhaled heavily.

"So, this is it. Our time has come to an end," she whispered.

"We must retreat now, Janace." Mattas's voice was filled with emotion. "We must see him! I, too, need guidance."

"And we must take Aura with us." She wiped a tear away.

Mattas kissed her forehead. "Do not cry, my Janace," he whispered. "This is not the end! It is just the beginning of a new challenge for us."

"Are you certain about that?" she asked, although she already knew the answer in her heart.

"Themis is deaf to my advice. My words have been greeted by a brick wall. I cannot be at the service of one who does not listen. I must seek guidance, and once I return, I will be better prepared to serve Green Valleys," Mattas whispered.

Janace closed her eyes and inhaled deeply, exhaling slowly as she opened them. The tears were gone.

"I understand you do not wish to leave Adira here. However, she might be the only one who might advise Themis wisely." Mattas closed his eyes for a moment. "It is not my wish to leave just as we face such a tough moment. Nevertheless, we are not much of a help if we stay."

Janace didn't reply. She glanced at Mattas and nodded.

"It is time for us to go home, Janace. It is time for Aura to learn the ways of her people. And for you..." He paused for a moment.

"And for me what, Mattas?" Janace asked.

"You will teach Aura the ways of the North!"

Chapter Thirty-Two

Memories of the Past and Visions of the Future

Although the heavy, navy silk curtains were closed in the master bedroom, Themis knew it was morning. His eyes were closed as visions of a crib floating in the air filled his eyes and heart with joy.

"A new beginning," he whispered with his eyes closed. "A new life. My redemption."

"I will give you a grandson to continue your bloodline." Faron's words echoed in his head.

The Magistrate thought about his own babies. *Tiny things they were,* he thought. He could see their little hands. He could see their little fingers moving in the air as if they were touching an invisible object. Their tiny feet. Themis grinned, thinking about how much he loved kissing them. He inhaled deeply. He could almost smell their sweet baby aroma.

The vision of Anandy sleeping in his crib appeared in front of his eyes. A white baby blanket covered his little body. His fair hair and red cheeks ornamented his angelic face.

"You are only sleeping, Anandy." A tear rolled down Themis's cheek as the crib slowly faded away, revealing the bloody golden pocketknife. "You are only sleeping, Anandy," he repeated, trying to bring back the vision of his sleeping baby.

"Not sleeping, you fool. He is dead," his father whispered.

"No! No! No! *You* are dead! Go back to Hell where you belong, you old devil!" Themis barked, clenching his fists. He could feel all the muscles in his body tensing up. The fear mixed with anger made him bury his fingernails deep in his skin.

"Ha! Ha! Ha!" The metallic laughter filled the room with darkness and a musty smell.

Themis opened his eyes. He scanned the luxuriously decorated room. The large bedroom felt bigger than usual. Themis could feel the spacious bed swallowing him into an abyss.

"I can't do it!" he whispered, feeling suffocated. It was as if he was falling. He tried to hold on to his sheets, but they were slippery.

"You can't. Give up and end your misery, Themis," the voice replied.

The Magistrate felt the sweat dripping down his spine. He put his hands to his head but stopped halfway. The shock made his heart skip a beat. Themis trembled in fear as he saw that the sheets were covered in blood.

"What in heavens?" he murmured, finding himself in a bloody puddle. "Is it my blood?"

Fighting his growing fear, he put two fingers to the once-white cotton sheets soaked in that dark red liquid. It felt warm and sticky. Themis looked at his hands. They were shaking uncontrollably. As his gaze travelled down, he saw blood pumping out of long, deep vertical cuts on both of his wrists.

"How...what?" he whispered, feeling the life leaving his body.

"I am proud of you, son. You finally ended your misery," the voice said. *"You freed your family from the burden of caring for you."*

Themis's confused eyes found the golden pocketknife covered in blood next to him in bed.

"It is my blood!" he murmured, gazing at the trace of blood going down his forearms.

Then the bedroom was gone. The bed. The pocketknife. All was gone. There was no longer a Magistrate. Themis was gone. All that was left was a white, blank room in front of him.

Themis heard laughter and celebration. The white, blank room slowly began to hum with voices, music, and cheerful laughter. Faces popped up. He could see Mattas, Janace, Faron, Aura, and Adira.

What are they celebrating? Themis thought as he tried to get closer to them.

"My family and friends! I am here!" He heard himself saying. His voice was weak and distant.

They didn't hear him. There was joy in their voices. Themis could see a multi-colored bubble engulfing them.

"This is happiness! Their life is better without you, boy," his late father hissed.

As Themis forced his way to approach the bubble, he saw something that made his blood run cold.

"Aura!" he gasped. "She is pregnant!"

His lips quivered as he watched Faron lay his hand on his daughter's pregnant belly.

"A grandson to continue your bloodline," Faron said, looking directly into Themis's eyes. His beautiful turquoise eyes reflected something disturbing. His lips curled into a malicious smile. *"I am the Magistrate. The Leader of the South. I am the Law! I am War! The most powerful man in Green Valleys. I am a God!"* His laughter echoed in the white blank room, hurting Themis's ears. He felt as if something was breaking inside them. He covered his ears with his hands.

Faron's evil smile dissipated in front of Themis's incredulous eyes. Everyone in the room slowly faded away. He blinked several times, watching unfamiliar shadows gaining form in that white room.

They were foreign ships anchoring on the shores of Green Valleys. Warriors with bearded faces and long hair jumped out of them. They carried foreign weapons, never before seen by Themis. There was a shadow covering their eyes. The shadow covered their ships as if it was hiding them.

Themis felt the ground rumble beneath his feet with each step the warriors took. They walked at first. Then they ran. The ground trembled. Themis fell to his knees. He grunted in pain. When he lifted his head, he cried at the sight of violence and destruction in front of him.

"No! No! We are being attacked! How? We are the most powerful Society in the world! The clans around us fear us!" he screamed in despair as he watched the foreign warriors burn houses, kill the men, and take their women and children to their ships. He heard the desperate pleas of women. The heartbreaking cries of children. Themis heard his own cries of despair and madness.

The white blank room was a battlefield now. The sky was red. It was the blood of Themis's brothers and sisters. The crows flew in circles as they sang their somber song of death. Themis looked at that field of desolation and saw the dead bodies of the people of the Central Lands. As he watched the battle unfold in front of his eyes, he could hear Dansa's voice giving orders to warriors.

"Dansa!" he yelled as his eyes tried to find the well-known form of the Leader of the Central Lands.

There he was, ahead of a group of warriors. He wore his war armor. He turned his head to face Themis. Dansa's eyes were lifeless. The Magistrate screamed in terror, taking two steps backward. Dansa's torso was split in two by a long, diagonal sword cut from his neck to his hips. Themis watched in horror as Dansa fell dead into the big pond of blood that was once the streets of the City.

Slowly, his corpse faded away, revealing vast crops trampled.

"The East!" he yelled. He could feel the hair stand up on the back of his neck. He could feel the evil lurking in those lands.

The vast green fields of the past were now dead and infertile. There were no longer crops, only death and destruction. Themis walked in the burned fields. He walked among the burned houses. He walked toward the trees of the East. There was a shadow encompassing them. They looked different. There was something unusual about those trees. Something was hanging from them. Themis's feet refused to take another step.

"No!" He put his hands to the sides of his head, screaming. "This is madness! This is evil!"

The hanged bodies of Gilbride and all his family were swinging almost rhythmically.

"Even the women and children!" Themis closed his eyes, disgusted. "Who would do something so despicable to women and children? Why?" He wept.

A warm breeze blew on his face. Gulls screamed above his head. He hesitated to open his eyes.

"I can't," he murmured.

"You must see." A woman's voice echoed in his ear.

Themis reluctantly opened his eyes.

His voice was barely audible as he whispered, "The sailors in the West."

The blood of the Westerners covered the Great River. Themis was horrified when he saw Ansel and his son's lifeless bodies suspended from the West Lands Leader's ship, a macabre display. The shadow surrounding the ship had grown stronger. Its silhouette reminded him of something, but he couldn't make sense of what it was.

Themis closed his eyes. Tears rolled down the Magistrate's face as he felt the dagger of guilt and shame stabbing his heart.

It is my fault, he thought, weeping bitterly.

The well-known war chorus of the South interrupted his thoughts. It started low and distant. But it was getting louder. They were getting closer.

"The warriors! The army!" He allowed himself to feel hope. "We will fight the foreigners! We stand a chance!"

Themis opened his eyes, expecting to see the greatest army in Green Valley's history. His jaw dropped. There was no army. The war chant was coming from all corners of the room. It was vibrating on every wall. Themis could feel its vibration inside of his head. But there was nobody. Only Faron.

Faron was sitting on a golden throne ornamented with skulls. He had his right hand on a well-preserved skull, patting it. Themis trembled at the sight. The Leader of the South drank from the golden cup. He emptied it in one gulp. A shiny red liquid dripped down the warrior's chin. Faron placed his eyes on Themis. They were no longer of the pleasant color of turquoise. They were dark, almost black.

"The blood of our enemies! The blood of our people! Your family's blood, Themis!" Faron smiled, revealing red teeth. He raised his golden cup to Themis and broke into laughter. It was an ugly sound. An inhuman sound.

The Magistrate fell to his knees in despair, watching the shadow rising behind Faron's throne of skulls. It was gigantic. The smell was terrible. It was diabolical. But it lasted only for a moment. It disappeared and took Faron with it.

"The Society is broken. The clans are no longer united," the woman said.

Themis raised his head in confusion. He tried to find where her voice was coming from but found himself alone in the white, blank room.

"Look again, Themis," she said. Her voice was coming from a distant place.

The man raised his head. He saw the coat of arms on the warriors' armor. He saw clan fighting clan.

"We are fighting ourselves," he murmured. "That is how the foreigners attacked us. We weakened ourselves!"

"Fear, madness, greed, evilness, and dishonor broke the Society. The Balance is broken, Themis."

"Please! Please! I beg you! Help them! Help my people, for I failed them! They are innocent!" He wept copiously. "I failed my people! I failed my family! My madness! My curse ended my bloodline. It was the ruin of my people! Please, help them, for I am now in the Realm of the Dead!" Themis knelt in that white, blank room. He buried his face on the floor in complete surrender. There was no place for pride in his heart. He was not the Magistrate anymore. He was only a man. A man in despair. A man pleading for help to save his kin.

"The skies were painted red. They are red with the blood of our people," she said.

"Spare my people and my family! Take me instead! Punish me! Imprison me in Hell! I have spent my life in darkness and madness! I am the cursed one! Save them, please! I beg you, honorable lady! Venerable elder! Please, have mercy!" the Magistrate pledged, remembering the elderly man who had offered him water in his dream.

There was silence. Themis allowed his body to melt onto the floor. His face was buried under the palms of his hands. The Magistrate lay in the silence of that white, blank room for what seemed an eternity.

"I brought darkness to Green Valleys," he whispered. "I did not intend to break our Society. I no longer care about myself. Nevertheless, I care for my people, for they are innocent creatures. They should not suffer for my sins. Please protect my people, Venerable Elder. Honorable Lady. I implore you with the humility of a hopeless man."

"Rise, Themis," the Venerable Elder said.

The Magistrate slowly lifted his head, feeling something soft kissing his cheeks.

It is snowing, he thought, opening his eyes. He saw fresh snow on the ground.

Themis slowly stood up, and the vastness of the Northern Lands greeted him. The Mighty Mountains stood in front of him with their peaks covered in snow.

"The White, Soft Blanket of the North," he whispered in awe.

As Themis stood in that snowy wonderland, he allowed himself to see the North with his heart for the first time. He had been to these lands several times, but it was the first time he could actually *see* it.

The snow felt fluffy under his feet. The Mighty Mountains surrounded the North like a protective wall. Their vastness and height were admirable. Themis saw the northern horses running free toward the mountains. Their muscular bodies looked as if they were levitating in the air.

Themis heard a noise from behind him. As he turned, he saw a majestic brown horse. It locked eyes with him. The noble creature bowed its head, allowing Themis to touch its forehead. He felt the warmth of the animal's body greeting the coldness of his own skin. At that moment, he noticed he was no longer bleeding. The deep cuts on his wrists were gone. The horse bowed again and glanced at him one last time. Its eyes were full of compassion and peace.

"Thank you for greeting this hopeless man, noble creature!" Themis bowed to the animal, which gracefully ran toward the Mighty Mountains. He watched the horse until it disappeared.

"The northern horses are peaceful, noble creatures, Themis." The elder's voice was coming from behind.

Themis turned to face him. He stopped for a second as he saw the familiar image of the Venerable Elder standing behind him. His clothes, unconventional for Green Valleys' fashion, were white. He was holding a white cane. His shaved face and short white hair matched the snowy scenery. He had a kind smile on his face and green eyes. A tall, slender woman stood by the man's side. There was something about her that made the Magistrate tremble.

"Majestic," he murmured as his brown eyes met her gray eyes.

The wind tousled her rebellious wavy blond hair. Her gaze was fixed on his.

"You have been living in darkness long enough, Themis." Her voice was deep and distant at the same time.

Themis felt something inside of him that was broken for a long time come together. He could feel the relief as a weight was released from his shoulders. He reverently bowed to her. It was the first time the Magistrate had bowed to a woman. The first time a man had bowed to a woman in Green Valleys. Themis didn't think about it. He felt compelled to do it. Her simple form inspired reverence and respect.

"Forgive me, Venerable Elder. My ears were closed to your wisdom. I fell into the depths of despair." There were honest tears of regret in his eyes.

"Your despair opened the gates to ghosts from the past and to something worse, which took pleasure in tormenting you," the Elder said.

Themis lowered his eyes, ashamed. Words were of no use. Excuses were of no use.

"We came to you to show you what the future holds for Green Valleys," the Elder said.

"Please! Help my people!" Themis pledged.

"Your selflessness brought us to your aid, Themis," the woman said.

"Thank you, Honorable Lady!" Themis humbly murmured.

"We will show you the way, Themis, but you are the one who will walk the path," she said.

"I will do whatever it takes to protect my family and my people."

"Open your ears and heart to goodness. Be brave. Believe in yourself," the man said. *"Especially in the light of difficulties and sorrow. Do not allow despair to make its home in your heart."*

Themis nodded. His eyes were wide as he watched the light emanating from the man and the woman.

"Above all, Themis," the woman said, *"fight the monster that inhabits your mind and your heart. Defeat it, and you will lead your people to greatness."*

The Magistrate inhaled deeply, and a wave of pain hit his chest as he thought of Anandy.

"Anandy...my son is gone," he whispered.

"There is always hope, Themis." Her gray eyes were shining as bright as the snow around them.

Themis saw Anandy as a baby sleeping in his crib.

"He is only sleeping," the lady murmured.

The Magistrate felt his heart getting full. It was an unusual feeling, something he hadn't experienced in a long time.

"It is hope, Themis." The lady smiled, and for a moment, the world became brighter.

"Thank you, my lady." Themis reverently bowed again.

"Allura," she whispered.

★ ★ ★ ☾ ★ ★ ★

"Father! Father!" Aura called gently.

Themis slowly opened his eyes and smiled at the sight of his daughter.

"I am sorry to wake you up. But breakfast is served."

The Magistrate didn't reply. He took her hands in his while he examined her face. There was love and peace in his eyes.

"Are you fine, Father?" she asked.

Themis inhaled deeply. "Yes, daughter. For the first time in my life, I am fine."

Aura's eyes shone with happiness.

"I love you, Aura," Themis whispered, kissing her forehead.

Chapter Thirty-Three

The Children of Allura

Adira quivered. She clenched her jaw and blinked back the tears as she stood at the threshold of the master bedroom. *Have my ears betrayed me? Did Themis indeed call Aura by her name?* she thought, watching how Themis took Aura into an embrace full of love and protection. An embrace different from every other one she had witnessed between father and daughter. There was love, fear, and regret in that embrace.

"Good morning, wife." Themis grinned. "Please, come in and close the door. There is much to talk about."

She closed the door and walked toward the bed. The air in the room no longer had the heavy musty smell from the previous night. She couldn't understand how that awful smell hadn't bothered Themis at all the night before. Adira wondered if Themis had opened the windows during the night. The air smelled fresh. There was a light floral scent in the room.

"Did you sleep well in the guest room?" Themis was still smiling.

Adira stopped for a moment to admire her husband's smile. *Such a beautiful smile,* she thought as memories from their early days together came to mind.

"Yes, I did. My apologies for leaving you alone last night," she replied. "How did you sleep?"

"Do not apologize, please." Themis stretched his arms as he slowly sat on the bed. "It was for the best that you left. I had to spend the night alone to get some clarity of mind."

Adira inhaled deeply. She no longer felt like the air was pressuring her chest. There was a welcoming feeling in the air. Adira inhaled peace. She inhaled forgiveness. She gazed at Themis. He was in good spirits. His smile was a marvel to contemplate. Her heart was full once again.

Aura observed her parents for a moment. "I will help in the kitchen," she said, standing up. "I will meet you downstairs, Father."

Themis's hand took Aura's wrist gently while his voice carried a gentle plea. "Stay, Aura, please."

"Oh! Father! I heard you right the first time! You just said..." she gasped, looking at Themis in horror.

"Yes, Aura. I said your name. It is a beautiful name."

Aura looked, stunned, at Adira and back to Themis. She had to rub her eyes and shake her head several times to make sure she wasn't dreaming.

Themis chuckled. "You are not dreaming, Aura."

Adira raised an eyebrow. *I do not recall the last time I saw Themis laugh,* she thought.

"Don't raise an eyebrow at me," Themis joked.

Adira didn't reply. She nodded suspiciously.

"Come. Have a seat next to me." Themis's lips trembled for a second. "Adira."

Aura gasped again, covering her mouth with her hands. "I will call Doctor Valens, Mother! Father is delirious!" She had to hold on to the tufted headboard for balance, feeling lightheaded.

Themis laughed heartily. Both women looked at him in terror. Adira nodded at Aura in approval.

"Send word to Doctor Valens to come at once," Adira said, placing the back of her right hand on Themis's forehead. "His forehead is warm to the touch. Call the servant, Aura. Tell her to bring a bowl with cold water and a towel. I will try to lower his fever."

Aura nodded and turned on her heels, making her way to the door.

"Hold on!" Themis wiped a tear from the corner of his left eye. "Hold on!" he repeated breathlessly.

The women were speechless. They dared not to utter a word as they watched the man trying to recover from his burst of laughter.

"I am not delirious, Aura!" the Magistrate finally said. "I know I shocked you and your mother. My apologies!"

"Oh!" Aura almost fainted. "Father is apologizing to us, Mother! I will get the servant to send word to Doc—"

"Please, Aura! Don't be so dramatic!" Themis interrupted her. "Let's have some patience and talk about important matters before bothering Valens with nonsense!"

"I am sorry, Father." Aura lowered her eyes, blushing.

"I understand you are concerned about my sudden change of behavior. This is understandable due to my recent lack of discernment." Themis offered his hand to Aura. She hesitantly came back to his side, placing her pale hands on his. "Please, give me the chance to speak. I want to talk to both of you before we join our guests for breakfast."

Aura and Adira exchanged worried looks and nodded. Themis could read the suspicion on their faces. They were hesitant, as if they were expecting him to have a breakdown at any moment.

I don't blame them. My latest actions were a source of trouble and distrust. I put myself in this situation, he thought.

Themis slowly made his way out of the high king-size bed. As he stepped barefoot onto the warm wooden floor, he felt centered and supported.

"Please, join me at the table." He pointed at the circular wooden table by the large window.

Themis walked without difficulty. *My legs are strong today. I feel good,* he thought, opening the silky curtains to allow the sunlight to enter the room. "Please, sun, wash away the reminiscences of darkness in this room," he murmured inaudibly.

"Please, take a seat, my wife and my daughter." Themis turned to the ladies and pointed at two long wooden chairs. He took a seat in a third chair, gazing at the empty fourth one. A stabbing wave of pain inflicted his heart. It lasted for a second.

"He is only sleeping, Themis," Allura whispered in his ears. Her voice was coming from the sunlight illuminating the room.

Themis smiled. He could see Anandy sleeping in that white, blank room. He was on a heavy, light-colored wooden bed. A heavy blanket was covering him.

He is only sleeping, Themis thought as tears filled his dark eyes.

The Magistrate watched as Aura shivered. She looked around the room as if she was looking for something or *someone.*

"Can you hear her voice, Aura?" Themis caught himself asking his daughter.

Aura froze for a moment at the unexpected question. She looked at her mother and lowered her eyes.

"You would not tell me," he whispered. "I always instructed you and your mother to dismiss your visions." The Magistrate touched his daughter's elbow. "I can *hear* her," he whispered.

Aura's heart skipped a beat. "Can you?" she asked hesitantly.

"Yes. She visited me last night," Themis said.

"She? Who are you talking about?" Adira's gaze traveled from Themis to Aura.

Themis turned his gaze to Adira. "The Honorable Lady. The tall, slender lady."

Aura shivered. She felt as if her heart was about to stop beating. *Is it possible he saw her?* she thought, fighting to sit still.

"Rebellious wavy hair falling free to her hips. Majestic gray eyes that can see deep into your soul." Themis's eyes were fixed on Adira's. His voice sounded as if it was coming from a distant place.

"Who is she?" A chill ran down Adira's spine. She couldn't hide her consternation.

Themis placed his gaze on Aura. He didn't have to utter the words. She knew it. Aura looked deep into her father's dark eyes. There was a flame shining inside them. It irradiated light and warmth directly to her.

"Allura." Aura's blue eyes shone in the light from the same flame inhabiting Themis's eyes.

"Allura." He felt the power of that name in every fiber of his body. He shivered, welcoming that feeling in his heart.

"Allura?" Adira quavered. "D–did she visit you, Themis?" She trembled, pressing her hands against her lap.

"She did," Themis assented. "Allura and the Venerable Elder released me from the darkness." He paused for a moment, taking a deep breath to give him the courage to talk. "They showed me the path. However, I am the one who should walk it." His voice was somber. The heaviness of his visions still haunted him. The uncertain future also haunted him. He knew his weaknesses. He knew his path wouldn't be an easy one. Still, he needed the courage to walk it, for he no longer walked alone.

Aura remembered her conversation with the Man in the Garden. *That cannot be! How can Father possibly have the sight?* she thought, glancing at her mother. There was confusion in Adira's eyes.

Aura turned her gaze back to her father. There were signs of doubt, but also resolution in his eyes.

"Father," she called, "you no longer walk alone, for the Good Friends guide you." She couldn't believe what she was saying. It never crossed her mind that she would ever talk about the Good Friends, let alone tell her father about them.

Themis smiled, revealing his white teeth. He nodded. There were tears of relief in his eyes. Aura kindly touched his hands. There was empathy in her eyes. She knew what her father was feeling. She could understand the shock. The confusion. The fear. The doubt in Themis's heart. She squeezed his hand gently. Her eyes told him she was there for him; Themis no longer walked alone. Aura no longer walked alone. They would walk together. The Good Friends would walk with them. Allura would walk with them.

"I have been living in the darkness for a long time, my loved ones." Themis took the hands of both women. "A monster took residence in my mind and in my heart, dragging me into madness and instability."

A monster! Aura thought. Her blood ran cold. The vision of the shadow coming out of the ground in the Main Plaza was vivid in her mind.

"My actions were a source of sorrow and chaos for our family and Green Valleys." Themis inhaled deeply and exhaled slowly. It was new for him to allow the feelings to flow in his heart and through his words.

Adira didn't utter a word. Her eyes were moist from tears. She simply squeezed her husband's hand.

"I love you, Adira," Themis uttered the words he had longed to say for so many years, but he never had the courage to utter. Just like the word "fear," the word "love" was forbidden to the men of Green Valleys. Love is a sign of weakness. Love is for women and children. Men don't talk or think about love. Men have their duties to fulfill within the military and the Society.

Themis had loved Adira since the first day he saw her in the Northern Lands at the Winter Celebration. As the son of the Magistrate, Themis had to accompany his father on all his political duties. It was his first time in the North. He remembered being in a corner by the big fire at the center of the main plaza, trying to warm up. Coming from the temperate Central Lands, the cold and the snow deeply bothered him. As he was trying to get warm, he watched a group of northerners come toward the big fire to dance and sing. Themis started to walk away, but he found himself paralyzed by the vision of this girl. As she twisted and span around with her arms wide, her golden straight hair flew around her face. Her smile was magical. Her blue eyes shone as bright as the clear sky above their heads. She was Adira, and Themis loved her at that moment, even before their eyes met for the first time. The young Magistrate's son felt his heart stop beating for a second when her gaze met his and she smiled at him. He gathered all his courage and invited her to dance. At the end of the celebration, he presented his marriage proposal to her father. And yet to this day he had never told her those three little words.

"I love you, Themis!" Adira whispered. Tears of happiness bathed her cheeks.

Themis drew her closer and kissed her lips. Aura lowered her eyes. Adira's heart was full of love. Her head, however, was full of questions, doubts, and fears. She feared it was a dream. She feared the future. She feared for Themis and Aura. She feared for Anandy.

"Please, forgive me, my loved ones! I was weak! I was controlling! My love for both of you was more than I could bear in my heart. I did not know how to express it. I was jealous and manipulative! I caused so much pain to you two and Anandy." He covered his face with his hands, allowing the tears to wash away his sorrow and guilt.

"Themis," Adira called out, her voice echoing through the air, "there is no point in dwelling on the past."

She gently wiped his tears with her yellow pocket handkerchief. Themis looked at it and saw the emblem of the Central Lands. He had given it to her on the day he left the Northern Lands.

"You are right. We must talk about the present and plan for a better future." Themis felt a chill running down his spine as the image of a broken and destroyed Society was vivid in his mind. "Allura and the Venerable Elder showed me the consequences of my actions."

"Allura," Aura said, "could you see her, Father?"

"Yes." Themis smiled at the thought of her face. "She is an honorable lady. When she gazed upon me, I felt as if the world got brighter." Aura could see Themis's face lightening up.

"Mother," Aura called, "can *you* see Allura?"

"No, Aura. I cannot." Adira lowered her eyes, ashamed.

"But you know her face! How could you not tell who she was when Father described her?" Aura almost jumped out of her seat.

"No, daughter," Adira answered. "I do not know Allura's face."

"Of course you do!" Aura insisted.

Themis was confused as well. "Adira." The sound of her name was like honey on his lips. He grinned. "You once told me you were the daughter of Allura."

"Yes, Mother!" Aura agreed. "Allura is my grandmother, isn't she?"

Adira looked at her husband and daughter for a second. Then she burst into laughter. Aura and Themis exchanged confused looks.

"Oh! I am sorry, my loved ones!" Adira was still laughing. "Allura is not my mother." She took a deep breath as a way of regaining her composure.

"But you said you were Allura's child," Aura said, biting her lower lip in apprehension. She thought of how eventful that morning had been. *And all before breakfast!* she thought, hearing her stomach's first complaints of the day.

"Oh, my love!" Adira put a hand on Aura's arm, bringing her back to reality. "We are all the Children of Allura. She is the Founding Mother of our Society. The Unifier of the Five Clans. She is our Mother! She defeated the evil walking among men thousands of years ago. Allura is the Protector of the North and of Green Valleys." The chilly feeling was growing stronger inside her with every word she uttered about Allura. Adira was proud of her people. Proud of her Mother. Proud of being a Northerner. But, above all, Adira was proud to tell Aura the untold story of Allura and the Society.

"No!" Themis objected. "The Founding Fathers created the Society! They unified the Five Clans! The statues and books tell us that!" The doubt in his eyes betrayed the certainty in his voice.

"No, Themis, my love." Adira's eyes were shining. "The statues and the books are wrong. They were made and written by the same men who betrayed Allura. They killed her. Her daughters were ostracized. That is the reason women are nameless. Those men feared our Mother's power. Those men feared her daughters."

Aura felt a chill run down her spine. She could sense Allura's energy vibrating in every word Adira uttered. Themis also shivered. He could sense her presence as well.

"Men like me." Themis lowered his eyes. For the first time in his life, he was ashamed of being a man. A husband. A father. The Magistrate. "I, too, ostracized women. I did it to you, my wife and daughter." He looked through the window and watched a lonely eagle soaring in the sky. "Our Society." He gazed at the eagle. "Our Society...was based on lies!"

"Indeed," Adira agreed. "Lies told by weak men."

Aura watched her mother's lips twisting in disgust. She lowered her eyes, feeling a pinch of sadness.

"You said you belong to the blood lineage of Allura. The purest one. The highest one." Themis recalled their conversation of the previous night.

"That is true. I believe it is a reason Aura has the gift of the sight." Adira smiled. The thought of having Allura's blood running through her veins made her proud.

Aura didn't like the pride in her mother's eyes.

"However, it does not explain why I was gifted." Themis's gaze was placed on the wooden table.

There was a moment of silence. Themis seemed lost in his thoughts. Aura's face lightened. "Father! The Good Friends came to your aid because you are the Magistrate! You have the power to change the future by changing the present."

"Changing the future by changing the present," Themis repeated, meditating on his daughter's words.

"Aura is right," Adira stated. "You are the most powerful man in Green Valleys. You have the means and the power to make changes."

"I am unstable and cursed by darkness." Themis's eyes were still fixed on the table. "What Allura showed me shook me to my very core. The visions of a catastrophic future will haunt me until the end of my days." He closed his eyes as the visions of the previous night came back to his mind.

"You no longer walk alone, Father." Aura touched Themis's chin, guiding his gaze to meet hers. "Allow Allura to guide you. Allow yourself to step into your *true* power."

The Magistrate trembled. These words resonated in his heart. He looked into Aura's blue eyes and saw goodness and purity in them.

"I always thought that being the Magistrate of Green Valleys was the epitome of power. However, I can see it through now. True power does not dwell in politics. True power dwells inside us." His voice was distant as his gaze was lost in his daughter's eyes. Aura saw a spark in Themis's eyes. He grinned. "I know my journey will not be easy. I am certain I will have my moments of weakness and doubt, but I will do whatever it costs to fulfill my duty of establishing a balance in Green Valleys once again. Peace and equality will be the purpose of my life. I will do it for my family and for my people. May the sun, my family, the Venerable Elder, and Allura be my witnesses!" Themis closed his eyes. "Please, Good Friends, guide me on the right path!" he whispered.

The chill wind wafted into the room. It was soothing, bringing freshness and calmness.

"May Green Valleys once again welcome the Children of Allura!" Themis's voice was deep. His eagle eyes were sharper than ever. He could feel the strength that comes when you step into your true power.

Chapter Thirty-Four

Hope

As Mattas watched the soaring eagle, his heart longed for home. *The North waits for us,* he thought as he experienced a vision of the snowy Mighty Mountains. The advisor could almost feel the cold air blowing on his face, as if it was a friend greeting him after a long time apart. He missed the feeling of walking on freshly fallen snow. Mattas missed how the snowflakes seemed to kiss his face. Home was calling his name.

"Good morning, Mattas." Themis interrupted his ruminations.

The Magistrate was standing next to him by the dining room window. There was some color on Themis's cheeks and lips, and he smiled pleasantly.

"Good morning, Themis," Mattas replied, noticing how the Magistrate was standing without assistance.

"Good morning, Leader Faron," Themis said as the warrior entered the living room. "My apologies for the delay. Without further ado, let's eat! I believe we are all starving!"

"There is no need to apologize, Magistrate. I lost the sense of time as I had a pleasant stroll in your lovely garden." Faron glanced at Aura.

Aura blushed.

Mattas discreetly glanced at the warrior and the young lady. *Pleasant indeed*, he thought, struggling to keep a straight face.

"It pleases me that my humble garden was a source of happiness to you, Leader Faron." Themis pointed to the table. "Please, ladies and gentlemen, take your seats. I can smell all the delicious aromas from the kitchen."

The Magistrate rolled up his white long-sleeved shirt and placed a napkin on top of his black pants. "Please, my ladies, bring the food!"

The servant and Janace brought the trays of fruits, pies, olives, cheese, freshly baked bread, sausages, fried eggs, jugs of milk, and water.

Themis's ferocious appetite was back, Mattas and Janace noticed. Adira and Aura also ate more than usual.

They seem relaxed and happy, Mattas thought as he took a bite of bread.

The breakfast was silent; everyone seemed to be hungry, since it had taken longer than usual for the host to join the table.

"My dear ladies," Faron said, "please, once again, accept my compliments! The food was delightful!"

"Oh, Leader Faron!" Janace said in her characteristically cheerful way. "You, sir, are a delight to have at the table. Your compliments are very generous."

The warrior smiled at the old lady. "Magistrate," he called, "I would like to take this opportunity to thank you for your hospitality." He glanced at Aura. "However, it is time for me to return to the South Lands."

The girl felt her heart pounding. She placed her hands on her lap to hide a slight tremor. *He is leaving!* she thought with an unfamiliar ache in her heart.

Themis glanced at Aura. He could read the unease in her eyes. "Leader Faron," he said as he placed his gaze on the warrior, "you are welcome to stay as long as it pleases you. My house is your house!"

Aura quickly snatched a napkin, pressing it to her lips to conceal her wide grin.

"Your offer fills my heart with gratitude, Magistrate." Faron bowed slightly. His eyes met Aura's for a second. He was pleased to see the spark in her eyes.

What is happening? Mattas thought, fighting the urge to raise an eyebrow.

Themis slowly stood up. "Gentlemen, please join me in my office for some strong coffee."

"I will make it, Magistrate." Janace hurriedly stood up.

"In that case, Leader Faron," Themis said, smiling, "you are about to have the best strong coffee in Green Valleys."

"Oh, my!" Janace stopped at the kitchen door and chuckled. Her laughter echoed through the house.

"Could you bring the coffee to the office once it is ready, my daughter?" Themis asked Aura.

"Yes, Father," she replied.

"Thank you, my love."

The Magistrate walked energetically to the office and politely opened the door for the two men.

I have not seen this Themis in a long time, Mattas thought, murmuring some thankful words to the Magistrate once he entered the room.

"Gentlemen," Themis said, taking his seat behind the table, "I would like to apologize for my behavior last night. I understand I might have confused you with my poor state of health."

"There is nothing to apologize for, Magistrate," Faron replied, giving one of his pleasant smiles.

"Actually, I owe you my apologies, Leader Faron," Themis replied. "You made a proposition last night, and I left you without an answer."

Faron blushed for a second. Mattas could see he was caught off-guard. There was a knock at the door.

"Would you be kind enough to open it, Leader Faron? I am trying to save as much energy as I can." The Magistrate pointed to his legs.

"Certainly, sir," Faron replied.

The warrior opened the door, and there was Aura bearing a silver tray with the strong coffee requested by her father. As the girl saw the warrior, her lips shivered for a moment. Faron's eyes shone.

Clever old Themis, Mattas thought, covering a smile with his right hand.

The Magistrate observed as Faron took the tray from Aura's hands, murmuring how heavy it was for her to carry given that she was still recovering from her illness. He also observed how their eyes shone when their gazes met and how flushed their cheeks were. Themis pressed his lips together.

As Aura served the coffee, Themis and Mattas noticed the slight tremor in her hands.

"Enjoy your coffee, gentlemen," she murmured, avoiding the men's eyes as much as she could.

"Thank you," Faron replied as he tried in vain to take his eyes off her.

"Thank you." Mattas smiled kindly.

Aura motioned to leave.

"My daughter," the Magistrate called.

"Yes, Father. Do you need anything else?"

"Yes." Themis glanced at Faron. "Please stay, since this conversation also concerns you."

Here it comes, Mattas thought, standing up. "Please, take my seat. I will finish my coffee in the living room," he said.

"You should stay, my friend," Themis said. "I need my advisor with me."

"I do not wish to intrude into family matters, sir."

"You are not intruding, my friend." Themis sipped from his cup. "I need your wise, valuable advice on this matter."

"As you wish, sir," Mattas assented.

Aura awkwardly took Mattas's seat by Faron's side. She could feel the warmth emanating from the warrior's skin. She placed her trembling hands on her lap. Her eyes were glued to the floor.

"As I was saying," Themis said, "you made a proposition last night, Leader Faron."

The tension in the room was almost palpable. Mattas could read all the feelings on the young couple's faces. He bit his lower lip.

"I did, sir." Faron sat up, trying to show confidence. "I presented my marriage proposal to you last night." He looked at Aura. His face softened.

She looked at him from the corner of her eyes.

Themis observed them for a few seconds. "Indeed," he said. "I did not give you an answer due to my weak health last night."

Faron nodded, trying to keep his eyes on the Magistrate.

"After the events of the night and this morning," Themis said slowly as his gaze travelled from Faron to Aura, "I came to the realization that I am not the one who should give you an answer."

Faron and Aura looked at the Magistrate, puzzled. Mattas raised both eyebrows in disbelief.

"You, my daughter." Themis extended his hand to Aura. She placed her hand on his. "The marriage proposal is for you, my love. You are the one who should either accept it or not." Themis smiled at his daughter. "You are free to decide your future, Aura."

Mattas pressed his fingertips on his cup. Faron's eyes shone imperceptibly for a second.

Oh! Father just called me by my name in front of them! she thought, shocked.

Faron's turquoise eyes were fixed on Aura. She kept her head down. She didn't want to face his penetrating gaze. Her heart was racing. She tried to resist it, but she couldn't. Aura turned her head, and her gaze met Faron's. What she saw in the warrior's eyes surprised her.

Is it real? she thought as she felt a warmth growing inside her and filling every cell in her body. *Is it really what I see in his eyes? So many emotions!*

Faron had his lips partly open, looking intensely at Aura. He tried to focus and control his breathing and heartbeat, but it was impossible. All these feelings were new to him.

What if she rejects me? I cannot bear to lose her! I want her! I need her with me! Faron thought, feeling the energy from the cherry tree inside him.

"She loves you. She needs you. No woman would dare to reject a God." His father's voice whispered in his ears.

She is not an ordinary woman, Faron thought, losing himself in Aura's blue eyes. *She is special.*

Aura smiled at him. His breathing regulated. His heartbeat slowed. For the first time in his life, his answering expression was not that of a confident, pleasant, seductive man. It was the smile of a shy boy.

"Will you accept me as your husband, Aura?" Faron's voice was as shaky as his hands.

Aura looked intently into his eyes, as if she was lost in his gaze. Mattas held his breath. Themis was silent.

"Yes, I will," she said faintly. "I accept you as my husband, Faron."

Faron could not control himself. He placed his hand on hers. Aura didn't move her hand. She felt as light as a feather.

"It is settled, then." Themis gazed gravely upon Aura and Faron.

"Thank you, sir!" Faron said eagerly. "Thank you for accepting me, Aura. I promise in front of your father and Mattas that I will make you the happiest of all!"

Aura was so overjoyed that words betrayed her. She could not speak.

"Congratulations!" Mattas said sincerely.

There is affection between them. The beginning of love, he thought, feeling relieved. *One less worry for me.*

"Well!" Themis stood up and hugged Aura. "Congratulations, Aura. You will be the prettiest of the brides." He turned to Faron and hugged him unexpectedly. "Make my daughter happy. It is all I ask of you, Faron."

The Leader of the South Lands awkwardly hugged the Magistrate. "Thank you, sir," he murmured.

"Welcome to my family, *son,*" Themis said. "Now, you two go tell Adira and Janace the good news! And please, talk! You need to talk to get to know each other before the wedding! Do not be strangers! Take a walk in the garden and talk!"

Faron tried to regain the composure lost by Themis's warm hug and words. He was moved.

"Yes, sir! Thank you, Mattas! Thank you, Magistrate." He offered his arm to Aura. "Please, my bride, take my arm now and be by my side now and always."

Aura took her place by Faron's side. Mattas observed them standing together. *Their children will be beautiful*, he thought, watching them leave.

"Congratulations, Themis!" Mattas said.

"Thank you, my friend. I believe Janace will be of immense help to Adira in organizing the wedding." Themis sighed, thinking of all the preparations.

He is saying the women's names now, the advisor thought.

"I am afraid that will not be possible," Mattas said. "After much consideration, Janace and I have decided to return to the North for a while."

Themis felt like he was hit in the face. "Leave? Now?"

"Yes, Themis," Mattas said. "We believe it will be better for you to recover in peace without me as a burden to remind you of your political affairs." He paused for a moment in search of the right words. "We also believe Aura would benefit from a trip to the North. It will help her regain her strength. However, I also understand it might not be possible given the circumstances of Aura's engagement to Leader Faron."

"The North?" Themis could see the Mighty Mountains in front of him. The vision of the noble horse greeting him entered his mind.

"Yes, sir."

"Well, Mattas, I believe that is a great idea!"

"Oh! You do?" Mattas failed to hide his surprise this time.

"Yes," Themis replied. "As a matter of fact, I believe it would be good for me and Adira to join you on your journey to the Northern Lands. We have much to do, my friend."

"Much to do? I beg your pardon, sir?"

Themis walked across the table and stood in front of Mattas. His moves were those of a tiger. His eyes were those of an eagle.

The old Themis is back, the advisor thought.

"Yes, my friend and dear advisor," the Magistrate replied. "I need your help to find Anandy."

"Find Anandy? I thought you had given up on him! I thought you had lost your hopes of finding him!" Mattas felt the adrenaline rush in his veins.

"As a wise man once told me," Themis replied calmly, "there is always hope."

Chapter Thirty-Five

Hasty Ways

The young warrior carefully guided Gilbride to the Leader's office. The old man's eyes were lost in the air. His steps were heavy and slow. As he held the young man's arms, he murmured some inaudible words. The warrior nodded politely, pretending to hear what the old man had said.

"Here we are, sir." The young man opened the heavy office door.

"Thank you, young man." Gilbride's voice was faint. "To the armchair, please." He pointed to a large red leather armchair at the center of the room.

"Yes, sir." The warrior held Gilbride's arms, allowing the Leader to find his way down to the armchair.

"That is good! That is good, young man!" The Leader was out of breath when he sat down.

"Are you in need of any further assistance, sir?" The young warrior made sure to speak loud enough to be heard by Gilbride.

"That is all, young man. You may return to your post now. Do not allow any visitors. I do not wish to be disturbed." His eyes were partly closed.

"Certainly, sir!" the young man replied.

Gilbride closed his eyes, hearing the warrior's heavy footsteps leaving the room and the door being closed behind him. The old man sighed heavily as he stretched his arms and back. He heard his back and shoulders cracking. *Ah! That's better,* he thought, sitting comfortably. His cold gray eyes scanned the room and stopped at a corner. There was a spark in them.

"Come out. Come out now." There was a nasty smile on his wrinkled face. "You are good at hiding, but you cannot hide from me, boy," he whispered to the corner. His eyes shone in expectation.

There was short laughter. Gilbride grinned and rubbed his hands, satisfied.

"Well done, old man!" A thin man jumped from behind Gilbride's rustic, heavy wooden table and stood comfortably in front of the Leader of the East Lands.

Gilbride admired the man's clever face. His straight black hair fell to the sides of his forehead. Intelligence shone in his black eyes. Although he was dressed as a commoner, he had delicate features and manners. There was agility and ease in his ways. He walked up to the glass side table between the two red leather armchairs in the Leader's office, reached for the small liqueur bottle, and filled two glasses. His clever eyes were fixed on the old man. A dazzling smile was drawn on his lips. Although there was a beauty to his face, it was his hasty ways that drew attention.

"To your good health, old man." The young man offered the liqueur glass to Gilbride while he bowed exaggeratedly. "May you be granted many years of life!" He raised his glass to the Leader of the East Lands.

Gilbride snorted. "Do not make yourself a fool, Anwir."

"To the greatness of the East Lands!" The man raised his glass once again and gulped the liqueur.

Gilbride raised his glass and took a sip. His eyes never turned away from the man in front of him. "Any news from our friend?"

"I handed the envelope to him, as you instructed." Anwir placed the glass on the table and reclined comfortably on the armchair, crossing his legs. "He sent his warriors after me for interrogation."

Gilbride raised his eyebrows. "And they never found you..."

"Here I am! A stranger...a mysterious man delivering an enigmatic black envelope and leaving behind a troubled man."

Gilbride did not reply. He nodded while he took a second sip.

"I assume our friend hasn't made contact yet," Anwir murmured. He knew Gilbride had excellent ears. *The old crow can hear a troubled man's heart pounding,* Anwir thought, smiling at Gilbride.

"Your assumption is correct," Gilbride replied quietly. "It is just a matter of time before he does."

"What makes you believe he will?" Anwir leaned forward. He placed his left hand under his chin and his inquisitive eyes on Gilbride.

"Anwir," the Leader said, "he is a desperate man in need of redemption." There was a shadow in his eyes. "And redemption is what I am offering him."

Anwir looked around the spacious office. His eyes stopped at the window. It was the sunset, and daylight was leaving the room. He walked across the room, opened the first drawer of Gilbride's desk, and got out a large candle and a silver holder. The old man watched as Anwir lit the candle and placed the holder on the coffee table between the armchairs.

"Much better," Anwir said. "I would not miss a chance to observe your magnificent gray eyes, Grandfather." The young man smiled, bringing more beauty to his pale face.

"Your flattering ways only lose out to your hasty ways, Grandson."

Anwir sighed. "Well, Grandfather, as the middle child of your eldest son, I have developed my own ways of survival." He ran his fingers through his straight black hair, winking at his grandfather.

"Indeed, Anwir, indeed." Gilbride's eyes suddenly shone under the candlelight. "Do you believe you were recognized in your venture?"

"Ha! I am certain I was not, Grandfather. This is one of the many advantages of being a middle child." He turned his gaze to his grandfather. "We are invisible."

"An advantage you have used in your favor," the old man agreed.

"Indeed, old man."

Quite different from Gillion, Gilbride thought as he observed Anwir. *His mind is sharp and dangerous.* He took the last sip of his liqueur. The liquid burned his throat once again. *A viper in the making. I must exercise caution. Otherwise, this little viper will try to bite this old crow,* Gilbride thought, observing his grandson's eyes. There was darkness in them, to a disturbing extent. But Gilbride smiled at Anwir.

"Another drink, Grandfather?"

"No, my boy. That is enough for this old man," Gilbride replied. Although he would enjoy having another, he could not risk taking his eyes off his grandson. *One mistake,* he thought. *That is all it takes.*

It is never enough for you, old crow, Anwir thought, maintaining his pleasant countenance. *This old serpent does not die. Father does not die. My older brother and his children do not die...* He forced himself to stop thinking. *Easy, Anwir! Let them live their pathetic lives. It is much more fun to be in the shadows.*

"So, Grandfather," Anwir quickly engaged in a new conversation, "how are things going with Father? Is my old man enjoying being the center of your attention?"

"Your father has been a useful tool. Giving him some limited knowledge has been profitable for me and for the East."

"His loyalty was upgraded," Anwir said. "He feels valued."

"Indeed," Gilbride replied. "Although he still lacks perspective."

"Yes, he does."

"You are the only one in our family capable of playing the game."

"Who is flattering now, you old crow?" Anwir laughed heartily. "Let me get out of these filthy clothes before I find myself drinking cheap liqueur and playing cards in bars." He jumped up, bowing exaggeratedly once again.

"Before you go," Gilbride said, "you have probably heard of the Magistrate."

"Of course, I have, Grandfather," Anwir replied. "I also have my informers. He was finally affected by his family's madness. His only son is dead. His beautiful daughter is all that is left. News travels fast in the City."

"Faron proposed marriage to the girl," Gilbride informed him.

Anwir laughed. "That seductive bastard! I bet she must be madly in love with that pretty face of his!" He spat. "I assume the other clans will present their suitors soon enough."

"The West will present Usman, Ansel's son."

"He is a pretty thing himself. But not as much as Faron," Anwir replied sarcastically. "Will the boy from the North present his proposal?"

"No soul knows what the North is up to, Grandson."

"The North is full of secrets." Anwir repeated words famous among the clans from Green Valleys. "Will my baby brother take up the challenge of having such a cute little thing as a wife?" He burst into laughter.

"They would laugh at us if I sent that rabbit's face as a suitor." Gilbride smiled nastily.

"Well! I am up to this challenge. I just must make my wife and my children disappear." Anwir laughed as if it was a joke, but his eyes showed otherwise.

I am sure you would do it, Gilbride thought. *You have your peculiar ways.* A chill went down the old man's spine as he remembered his grandson's games. *Evil "games," indeed. A sadistic, evil seed in my garden. He can be useful at times but dangerous to have around.* Anwir's hasty ways were useful for Gilbride. His "peculiar ways," however, were quite disturbing, even for an old crow like Gilbride. Coming from a powerful family, Anwir had the luxury of his actions being ignored by his parents. Especially by his father. Gillion used to dismiss his son's behavior as "peculiar," or referred to his son as a "spirited lad," when in reality, he was just plain evil.

"I believe it will not be necessary, Anwir." Gilbride reclined in his armchair. "The East never publicly takes part in these sorts of affairs. Besides, we will have our puppet soon."

Anwir did not reply. He just nodded. Gilbride did not like what he saw in his grandson's eyes. *Pure evil and ambition.*

"You may leave now, Grandson. Send my regards to your wife and your three young children," Gilbride said.

"Thank you, Grandfather. I miss my beautiful wife and my children. She will be relieved to have me home to help her with our newborn son."

She will be relieved when you leave the Realm of Living, you little viper, Gilbride thought.

"Have a good night, Grandfather!" Anwir bowed. "A new day awaits us!"

Gilbride nodded and watched his grandson leave the room, closing the door behind him.

"He has left now," the old man said to the darkness.

"Yes, sir," a voice replied from the shadows.

"You may come out now," Gilbride commanded.

A large man with a scar cutting across the center of his forehead, going down his nose and right cheek, stepped into the candlelight. He had a sword in his right hand and a dagger in his left one.

"You will not need your weapons now, Evander." Gilbride pointed to the warrior's hands.

"Should I follow him?"

"No, it will not be needed." Gilbride's eyes were fixed on the door. "Walk me to my bedroom. Then be free to fulfill your High Captain's duties."

Evander nodded as he watched the Leader stand up by himself. He did not offer help. He knew Gilbride was not really a frail old man. As he stood impassive in front of the Leader of the East Lands, he could not help but feel sad for the missed chance of taking a life. The High Captain of the East Lands was a fearsome man known for his ferocious appearance and his skills as a warrior. But what nobody knew was that Evander was Gilbride's assassin, a task that would be considered an offence to any warrior in Green Valleys, but not to someone whose thirst for blood could not be quenched by daily training.

★ ★ ★ ☾ ★ ★ ★

Anwir left the office and walked down the dark hallway leading to his bedroom on the lower floor. The upper floors were reserved for Gilbride, his elder son, and grandson. The rest of the Leader's younger children and grandchildren were relegated to the lower floors.

The younger you are, the lower you are, he thought bitterly, walking down the dark hallway.

He stopped at the last door, his bedroom. He could hear his newborn son crying and his wife trying to soothe him. His two older children were singing happily. Anwir could hear their little feet stomping and running around the room. He wondered how many seconds it would take them to stop singing and dancing. He wondered if his wife would shiver at his sight. The thought made him smile.

Looking at both sides to verify he was alone, he carefully touched his golden dagger underneath his shirt. He could feel the cold blade on his skin. It made him tremble with pleasure while delightful visions popped into his mind.

"Ah!" he sighed. *Not today, my friend,* he thought. *No blood from the young or old will cover you, my beauty. Not today.* He opened the door and entered his bedroom. The singing and dancing ended. There was a moment of silence until the baby started wailing inconsolably. Anwir closed the door behind him.

Chapter Thirty-Six

Whatever It Takes

Adira beamed her approval as she watched the happiness emanating from Aura's face and Faron's eyes.

"Oh, my! A wedding!" Janace couldn't contain her excitement. "I can't believe it!" She wrapped her arms around Aura and Faron in a tight hug, kissing their cheeks. "May your happiness be endless, children!"

"I love you! Thank you for all you have done for me and my mother!" Aura embraced the older lady.

"Oh! I love you, too!" Janace said. It was at this moment that she realized Aura was no longer a child. The thought of holding Aura's babies brought tears to Janace's eyes. "Happy tears, my lovely!" the old woman said, looking at Aura's face, seeing her baby eyes, hearing her infectious baby laughter.

"Thank you for your kind words, my lady." Faron touched the old lady's shoulder kindly.

"Oh, my daughter! Although I have always dreamed of this moment, I never imagined it would happen this soon!" Adira had to fight back her own tears.

"Oh, Mother!"

"Welcome to our family, Leader Faron," Adira said. "May you be a loving, kind, and *understanding* husband to my daughter." Her eyes were scrutinizing Faron's.

"I am offering your daughter the best I can be." Faron held her gaze.

"Oh my! We have much to do and not enough time!" Janace clapped her hands. "We must start our arrangements right now! There is no time to lose!"

"Do not worry, my kind lady." Faron grinned. "I will send word to my servants in the South Lands to come as helpers. You will have as much help as you wish."

"Oh! You are such a darling!" Janace clapped her hands once again. "I will shamelessly accept your generous offer!" She burst into a peal of her characteristic laughter. Even though she knew it wouldn't be possible. Her last conversation with Mattas about returning to the Northern Lands was vivid in her mind.

Aura and Adira chuckled. Faron smiled.

"Will you stay until the wedding?" The old lady wiped a tear from the corner of her eye.

"I must return to the South Lands soon, as I have not made any sort of arrangements for a longer stay in the City. I originally thought it would be a one-night trip." Faron touched Aura's hand. "However, I am glad it turned out to be a long one."

"You are welcome to stay as long as you wish, sir," Adira replied, observing how Aura's eyes shone when Faron touched her hand.

"That is very kind of you, my lady." Faron slightly bowed.

"Yes! Yes! You should stay!" Janace agreed. "And we should leave the lovebirds in peace. Come, my lovely! Let's go to the kitchen to start the wedding preparations! I have everything figured out."

"Already? When did you have time to figure out the wedding preparations?" Adira was surprised.

"I have five children. All of them are married! I have plenty of experience organizing weddings! After all, I was the one organizing their weddings and *yours*, Adira!" Janace took Adira by the arm and took her to the kitchen, happily bubbling about her children and their wedding parties.

Aura giggled at the thought of the two ladies planning her wedding. *Am I dreaming?* she thought, not believing how her whole life would change in one day. It was hard to conceive the idea of starting a new life. The warm touch of Faron's hand told her otherwise. *It is real,* she thought.

"You made me the happiest of men today, Aura," Faron whispered.

Aura blushed, thinking of how she could have said that herself.

"There is no need to blush, Aura." Faron touched her shoulders. "You will be my wife soon."

"In three months," she murmured, remembering the standard engagement time in the Society.

"Yes. Three months, my star!" His voice was warm, full of emotions that were new to Aura.

Aura glanced at the door. The excited voices of Janace and Adira making plans and the old lady's occasional loud laughter brought sadness to her heart.

"Do not worry, my love," Faron said as if he could read Aura's feelings on her face. "I understand you will miss her and your mother. Her laughter is infectious!" He grinned.

Aura smiled sadly, hearing Janace's laughter once again.

"The South Lands are very close to the City," Faron said. "You can come to visit them whenever you wish, and they will be always welcome at *our* house."

Our house? Aura thought as a chill travelled down her spine. It was the first time the thought of leaving her father's house and having her own place hit her.

"I have a big and comfortable house. You will be treated like a queen. You can have as many visitors as you wish, and you are free to go out and visit whomever you want, my star." Faron kissed her hands. Aura trembled at the touch of his soft lips on her skin. Words failed her.

"Aura," he called. "You will do as it pleases you. I just want to tell you I will impose nothing on you. As I promised you before, you will be Aura to me, and I will be Faron to you."

She nodded as Faron kissed her forehead. She trembled once again, trying to fight the burning fire growing inside her.

★ ★ ★ ☾ ★ ★ ★

"So, my lovely," Janace said, "will you tell me the reason you have a frown on your face?"

Adira did not have to reply to this question. Her eyes were fixed on the window as she watched Aura and Faron strolling in the garden.

"You don't approve of it, do you?" Janace's eyes were fixed on Adira.

Adira sighed. "It is not about approval, Janace. I can see the happiness in my daughter's eyes. I can see how Faron is pleased with the engagement. However, I don't know if the source of his contentment is love."

"If it is not love, what else could it be? Politics? Power?" Janace asked.

"I don't know, my friend. I could not bear my daughter's suffering. I could not bear it...now...that...Anandy..." She sobbed quietly.

"Why do you weep, Adira?" Themis asked.

The ladies turned their heads to the kitchen door and found the Magistrate standing next to Mattas.

Adira quietly wiped her tears, lowering her head.

"Don't cry, Adira," Themis said softly, handing her the yellow handkerchief, his first gift to her.

She smiled at its sight and wiped away her tears.

"Aura loves Faron, and he loves her," Themis said. "I can see it in his eyes." He paused for a moment, watching the young couple in the garden. "However, I believe everyone in this room will agree with me when I say that there is something else in his eyes. Something deeply disturbing."

There was silence. Mattas and Janace exchanged a worried look. Adira gazed through the window.

"That is why," Themis continued, "we must be vigilant at all times."

Janace and Mattas nodded eagerly. Adira gazed at the couple.

"Our journey to the North will be a good reason to prepare and to think of our next move," Themis said.

"Journey to the North?" Both women were caught off-guard.

"Yes, ladies." Themis smiled. "Our family will accompany Mattas and Janace to the North." The Magistrate looked at Adira. "The North is calling us. And..." He paused.

"And what, Themis?" Adira asked.

"And it is time for me to get up from the darkness in my mind and try to really find our son." He held his wife's hands. "I will not give up on Anandy! If there is a chance he is alive, even the slightest one, I will take it, and I will do whatever it costs to bring him home and to be a better father."

"Oh, Themis! Thank you for not giving up on our son!" Adira buried her face in his chest.

Mattas smiled and hugged Janace.

There was a heavy knock at the front door. They could hear the servant walking hurriedly toward it. There were voices in the living room. After a few seconds, the female servant showed up in the kitchen.

"He is here, sir," she told Themis.

"Tell him to wait for me in my office," Themis said.

The girl bowed before disappearing into the living room.

"But before we start our journey," Themis said calmly, "I must make some arrangements."

"Who is here?" Adira asked suspiciously.

"A friend? An enemy? An ally?" Themis's dark eyes shone mysteriously. "The outcome of this conversation will answer your question, Adira."

"Good luck, Themis," Mattas replied gravely.

"Thank you, my friend," Themis replied. "I will ask you to stay here with the ladies, since this is a conversation I should have in private."

Mattas and Janace nodded. Adira glanced at Themis before taking her gaze back to the garden, frowning. The Magistrate left with a last glance at the young couple in his garden, walking hand in hand. He pressed his lips together, making his way to his office.

Themis stood by his office door. *It is dead quiet inside,* he thought apprehensively. *Allura, Venerable Elder, Good Friends, please be with me. Guide my words and actions!* He inhaled deeply and exhaled slowly. He opened the door and stepped confidently into the room.

"Greetings, Magistrate!" Dansa was standing by the bookshelf, pretending to be interested in the books on the shelves.

"Greetings, Leader Dansa," Themis replied politely. "Thank you for coming on such short notice. Please, have a seat." He pointed to the chair by his desk.

"Thank you, Magistrate!" Dansa replied, sitting on the appointed chair. "It fills my heart with happiness to see you on your feet."

Does it? Themis thought, but he quickly swept that thought away. *It will not be of any help if I plant distrust in my heart.*

Themis nodded, trying his best to draw a polite smile on his face. "Would you like anything to drink?"

"No, thank you." Dansa's eyes were shining with expectation and curiosity.

"Of course." Themis recalled how Dansa did not fully appreciate pleasantries. "First off, I would like to offer you my deep gratitude for managing the City's affairs so competently during my absence."

"It was a pleasure, indeed!" Dansa replied. "I believe you invited me here so I could update you on the City's latest developments."

"As a matter of fact, Leader Dansa," Themis said, "the reason I invited you here today was to request your further assistance in the City's management."

"My further assistance?" Dansa frowned.

"As I am certain, you are aware of my son's disappearance. My daughter and I fell ill. And this is my second day on my feet," Themis said.

"I am sorry to hear about your son, Themis." Dansa's eyes softened as he saw vulnerability on the Magistrate's face.

"Thank you, Dansa." Themis smiled sadly. "I am not fit to exercise my duties properly. Thus, your help would be truly appreciated."

The Leader of the Central Lands nodded, witnessing in dismay that the warm feeling growing inside him was fading away.

There is something in Themis's eyes, he thought. It *reminds me of...* He forced himself to stop thinking. *No good will come from revisiting the past, Dansa,* he thought.

"I assume I can count on you," Themis said after a few moments of silence.

"Of course, Themis," Dansa replied faintly.

"I am glad you assented. You are the only leader I trust."

"Am I?" Dansa laughed in disbelief.

"Yes, you are. You are my only childhood friend. Our friendship made the hardship of the army camps bearable." He paused for a moment, as if he was searching for the right words. "Although we have grown apart over the years, and even became antagonists, I still hold you as a dear friend."

Dansa trembled as stubborn memories revisited his mind. He could see Themis's beloved boyish face under the moon. His bright smile under the stars. His heart ached. The same ache he had experienced all those years.

"Themis," Dansa called, "I would *never* do anything to harm you or your family!" A feeling, forgotten long ago, emerged in Dansa's heart. It was tenderness. It was genuine affection.

"I believe you, Dansa." Themis knew in his heart it was true.

The Leader's heart raced. He knew it was time. He knew what he had to do.

"I must tell you something, Themis." Dansa placed a black envelope on the desk.

Chapter Thirty-Seven

Withstand the Storm

The clouds formed a big white blanket. Although the sun had not yet made its appearance, it was a bright day.

"It will snow soon." She was standing in front of Usman, but it felt as if her voice was coming from a farther place, somewhere beyond the land of dreams.

The warrior stood mesmerized at the sight of her. She was dressed all in white. Her long blond curls were falling loose down her back. She was barefoot. Her dress and curls were waving in a sort of melodic, slow dance. It was beautiful.

"Are you coming with me, Usman?" She extended a pale hand to him. Sorrow darkened her blue eyes. Usman noticed how her lips were moving, but her voice was coming from a different place.

Usman felt as if the sight of her hypnotized him. He placed his tanned hand on top of hers. The coldness emanating from her fingers almost made him retrieve his hand from hers. However, he stayed still, allowing the beautiful girl to guide him through the empty streets of the West Lands.

How can she be barefoot? Usman thought, glancing at her delicate feet stepping on the cold grass.

"Does the cold bother you, Usman?" she asked, guiding him by the hand.

"Yes," he heard himself saying. "It does not snow in the West. It gets chilly, it gets wet, but it does not snow."

She smiled at him as the first snowflakes fell from that blank white sky.

"It is snowing, Usman." Her smile was sweet but sorrowful at the same time.

He placed his hands on his face in dismay as the cold snowflakes caressed his cheeks. He watched the grass being covered by the white carpet of winter. He witnessed the Great River being greeted by the fresh snow. He felt it on his naked arms. It was cold but soothing.

"It is beautiful!" he whispered, smiling. "Thank you, God! Thank you for allowing me to witness your magnificence!" He tilted his head back, closing his eyes. The snowflakes touching his skin were a relief. The cold no longer bothered him.

"It is God's glory!" he murmured as a tear of gratitude rolled down his cheek.

"Do you feel God is with you now, Usman?" the girl whispered. Her voice was distant, as if it was coming from beyond the Great River.

"Yes! Always!" He did not hesitate. His eyes were still closed as more tears rolled down his cheeks.

"Is God talking to you now, Usman?" Her voice was no longer coming from beyond the Great River; it was coming from a place closer to him.

The warrior opened his eyes. His head was still tilted back so he could still see the sky. The snowfall was heavier now. It was hitting his face, covering his eyes and nostrils. He kept his eyes open and inhaled the cold air into his lungs. He gazed at that white blanket sky.

"Yes." There was no hesitation in his voice. "God always talks to me."

"How?" she asked. Her voice seemed closer than it was before.

"It is a warm feeling inside me." He was still gazing at the sky. "My mother says this feeling is God talking to me. I know it is true. I can feel His presence."

"What is God telling you now, Usman?" There was sorrow in her voice.

He didn't reply at first. He lowered his eyes. The warm feeling was there once again. It was inside him. He could feel it.

"I don't know," he murmured, gazing at the snow underneath his feet. It was covering his boots now.

"Listen carefully and you will know, Usman." Her voice was coming from right next to him. He could feel her standing by his side, but he didn't look at her.

Usman closed his eyes. He tried hard to focus on that warm feeling.

"I must listen," he told himself silently. "Please, God! Talk to me. I am listening." He exhaled heavily.

Usman trembled as a chill of horror went down his spine. He opened his eyes and placed his gaze on the girl standing next to him. There were tears in her eyes. He felt it in every inch of his body. It was there. Usman felt the tremor coming to his hands, then to his legs. Soon, it was in his entire being.

"Did you listen, Usman?" Her voice was shaky.

"Yes," he murmured. He listened to it. He knew what it was. It was taking over his body. It was fear.

The icy wind blew snow violently against his face. Usman struggled to keep his balance. His legs shook as he tried to bury his feet in the snow and engage his leg muscles and core to resist the wind's strength. The wind blew once again. His legs failed him. He was thrown against the ground. A wave of pain ran through his body as his back violently struck the icy grass. Usman tried to jump up. He knew it would get worse if he stayed on the ground. He placed his right knee on the ground and used his hands for support. The wind gusted again, this time stronger than before. Usman fell once again and rolled twice as if he was a ball on a grassy field. The young warrior buried his fingernails in the snow. He could feel the cold burning his skin.

"The wind is keeping me down! I can't get up!" he yelled. He shivered, feeling his fingers getting numb.

A slim shadow walked toward him through that snowstorm. There was grace and firmness in her moves. It was as if the storm could not harm her.

"God wants you to stand, Usman." The blond girl's voice was clear. "Stand in the storm, Warrior!" Her voice was coming through the wind. "Stand and fight!" Her voice echoed through every corner of the West Lands.

Usman felt these words resonating in every cell of his body. Her words struck him with the force of a physical blow. He closed his eyes, inhaling deeply.

"Show me my true strength, God!" he yelled to the storm, fighting the fear and the pain.

The warrior buried his nails deeper in the snow in front of him and groaned in pain as he fought the wind to make his way to his knees. The unmerciful wind blew wickedly into his face. His torso shook. Usman screamed in pain as the wind whipped his face, his arms, his torso, and his legs. Blood was dripping onto the fresh snow, painting it red. The snowflakes were burning his skin. He screamed in pain again as he collapsed face-down on the ground. Usman felt tears of agony falling down his cheeks. The once soothing snowflakes were like a whip on his flesh. He could feel the blood dripping from his face and limbs. He looked at his muscular hands, watching the blood running from the back of them. Usman inhaled again, looking at his red fingers. He closed his eyes and took two deep breaths before burying his fingernails as deep as he could in the snow.

"I will stand!" he grunted at the girl as she watched his suffering. Tears bathed her face.

"Stand in the storm, Usman!" she said. Her voice came as a whisper in his ears.

The storm worsened. Usman felt the whiplashes multiplying on his skin. He screamed, fighting not to roll on the snow once again.

"Not today, wind!" Usman yelled, gathering all the energy left in his body. "Today, I, Usman, son of Ansel, a warrior and server of the West Lands, will stand for God's glory! For the glory of Green Valleys!"

Usman steadied himself on the ground, planting his feet firmly side by side and pushing his hands forward until he was standing upright. The wind blew again. The warrior's torso bent, but he did not fall. Stepping firmly on the snowy ground, Usman stood against the storm. His body was burned, covered in blood. He shivered in pain and cold, but fear did not take its place in his heart.

"God spoke to me today," the warrior groaned.

The girl stood motionless in front of him. She didn't utter a word but wept silently.

Usman gasped for air as he placed his gaze on the Great River. Once it had been his people's blessing. Now it was painted red.

"The blood of my people." He felt his knees falling, but he stepped firmly on the ground once again.

"Yes, Usman," she replied.

"What is happening?" he asked, out of breath. "Why is it happening?"

"There is nothing happening." Her eyes were wide open. The tears were gone from her eyes.

"*This* is happening!" He pointed to his bruised body and to the river covered with blood.

"Oh, Usman!" she replied calmly. "It is only a dream!"

"What? Am I dreaming?" Usman looked amusedly at his limbs, watching the cuts and burns disappear. As he turned his attention to the Great River, he witnessed the blood and the snow dissipating.

"It is only a dream," she repeated. "A dream of a future where you do not withstand the storm."

Usman's lips shivered. Words refused to come out of them as he looked in disbelief at the thin girl standing in front of him.

"Come to me," she whispered inside his head. "I need you to withstand the storm by my side."

"Who are you?" Usman asked.

"I am Aura." The girl smiled. "Withstand the storm and fight, Warrior! Come to me!"

★ ★ ★ ☾ ★ ★ ★

"Son! Wake up!" his mother called.

Usman opened his eyes. He found himself safely in bed. His mother was standing at his bedside, her face grave with worry.

"Oh, my baby!" she murmured. "I heard you screaming. You had a nightmare."

"Yes, Mother," Usman said faintly. "My apologies for waking you up." He looked around to make sure he was indeed in his bedroom.

"Don't be silly! I was already up. It is morning. The girls and your father are still sleeping," she said. "Oh! Your shirt is soaked!" His mother pointed at his wet shirt.

"I must have sweated during the night," he murmured, still confused.

"Take it off before you get sick!"

Usman slowly sat down on his bed and took off his sweaty shirt. His mother got a small white towel and wiped the sweat from her son's arms and back.

"I will bring you some warm milk, Usman." She collected his sweaty shirt and the towel. "Meanwhile, get into dry clothes! I will be right back."

"I guess I will be up for the day." Usman rubbed his eyes. "I will get dressed and meet you in the kitchen, Mother."

"As you wish, son." She smiled as she quietly left the bedroom.

Usman exhaled heavily, making his way to the large window. He opened the heavy curtains.

"Right before the sunrise," he whispered, watching a group of fishermen returning from the Great River. Their nets were full. The image of the river covered in blood was vivid in his mind. He noticed a slight tremor in his hands.

The blood of my people, he thought, trying to sweep that image away. *It was only a dream.* He tried to believe in his own words.

Usman stepped away from the window and opened his wardrobe. He motioned to get his light armor, but he changed his mind. Instead, he got out a green light shirt and green light pants. As he watched himself in the mirror, he touched the emblem on his shirt.

The fish, the river, and the hand, he thought. *The hand is our people. Our true wealth. They are the reason I must withstand the storm.*

★ ★ ★ ☾ ★ ★ ★

After a few minutes, Usman was completely dressed in his non-warrior clothes. His face was washed, and his brown hair was neatly combed.

"Oh! Look at you!" his mom said. "You look even more handsome when you are not wearing that light armor!"

Usman kissed his mother's forehead.

"Take a seat and have some bread, Usman." His mother pushed a plate of bread, cheese, olives, and grapes toward him. "Be careful! The milk is hot!" She placed the mug on the table. "I will make some eggs and sausages as well."

Usman took a seat, said a prayer, and started working on the food in front of him.

"How is everything?" His mother took a seat across from him, postponing the eggs and sausages.

"Perfect as always, Mother." Usman placed his tired green eyes on hers.

"Are you ready to talk to me about that dream?" she asked softly. "Last time you had a nightmare, you were a little boy." She smiled. Her dreaming eyes were lost in the air while her mind revisited some beautiful moments from the past.

Usman hesitated for a moment. He didn't know what to say, but something in his mother's eyes gave him the confidence to speak up.

"I dreamed..." he started, "it was God talking to me, Mother."

His mother raised her eyebrows curiously. "Tell me about it, my son."

"There was this girl," he said. "She asked me to go to her and stand in the storm together." His eyes were fixed on his mother's. "But I don't know who she is or what that dream meant."

"Usman," his mother said, "do you truly believe this dream came from God?"

"Yes, Mother," he replied without hesitation.

"Then go to this girl." Her brown eyes were shining intensely. "And stand in the storm, Usman."

"How?" he asked, confused.

"Trust God! He will guide you to her." She smiled. Usman's heart warmed. "You will know in your heart when the chance to meet her arises."

"Good morning, family!" Ansel said from the hallway. He had the custom of speaking before entering the room as a way of announcing himself.

"Good morning," Usman and his mother murmured, startled.

"Well! It is the day of our journey, Usman," Ansel announced happily.

"Oh! I forgot you two are going to the City today!" his wife said hurriedly. "There is so much to do."

"Don't worry, wife!" Ansel said. "We need little for our journey."

She kissed her husband's right cheek.

"Are you ready, Usman?" Ansel asked.

The warrior didn't reply, his eyes unfocused. His lips were partly open. Usman's heart was pounding. There was a soft, almost inaudible breath in his ear, whispering the word "Aura."

"Usman?" Ansel insisted.

His son blinked many times, as if he had just woken up from a dream.

"Yes, Father," he replied faintly. "I am ready to go to the City."

★ ★ ★ ☾ ★ ★ ★

In the Central Lands, Aura was sitting on her bed, gazing at the darkness in her bedroom. She was shaking uncontrollably. Her lips were shivering. Her heart was racing.

She watched as the first sunrays brought the morning light into her room. Aura's lips shivered as she whispered, "Stand in the storm, Usman."

Chapter Thirty-Eight

The North Is Full of Secrets

Her warm, gentle hand wiped the sweat from his forehead. He could feel the softness of her skin when she delicately touched his chin and turned his head to the right. She was singing a beautiful foreign song. Her voice resonated clearly throughout the room. He tried to open his eyes. There was pain. He groaned.

"Shh!" she said. "Stay still. It is almost over." There was kindness in her voice.

He tried to move, but his body didn't obey his commands. He felt the urge to open his eyes and view that singing angel in front of him.

"I–I can't move," he murmured.

"It is almost over," she whispered. "Just follow my voice." She resumed singing that foreign song.

Although he couldn't understand the words, it was the most beautiful song he had ever heard. It was pure. It was clear. It was peaceful. There was ancient wisdom in that slow melody. *This must be how angels sing*, he thought, allowing her voice to guide him. It echoed in his mind, taking him to different places, different times.

It took him to his boyish years. He found himself hiding behind his mother at the sight of a visitor in the house. He could see her kind eyes, her smile as bright as the stars. His heart ached as her face dissipated into thin air. A tear rolled down his cheek. "Mother!" he gasped, feeling his face moistening with tears. He missed her. He missed being a little boy. He missed having the innocence of a child.

"It is fine. Stay with my voice." The girl wiped his tears with a white handkerchief and took his hands. Their fingers entwined. He felt the warmth emanating from her skin, travelling through her fingers straight to his. It was soothing. She whispered something. He forced himself to focus on her words, but they seemed to vanish as soon as she uttered them, leaving behind a feeling of something lost long ago. Something precious but lost.

"Argh!" he howled in pain, feeling his chest being stabbed by a thousand daggers.

He felt her fingers on his chest. The soothing, warm feeling was there, once again travelling through his entire body.

"It is almost done." Her voice was mellow but powerful. "Let my voice guide you." She whispered a few words that had a rhythm in them. Her tone rose or lowered at certain words.

Is it a foreign language? he thought, feeling the pain diminishing. He felt warm. The pain was gone. He sighed, relieved.

"Sleep now." She kissed his right cheek, giving a last squeeze to his hands.

He clung to her hands. *Should I open my eyes?* he thought indecisively.

She didn't take her hands away. She patted his twice.

Yes! I must see her! He slowly opened his eyes, trying to get used to the blinding light in the room. Once his eyes were accustomed to the light, he saw her.

A young lady sat at his bedside. She smiled as her light blue eyes met his. Her long, straight blond hair was braided. She wore a long white dress. The light in the room emanated from her. Her body was engulfed in a sort of arc of light. He could see it perfectly. It was the color of amber, warm and healing. He saw the light leaving her fingers and travelling to his hands. *She is an angel!*

"Welcome!" Her smile brightened the room further.

"Am I dead?" he asked. "Are you an angel?" He marveled at the light emanating from her body.

She laughed. The sound was so pure, like a child's mirth. It made him want to laugh as well. He blinked. The light started to fade away. He blinked again. It was gone.

"No, I am not. I am only human. I have been nursing you back to strength," she said.

He scanned the room and found himself in a white bedroom. A heavy blanket covered him. There was a fireplace and a large window above it. His gaze stopped there to see small snowflakes falling. He tried to move, but a stabbing pain came from his shoulder.

"Is it snowing?" he asked, confused.

"Yes, it is." Her eyes followed his to the window.

"What? Wh—" He stopped himself. "Oh, I forgot my manners," he said slowly. "Please, allow me to introduce myself. I am—"

"I know who you are." She cut him short.

He felt his cheeks blush. "Thank you for taking care of me, girl."

"Minna," she whispered. "My name is Minna. We have names here!"

"Oh!" he hesitated. "Here? Where? What is this place?" He thought it was awkward to have a woman clearly stating her name to a man, but he kept it to himself. He didn't want to be disrespectful. After all, she was taking such good care of him.

Minna smiled proudly and looked at the bedroom door. A slender figure stood against it. The dark hallway hid his features.

"Welcome to the North, *Anandy*, son of Themis," the slender figure said solemnly.

"The attack! The mercenaries!" Anandy exclaimed as flashbacks of that fateful day echoed in his mind. He tried to sit up, but another wave of pain stabbed at his chest. He groaned.

Minna placed her hands on his chest, rubbing it. "Easy there, Anandy." She turned to the man standing by the door. "Don't startle him like that. He is still recovering."

Anandy didn't hear her words or feel Minna's warm hands on his chest. His mind had taken him somewhere else. He was back at the borders of the Central and the South Lands. The vision of the mercenaries attacking him, their arrows, cutting through his flesh, the pain, the fear! It was all so vivid. He instinctively lowered his gaze and found his naked chest carefully covered in a bandage. He was wearing a light white cotton shirt. He lowered his blanket and saw his right thigh was wrapped in a white bandage. The right leg of his white pants was cut up to right below his hip.

"I cut it to treat your wound," the girl explained, taking her hands from his chest.

Anandy blushed at the idea of Minna seeing his body. He didn't sustain her gaze. His eyes were fixed on the man. The vision of him jumping and fighting the mercenaries in that unusual way popped up. *He saved my life and brought me here for treatment,* he thought as he studied the mysterious man. *It wasn't possible for him to do it by himself. He had help,* Anandy thought, observing the small silhouette standing by the door. He tried to make sense of it all, but darkness covered the man's features.

"Minna is a skillful healer," the man said. "We brought you here after the attack, for you needed northern treatment for your wounds. You were half dead when we arrived at these lands." There was calm and self-control in his voice. Anandy thought of Themis's constant reminders of "restraint." Then it hit him. He remembered!

"I know your voice!" Anandy said, startled. He fixed his gaze on the door, watching the slender figure entering the room. "*You!*" he exclaimed, perplexed. "No! What sorcery is it? Was it *you* who saved me?"

The young warrior could not believe his eyes as he saw Conrad, the Leader of the North, walking into the room.

"There is no sorcery, Anandy. It was me you saw fighting the mercenaries." He slowly lifted his white shirt, revealing a long black wound on his ribcage.

"I can't believe it!" Anandy said, trying to reason how a non-warrior could fight and defeat a group of trained assassins. It seemed unbelievable. His eyes were fixed on Conrad's muscle definition.

"Conrad got a broken rib," Minna explained as she lifted the Leader's shirt and touched his wound. "I will go to your bedroom tonight for further treatment."

Anandy turned his eyes away, twisting his mouth in disgust. He didn't feel comfortable watching a young woman touching a young man so intimately. That was wrong.

"Minna is a healer," Conrad said, noticing the disapproval on Anandy's face. "Besides, she is my sister."

The warrior blushed and lowered his eyes, feeling silly. Minna laughed once again. This made him blush even more.

"I will leave you two alone," she said. "You have much to talk about." She glanced at Anandy and smiled.

"Thank you, girl," he murmured.

"Call me Minna," she replied. "Women are called by their names in the North." And with these words, she left the room, closing the door behind her.

"What did she say?" Anandy's heart was sprinting. "Did she say that women are called by their names in the North?"

"Why wouldn't they be called by their names?" Conrad grinned. "What is the reason behind giving someone a name if you will not use it?"

Anandy didn't reply, watching the snowflakes gently kissing the window.

"Heavy snowfalls are common in the North," Conrad pointed out.

"I have so many questions," Anandy said as if he was coming out of a trance.

"You certainly do," Conrad agreed, glancing at Anandy. Then he took his gaze back to the snowfall.

The young warrior tried to make sense of time. "How long have I been here?"

"Fifteen days."

"Fifteen days?" Anandy almost jumped out of bed. "Where is Father? Could you call him, please?" His eyes swept the room, searching for any familiar face.

"I am afraid it will not be possible to summon the Magistrate," Conrad replied gravely.

Anandy's blood ran cold. "Am I a prisoner?" he asked, imagining he was the centerpiece in a cunning political scheme. His mind tried to trace an escape plan as he ran his eyes around the room, trying to find a way out.

"On the contrary," Conrad replied. "You are a guest and free to leave when it pleases you."

"Why isn't my father here?" Anandy frowned, still trying to figure out an escape plan, but nothing came to mind.

"Because he does not know you are alive." Conrad lowered his eyes. "He believes you are dead."

"Dead?" Anandy felt his heart sink. "Father must be looking for me."

Conrad lowered his eyes, remaining silent.

"Did you send word to him about me?" Anandy asked.

"I did not," Conrad replied. "As I told you, when we brought you here, you were half dead. We put all our efforts into saving your life."

"And I am grateful for your kind gesture, Leader Conrad," Anandy replied. "However, I cannot understand why my father is not aware of it."

"Because we did not want to risk your life." Conrad's eyes were fixed on Anandy's. "Someone paid those mercenaries to kill you, Anandy." He ran his fingers through his straight blond hair. "If word got out that you had survived the attack, you would be in grave danger. We kept the truth from your father to protect your life."

Anandy didn't reply but took a few moments to study the young leader's face. *He seems younger than me,* he thought. *However, he possesses a kind of ancient wisdom in his words and movements. The same wisdom from the girl's song,* he thought, remembering the vision of the amber light emanating from Minna's body.

"Leader Conrad," Anandy said, "I must return to the City. I must be reunited with my family. Thank you for all you have done. But it is time for me to leave."

Conrad didn't move. He stood by Anandy's bedside, watching him for several moments, expressionless. "Anandy," he finally said, "there are a few missing pieces in this puzzle."

The warrior raised his eyebrows in confusion.

"We have a series of events which are linked," Conrad explained. "First, the concerning numbers presented at the Council. Then the mercenaries who tried to kill you."

"Do you believe there is a connection between these two events?"

"I am certain of it." Conrad looked deep into Anandy's eyes. "The same person who manipulated the numbers was the one who paid those mercenaries to take your life."

Anandy felt his blood boil. "Then this man will have a taste of my iron!"

"That would not be prudent, young Anandy," said a man standing by the window.

The warrior trembled as he heard the man's voice. *How did he get in? The girl closed the door behind her.* He replayed the scene of Minna leaving and closing the door behind her.

Anandy watched in horror as an older man walked toward him, standing next to Conrad. The warrior took a few moments to observe the man's face. He had straight gray hair, light blue eyes, and a slender figure. *They look alike!*

"You will see soon enough, young Anandy," the man said, "that being dead has its advantages. Especially when it comes to confusing your enemies." He smiled.

"And," Anandy hesitated, "who is this one I have the pleasure of talking to?"

"I am Daman."

Anandy felt he would faint. "Daman?" he asked, petrified. "Leader Daman from the Northern Lands?"

The man nodded. "Indeed. In my previous life, I was the Leader of the North and Conrad's father." The old man placed a hand on the young man's shoulders.

"What sorcery is it?" Anandy's voice was weak. "What kind of place is the North? Women have names, a healer whispers foreign words, an unknown fighting style...and...and...the dead walk among us!"

"You are talking about the invisible North, pretty boy!" a voice said from the place behind the door.

Anandy had to blink several times to make sure his eyes weren't playing tricks on him. There were two other men in the bedroom. He couldn't believe how he had failed to notice them.

"The invisible North. Covered by the Mighty Mountains. Hidden by the Sankul Woods," the second man said.

Anandy was in shock, not because he had failed to notice those two men, but because of how they looked. The man who was first to speak was short and thin. He was around Themis's age, but he was different from any person Anandy had ever seen.

His eyes! I have never seen eyes like that before! Anandy thought, observing his almond-shaped red eyes. His straight red hair fell free, covering his heart-shaped shaved face. He was dressed in black pants and a long-sleeved black shirt. There was a light black sword hanging from his belt.

"You mentioned the unusual fighting style," Conrad said. "Please, allow me to introduce you to Inalef, my Master of Arms and my Mentor."

The red-haired man winked at Anandy. "Hello, pretty boy!"

The young warrior frowned at him.

"Ah! Don't worry. You are not my type," the man replied. "I don't like the big men from Green Valleys. I am already taken, sweetheart." He laughed. His laughter was strident, like his voice.

"Don't scare the boy with your flirting, Inalef," the second man said.

Anandy placed his shocked gaze on the tall man standing in front of him. *His skin! It is painted in black as the night sky,* he thought, observing the bald man dressed in fur.

"Welcome to the Northern Lands, boy." The man fixed his golden eyes on Anandy.

"Thank you." Anandy trembled at the sight of those magnificent eyes. *They shine like golden coins.*

"This is Batoor," Daman said. "The best hunter and warrior in his clan. And a great friend of the North."

Batoor nodded. He never smiled. Anandy thought he seemed young at first, then he looked older. It was hard to tell his age. One thing, however, was easy to tell: his eyes were not human. Inalef's eyes were not human, either. Anandy felt like he would faint.

"Batoor and Inalef fought the mercenaries by my side. They also saved your life," Conrad explained.

"Who are they? What are they?" Anandy murmured. "Are they human? I have never seen people like them in my life."

Inalef laughed loud, shaking his head. Batoor gazed at Anandy, who trembled even more. Conrad glanced at Daman, who nodded in approval.

"The North is full of secrets, my new friend." His eyes were shining like two precious gems. "Come! Allow me to show you some of them!"

Epilogue

The immensity of the open grassy field unfolded in front of my eyes. The warmth of the sun directly above my head was soothing on my tired body. I stood alone in the middle of that field. As old feelings revolved inside me, I tried to focus on the end of my journey.

"This is just the beginning," the ghost from my past whispered through the gentle breeze.

I remained silent. I chose to ignore that voice long ago. I chose to leave that field long ago.

"So, we meet again," it said. I could hear the delight in his voice, as if he had expected to find me in that field.

I didn't utter a word. I was in control of whom I spoke to or where I went.

"You have returned, my old friend." His voice was no longer in the breeze. Instead, it was coming from the warm grass underneath my boots.

"I know your games. Reveal yourself!" I commanded.

"Who are you to command me, mortal?" it barked above my head from the blue skies.

"Who are you to play games with me?" I replied.

I heard steps. It was behind me. I turned in a jump, and I saw it. There it was. That creature, which did not deserve to be called human. His skin was golden. His face and features were unknown to me. It was as if there was a shade covering them. I gazed at its face, but it was blurry. All I could see was a golden humanoid shape standing in front of me. I would call it humanoid, because it resembled us. It had a head, two legs, two feet, two arms, and two hands.

"I remember when you were a little thing and our games very much impressed you!" His voice was metallic.

I trembled as visions of my earliest days revisited. I could see myself as a little child, crying and screaming. The fear running through my veins. I could see my mother holding me in the dark, her sweet hands caressing my hair. Her gentle voice singing. And I could see it. It was there. It had been there my entire life. A smile in the darkness. There was deceit in its words. There was a malefic reason for each word it uttered.

"I walked away from you once," I said. "I can do it again." I tried to believe myself. I tried to sound, at least, as if I believed myself.

"No, you cannot, child."

The sound of its laughter pierced my heart like a knife. I covered my ears as I howled in horror. I could make out the faintest hint of a smile through the blur of its face.

"You are here again because you belong to me. You are my servant."

It laughed again. I felt to my knees, desperately trying to block its deafening laughter.

"No!" I yelled. "I do not belong to you!"

"Oh, child!" It laughed once again. I felt as if an invisible arm had punched me directly to the ground. I groaned in pain.

"You will be a good child and work for me," it said calmly. "Do as I say, and I can make the pain go away."

I tried to yell again, but my voice was stuck in my throat. I tried to make my way to my hands, but my arms refused to work.

"You will spread my work among your peers," it said. "And I will make you powerful again! Do you remember the things we achieved *together?*"

I closed my eyes for a moment as tears of pain bathed my face.

"Enough!" she said.

My heart almost stopped when I heard her voice. "That is her!" I whispered, feeling my face moist with tears. "The Fair Lady from my childhood! The Beautiful Queen!" That's what I used to call her. "She always comes to my rescue!" My heart was full of joy at the sight.

She stood magnificent in her white dress as the gentle breeze played with her fair hair. She raised her white left arm. There was a blue light emanating from it.

"Come to me!" she told the evil creature. "Come to me, brother. Come to the light! Let me help you!" Her voice was a kind whisper.

The creature crouched in fear. It raised its golden arms, protecting its eyes from the light emanating from the queen's arms. It emitted a high-pitched sound and faded away. There was sadness in her eyes as she watched it disappear.

With difficulty, I made my way to my feet. She was standing a few feet from me. I awkwardly bowed to her. The Lady's presence evoked reverence and respect.

"Do not bow to me, child," she said.

"Thank you for coming to rescue me, o Fair Lady!"

"You remember me."

I lowered my eyes in shame and nodded. I remembered her from my childhood. I remembered her and the many others who populated my nights of torment and fear.

"I am sorry for walking away from you." My eyes were fixed on the ground.

"Look at me, child," she said softly.

I did as she said. I marveled once again at the sight of her spectacular long wavy blond hair. Her gray eyes were fixed on mine. I knew she could see deep into my soul. I shivered.

"There is nothing to forgive, child," she said. "You were little and scared. You did what you believed to be the right thing to protect yourself."

I gasped as tears inundated my face. I nodded. It was true! I was trying to protect myself!

"You are no longer a child," she said.

"I am not," I assented.

"Will you reject us once again?"

I could feel her gray eyes searching my soul for an answer.

"I will not, Fair Lady."

"It is true," she said, as if she could hear my mind. "Once you accept us, they will come." She pointed to the place where once stood the golden creature.

I trembled. "What should I do? I do not wish to see them."

"But you will," she said. "They are attracted to the light. You are the light."

"I am not," I whispered, lowering my eyes again in shame.

"Be brave and wise," she said. "Listen to the right voices. Ignore the others, for you are not in a position to help them."

"I am listening to you, my lady," I murmured.

"Good! We need you!"

I dared to meet her gaze. I shivered with the cold emanating from her eyes.

"How can I help you?" I asked, confused.

"You will help defeat a monster."

"My lady?"

"Allura," she said.

A chill went down my spine. Every fiber of my body trembled at the sound of her name.

"Allura," I repeated.

She smiled a third time, and the world became as bright as the sun.

"Are you ready to defeat a monster, Anandy?" Her voice came from a distant place.

I nodded.

"Wake up, Child of Allura!"

★ ★ ★ ☾ ★ ★ ★

Anandy opened his eyes. He was no longer in the grassy field. He was in the white bedroom in the Northern Lands. He inhaled deeply and looked through the window. It was almost morning. It was snowing.

"Things just got interesting!" He smiled as the name Allura echoed in his mind.

The story continues in THE SECRETS OF THE NORTH

Book two (2) of the Green Valleys series

Acknowledgments

"The Children of Allura" wouldn't be possible if it wasn't for my husband, Xhulio. Thank you for your constant encouragement and for convincing me to publish this book. Thanks to you, the citizens of Green Valleys can share their tales with the world. Your honest feedback since the early drafts and your views on the cover helped me stay true to my story.

I would like to thank my son, Axel, for keeping me accountable by asking me the same question every day at pickup time at school: "How many words did you write today, Mama?" Your passion for numbers helped me push myself to work harder.

My parents, Moacyr and Eliane, played a huge role in my love for the art of crafting stories. They were the first ones who believed in me. They have been reading everything I have been writing since I was a child. Watching the light in their eyes at the end of every story motivated me to keep writing. Their encouragement was beyond words. Obrigada, mamae e papai!

I want to extend my gratitude to my editor, Allister Thompson, for polishing this story while keeping my voice behind it. Thank you, Betty Martinez, for designing a beautiful cover!

And thank YOU, my dear friend, for joining me on a journey to Green Valleys. See you in the Northern Lands!

Also By

Thank you for purchasing a copy of my book. I hope you really enjoyed the tales of Green Valleys! While we are waiting for the second book to come out, "The Secrets of the North," I would like to offer you a gift for your support. Please, sign up for my newsletter by scanning the QR code below and get a **free** short story from the Green Valleys universe. It is a fun project I have been working on for the past few months. Please, join me and Aura into a world of magic through the pages of "Aura's book of fairytales."

About Author

Elaine Santos is a teacher by trade and a writer by heart. She writes stories that depict strong, relatable characters. Nature, suspense, and adventure are recurrent elements in her works.

Elaine lives in Ontario, Canada with her husband, son, and two cats. She loves hiking, fitness, yoga, meditation, and baking. Her perfect evening would include quality time with her family, enjoying the pages of a great book, and the soothing scent of her favorite tea. Her perfect day? Hiking and writing!

Printed in Great Britain
by Amazon

32187161R00155